The Pendragon's Quest

The Last Pendragon Saga

The Last Pendragon
The Pendragon's Quest

The After Cilmeri Series:

Daughter of Time
Footsteps in Time
Winds of Time
Prince of Time
Crossroads in Time
Children of Time
Exiles in Time
Castaways in Time
Ashes of Time

The Gareth and Gwen Medieval Mysteries

The Bard's Daughter
The Good Knight
The Uninvited Guest
The Fourth Horseman
The Fallen Princess

Other Books by Sarah Woodbury

Cold My Heart: A Novel of King Arthur

Book Two in *The Last Pendragon* Saga

THE
PENDRAGON'S
QUEST

by

SARAH WOODBURY

The Pendragon's Quest
Copyright © 2011 by Sarah Woodbury

This is a work of fiction.

Cover image by Christine DeMaio-Rice at Flip City Books
http://flipcitybooks.com

To my Dad
who loved Cade and all his friends

Pronouncing Welsh Names and Places

Aberffraw – Ah-BEAR-fraw

Annwn –ANN-oon

Bwlch y Ddeufaen – Boolk ah THEY-vine (the 'th' is soft as in 'forth')

Cadfael – CAD-file

Cadwaladr – Cad-wall-AH-der

Cadwallon – Cad-WASH-lon

Cai – 'ai' makes the long i sound like in 'kite' so Kie

Caernarfon – ('ae' makes a long i sound like in 'kite') Kire-NAR-von

Cymry – KUM-ree

Dafydd – DAH-vith

Dolgellau – Doll-GESH-lay

Deheubarth – deh-HAY-barth

Dolwyddelan – dole-with-EH-lan (the 'th' is soft as in 'forth')

Goronwy – Gor –ON-wee

Gruffydd – GRIFF-ith

Gwenllian – Gwen-SHLEE-an

Gwynedd – GWIN-eth

Hywel – H'wel

Ieuan – ieu sounds like the cheer, 'yay' so YAY-an

Llywelyn – shlew-ELL-in

Maentwrog – MIGHNT-wrog

Meilyr – MY-lir

Owain – OH-wine

Rhiannon – Rhee-AH-non

Rhun – Rin

Rhys – Reese

Sidhe – (from the Gaelic) Shee

Sion – Shawn

Taliesin – Tal-ee-EH-seen

Tudur – TIH-deer

Usk – Isk

Map of Wales

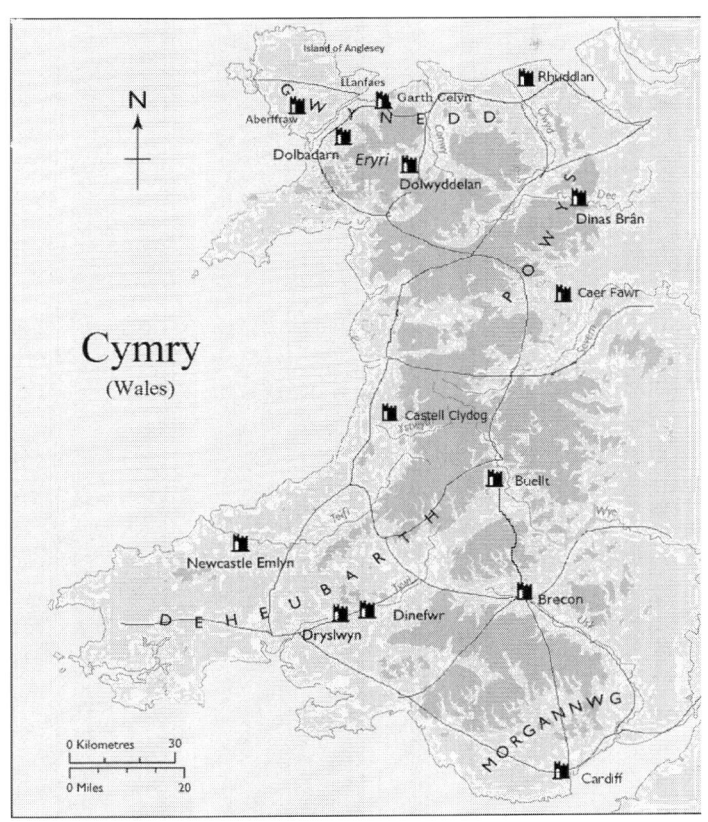

Cymry
(Wales)

Dear Reader,

Although I'm sure that many, many of you have perfect retention of the cast and plot of *The Last Pendragon*, I must report that my own husband failed to remember who everyone was and what had happened between the publication of the first book and the release of The Pendragon's Quest. I'm shocked, I tell you, shocked!

So, a refresher:

In *The Last Pendragon*, Cadwaladr ap Cadwallon (Cade), enters the court of Gwynedd after King Cadfael's men ambushed and killed all of his men, including Cade's foster father, Cynyr, on the road to Aberffraw. As Cadfael had married Cade's mother (Alcfrith), Cade had believed that Cadfael's overtures towards him were genuine. A mistake.

Rhiann, Cadfael's daughter (not by Alcfrith), rescues Cade from hanging and they flee Aberffraw. In the process, Rhiann learns that Cade has been changed by the goddess Arianrhod into one of the sidhe (of a sort, anyway). Eventually, they connect with Cade's men: Rhun (his foster brother), Goronwy, Bedwyr, Taliesin, his seer and bard, Dafydd, Goronwy's younger brother, and Geraint, one of Cade's captains.

Word comes from the south (Llanllugan) that Saxons are encroaching into Wales and Cade leads his men—and Rhiann—into battle. It turns out that the Saxon force has combined with demons, who've been released from the Black Cauldron by Arawn, lord of the Underworld, and are controlled by Mabon, the son of Arawn and Arianrhod.

Adventures ensue, including the defeat of this combined demon/Saxon force at Llanllugan, the capture and rescue of Cade at Caer Ddu, the crowning of Cade as King of Gwynedd at

Aberffraw, where he is reunited with his mother, and the assault on Arawn's lair underneath Caer Dathyl by Cade and his friends.

The Last Pendragon ends in a clearing outside of Caer Dathyl. Arianrhod has rescued them from Arawn's cavern and set them to rights. She visits Cade, tells him that Mabon has been returned to her, and blesses him.

Thank you for reading *The Pendragon's Quest*. Enjoy!

Tonight the hall of my lord is dark,
With neither fire nor bed.
I will weep a while, then still myself to silence.

Tonight the hall of my lord is dark,
With neither fire nor song.
Who will give me peace?

Tonight the hall of my lord is dark,
With neither fire nor hope.
Grief for you overtakes me.

Darkness descends on the hall of my lord
The blessed assembly has departed, praying
That good comes to those of us who remain.

—Taliesin, *The Black Book of Gwynedd*

Prologue

Arianrhod

"You can't rely on hope, Sister. You know that."

I leaned over the rail of the boat, trailing my fingers in the water and ignoring my brother, Gwydion, as I usually did. He might be a great warrior, and my senior by millennia, but what he didn't know about matters of the heart could fill Taliesin's great tome.

I grasped Gwydion's hand as he helped me onto the shore and then tilted my head to feel the warmth of the sun on my face. Mist had descended on the water as I'd made the journey across the sea, moving from the human world to that of the *sidhe*. But the sun always shone on my Isle of Glass.

"Arianrhod—"

"I am listening, Gwydion, but you have never been a parent and cannot know what it means to have a son. Mabon is my child—"

"You may wear a *glamour* in the human world," Gwydion said, "but I have never seen it cloud your thinking as it has in this case. You can't fix this merely by wishing. Mabon has left you, and if you can't find him before another does, he will face the greatest punishment our kind can inflict on one of its own."

"I know that," I said.

And I did. If the *Sidhe* Council, of which I was a member and which my mother and father had ruled through all the ages of the world, discovered that Mabon sought the Thirteen Treasures of Britain, they would strip him of his powers and condemn him to walk the earth as a human man. The Treasures were great gifts of the *sidhe* to the Welsh, the possession of only a handful of which would give Mabon enough power to usurp my father's seat.

My father, Beli, had described his command of the Council as akin to riding an untamed horse. With the coming of the Christian God and the failing of the old ways, it seemed at times as if he'd dropped the bridle. He would want to make an example of Mabon to prove that this was not the case.

Mabon might not survive such a fall from grace.

"What of your champion? This Cadwaladr ap Cadwallon— can he help?" Gwydion said.

"Not this time," I said.

Cadwaladr ap Cadwallon, the future High King of Wales, might prevail over his Saxon enemies and thwart my son's plans again, but I couldn't depend upon it, not without interfering in the human world myself more than my father would condone.

"Besides, he hates Mabon."

Gwydion snorted laughter. "For good reason. But Cadwaladr doesn't hate you. He has served you well in the past."

I had given Cadwaladr the power of the *sidhe,* and because of that gift, he had succeeded in banishing Arawn, Mabon's father, to the Underworld. Arawn, at least, wouldn't be interfering in human affairs for some time to come. In addition, Beli had spoken harshly to him of his foolish actions—of stepping beyond his mandate as the Lord of the Underworld. That Arawn had done so out of love for Mabon couldn't excuse the error. It was probably better not to dwell upon what my father might say about my own meddling, which admittedly, was unlike me. I hadn't had a true champion among humankind for centuries—I hadn't wanted one nor seen the need.

"Will you help me, Gwydion?" I said. "Will you find Mabon for me before our father discovers what he's trying to do?"

Gwydion gazed over my shoulder, towards Wales, though of course he couldn't see it from where we stood. For a moment his face was shadowed, as if a cloud had crossed the sun. But that couldn't be … could it?

"I have distanced myself from the human world of late. You know that."

"The bard, Taliesin—" I said.

"No longer *sees*," Gwydion said. "He is the last of his line. Given that, I've seen little use in furthering my patronage." He focused on me and though his face was bright, my memory of the shadow hadn't faded. "It is a fine line we walk, Arianrhod. I sometimes wonder why we ever desired interaction with humans at all."

I couldn't make sense of that so I changed the subject. "Speak to Taliesin now. He will not have forgotten you."

"I'll think about it," Gwydion said.

"What do you fear?" The words burst from me, though I'd never known Gwydion to fear anything.

"We are fading, Arianrhod. Our power wanes, even as Father strives to rule the council as he always has, hanging onto his dignity with both hands—while Mabon tries to take it from him."

"The sun still shines ..."

"Don't be a child, Arianrhod," Gwydion said. "A darkness has crept into the world, filling the chasm between us and this new God of the Christians. It stands now as a barrier between me and my servant, Taliesin."

"I don't believe it," Arianrhod said. "You are the son of Beli. You can do anything."

Gwydion pursed his lips. "If I do as you ask, if I renew my ties with Taliesin, you must promise me something."

"Anything." Hope rose within me. Gwydion was wavering.

"You must go to our father and reassure him of our loyalty. You are the goddess of battle, as well as time and fate. Look to your duties and stop trying to protect your son. He does not deserve your love." Gwydion's eyes bored into me.

"And Cadwaladr?" I said.

"Leave him to his fate." Gwydion turned away, ending the conversation. He strode away from me, into the mist.

"I don't know if I can do that." Though I'd allowed my brother to vanish before I answered him.

Part One

1

March, 655 AD

Cade

"Wake up!"

Cade had been dreaming of the battle in Arawn's cavern. His stomach hurt from clenching it in his fear and desperation. Even with Arawn's defeat, his people were still in danger. Geraint and Tudur would soon face a host of demons which Arawn had unleashed, in such numbers as Geraint could never hope to counter.

"Goddamn it, Cade, don't scare us like this." That was Rhun's voice. His foster brother had always been one for telling Cade what to do.

"Oh please, please, wake up, Cade."

Cade's eyes snapped open.

Rhiann gazed down at him, her face six inches from his. They looked at each other for one of her heartbeats before she threw herself at him and wrapped her arms around his neck. "I was so worried! It was as if you were really dead!"

Cade's arms came around Rhiann. He reveled in the feel of her, kissed her forehead, and patted her several times on the back, trying to get her to look at him again. Tears tracked down her cheeks as he brushed her hair out of his face with one hand.

After another reassuring look, Rhiann released him and sat back on her heels. Cade pushed onto both elbows, studying his friends who formed a circle around him: Rhun, whose deeper voice he'd heard; Dafydd, a bit wide-eyed, clenching and unclenching his large fists; Goronwy and Hywel, mirror images of each other, not in looks but in temperament, their swords out and half-turned away, ever watchful for potential menace; and Taliesin, who gazed at him reflectively while leaning on his staff.

"*From the seer who no longer sees, I, Taliesin, speak of Cadwaladr ap Cadwallon—who calls usurpers to account, who vanquishes demons, who, with his magic sword, banished Arawn to the Underworld—*"

"All right, all right. Enough." Cade scrambled to his feet. "Next you'll say something about escaping Aberffraw without help, or battling the storm that shipwrecked us in the world of the *sidhe* and saving you single-handed." He glared at Taliesin. "None of which would be true."

Cade's critique didn't seem to affect Taliesin. "You are not normally one to sleep."

"I haven't slept too long, have I? The sun isn't yet up, is it?" Cade checked the skyline above the trees that surrounded the clearing in which the companions found themselves. No light showed on the eastern horizon and Cade allowed himself a moment of relief. Then he noted the location of the moon, and stared at it, puzzled, for it was in the same spot it had been when Arianrhod had visited him after they defeated Arawn. He could have sworn their conversation had occurred hours ago, but if he'd really slept, perhaps that wasn't something he had the ability to gauge.

"Not for a long while yet," Rhun said. "Or, at least that's my feeling. I don't have a good sense of the hour."

"Nor I," Taliesin said. "And that disturbs me." He studied Cade some more. "Has something happened we should know about?"

Cade bit his lip. His friends weren't going to like this. "Arianrhod visited me." There was no good way to say it, except straight out.

Taliesin narrowed his eyes at Cade. "And ..."

"She apologized, not so much for giving me the power of the *sidhe* but for bringing us into such danger."

"She apologized?" Rhun said. "That's—that's—"

Taliesin finished for him. "Unprecedented."

"She also thanked us for doing what she could not," Cade said.

"You're being polite." Goronwy glanced at Cade, flashed a smile, and then looked away again. "She thanked *you*, you mean."

Cade had to acknowledge that Goronwy was right, though he hadn't wanted to say it. "If that was an oversight on her part, allow me to thank you now, if not for her, then for myself. I couldn't have defeated Arawn without you."

"Modesty at last," Goronwy said.

Cade ignored that, as Goronwy deserved. "She also gave me two gifts."

Taliesin took a step towards Cade, his face paling. "Don't tell me you accepted them! A gift from a goddess is never without price!"

Cade choked on a laugh. "Did I have a choice? Need I remind you how little control I have over the goddess?"

"That would be none," Rhun said.

Taliesin nodded and subsided, his expression grudging. "She made you so you could do her bidding. I have not forgotten."

"I would like to think these new gifts were in thanks and not in expectation of future services," Cade said, "although I suppose I'll have as little choice in the matter then as now, were she to ask more of me. As it is, she gave me the gift of sleep, as you saw."

"So you *were* sleeping!" Rhiann said. "I could hardly credit it."

"... and the ability to do this." Cade reached for Rhiann again, pulling her to him. She fit perfectly in his arms—as he remembered from their brief interlude underneath Caer Dathyl— tucked under his chin with her slender arms tight around his waist, holding on. Laughter bubbled in his throat at how natural it felt to hold her.

"So this means you can touch me now—can touch any one of us—without fear of doing us harm?" Rhiann leaned back to look into Cade's face.

"So it seems," Cade said.

Rhun stooped to pick up Caledfwlch, which lay on the edge of the blanket, a yard from Cade's feet. The companions gazed at the sword and Rhun held it out. Rhiann took it, with a wary look at Cade. "You told me when we first met that your touch had the power to kill. I've seen you use it. And struggle to contain it."

Cade had been unable to touch anyone—unless he meant to kill them—since Arianrhod had changed him from man to *sidhe* two winters earlier. From the moment he'd found Caledfwlch at the enchanted Caer Ddu, however, the sword had given him both a strength and a control over his power that he'd never known before. He'd only allowed himself to admit to loving Rhiann because of it, because the sword gave him a chance—a slim one, but a chance—at a normal life.

Rhiann drew the belt around Cade's waist and buckled on his sword, fumbling a bit with the stiff leather. He studied her downturned head and then looked at Taliesin. It was he who would best understand what Arianrhod had done to him and what she'd changed.

"I still have the power," he said. "But it's quiet, as if it's waiting for me to use it rather than waiting to use me."

"That's all to the good," Taliesin said, "but something tells me that Arianrhod isn't finished with you yet."

"And if she's not done with Cade, we're all in for it," Rhun said.

"I'm sure you have the right of it," Cade said, "but for now..."

"For now, we need to move," Goronwy said. While they'd talked, he'd surveyed the entire perimeter of the clearing. It was thirty feet across, surrounded by leafless trees. A fire pit sat at its center, the flames still burning brightly, though to Cade's knowledge, nobody had stoked it. "I, too, am confused about many things, but I do know that we still have the demons from Caer Dathyl to deal with. Geraint and Tudur need our help."

Demons came in all shapes and sizes, often with horns or fur: the manifestation of a child's nightmare, only worse. Much worse, because they weren't created in a dream, but were real, sent through the black cauldron by Arawn, Lord of the Underworld, to haunt the fields and forests of Wales. Few were able to pass as human, as Cade could, and he'd met no other demons who possessed his particular gifts, if one could call them that, nor his degree of power. It seemed that Arianrhod had bestowed his affliction only on him.

"Where are we?" Rhun said. "That remains our most pressing question, although some information as to how we got here wouldn't go amiss."

Cade checked the moon again. It still hadn't moved from its initial position. Come to think on it, the moon was nearly in the same place in the sky as when they'd entered the caverns underneath Caer Dathyl.

"As to how, we can certainly make a good guess," Taliesin said. "Arianrhod took us from the cavern, set us to rights, and has put us on a path of her choosing. As to where..."

"I know where we are." Dafydd turned slowly on one heel, studying the trees and the sky above them. "We're still in Arfon, not far from Caer Dathyl. I came through here when I fled the fortress after Teregad gave me leave to go, back before I fell in with you."

"He gave you leave to go, only to hunt you down afterwards," Goronwy said, correcting his younger brother, "but that's past and done. Are we near the road?"

"It lies a hundred yards to the west, no more." Dafydd peered at the skyline. "I believe Arianrhod has placed us just to the north of where Geraint and Tudur were supposed to set up camp."

"What—so now we can fly?" Rhun said.

Gone was the jesting tone of before. His words came out bitter and Cade catalogued the list of crazed events that had happened to them in the last twelve hours, wondering which of them most troubled Rhun and caused his anger.

"How helpful of Arianrhod not to put us in the path of the oncoming demons," Goronwy said. "Just think if she'd put us between them and Geraint's camp."

Cade eyed both Goronwy and Rhun, and then took charge before the others caught their discontent. "Lead on, Dafydd. It's likely we have very little time, if we have any time at all, before the demons reach Geraint's position."

Dafydd set off at once through the trees, Taliesin close behind, the little light on the end of his staff lighting the way. Rhiann, who'd found her quiver and bow and slung them on her back, followed with Hywel. Cade, Goronwy, and Rhun brought up the rear.

"What's gotten into you two?" Cade said, once the others had moved a bit ahead and the three of them could speak more privately.

He pushed through a blackberry bramble: the rich, sweet scent of sun-warmed berries saturated the air. In another life, Cade would have eaten them but now they would taste like nothing more than sawdust in his mouth. The bramble had found a niche at the edge of the trees, cascading over the edge of a rock as it sought sunlight, rather than thriving in the darker, shadier places, like raspberry or blackcurrant. *Or me.*

"This is *wrong*," Rhun said. "I may not be *sidhe*, but even I can feel it."

"Which part?" Cade said.

"Which part isn't?" Goronwy said.

Rhun made a dismissive gesture. "Not so much the goddess, though I'm none too fond of the way she's manipulated you—and through you all of us—these last weeks. But this is too easy; too pat."

"We defeated Arawn—"

"Begging your pardon, my lord," Goronwy said, "but we didn't, not really. You may be *sidhe* and by that power able to silence him for a while, but his actions against us—against Wales—

- 8 -

and our reactions, with the help of Arianrhod, are the start of what looks to me like open warfare between the gods—and maybe between the gods and men."

"That's exactly it." Rhun nodded and punctuated his words with a finger to the sky. "The gods haven't interfered in our world since the Romans came. They didn't even step in to save Vortigern as he lay dying and the Saxons overran all of Britain but our small corner. Why do they arise now? And what role do we have to play in it? Do we have to be on Arianrhod's side just because she made you? Are there other sides besides Arawn's or Mabon's?"

It had been Cade's ancestor, Vortigern, who'd invited the Saxons into Britain after the Romans left, hoping they would stand as a buffer against the even more barbaric Picts who raided Briton's shores at every turn. As he'd been fighting the Picts in the northeast, the Scots in the northwest, and the Irish along the coast of Wales all at the same time, one could hardly blame Vortigern for latching onto a convenient solution. He'd given up too much land to the Saxons, however, and was betrayed in the end by the very people he'd sought to befriend. Cade's people had been fighting these interlopers ever since, backing further into the mountains with every year that passed.

The Saxon lords had divided the Welsh into small pockets, with the western lands the last untouched bastion of Britain. As recently as two years ago, Cade's uncle Arthur, the great king of Gwent, had sent a lone rider from his seat at Caerleon to Bryn y Castell to warn of the events to the south. Like his northern compatriots, Arthur had fought many battles against the Saxons and feared the Welsh would be reduced to ever shrinking circles of land, fighting back to back as the invaders attacked from all sides.

Cade's birth father, Cadwallon, had formed an alliance with the Saxon King Penda of Mercia, in an attempt to forestall the attacks and regain land for the Welsh. Upon his death, the usurper Cadfael had pledged his forces to the same treaty. But the Welsh had gained nothing from either alliance but time.

Cade swallowed hard. "I'm sorry. I can't answer any of that. And Taliesin..." His voice trailed off.

"Doesn't *see* anymore. Yes, we know," Rhun said, "even if he tries to make light of it."

Cade didn't know how to respond to that either and they continued in silence, eventually gaining on their companions. Cade was both disgruntled by his friends' observations—since he'd been thinking things were going pretty well for once—and dismayed that he heard truth in their words.

Behind Cade, back in his more cynical, jaded, and ultimately humorous shell, Goronwy grumbled yet again about knights not walking.

Rhiann overheard, glanced back at him, and shot him a wicked smile. "You know, Goronwy. You say that knights don't walk, but since I've known you, you've done quite a bit of walking. Either knights do walk, or perhaps you're not a real knight?"

Goronwy growled back at her and Rhiann's eyes lit with amusement. She knew not to take him seriously and Cade's heart warmed to have her with him. That part of the world was going right at least. He was just happy to have all his friends in the same place and in one piece. Although Arianrhod hadn't realized it, that was reward enough.

As the companions trotted on, Cade kept checking the sky, expecting the sun to rise at any moment but it stubbornly refused to show itself. Normally, that would have pleased him, but the oddness of not being able to locate himself in the dark, or in time, only disturbed him instead.

He tried to pass off his disorientation as a result of the heavy cloud cover which had blown in since they'd left the clearing. And when it released its rain a few moments later, it only seemed inevitable, given the way the day and night had gone so far. In Wales, cloud cover in March was more normal than not. Cade told himself he was imagining trouble where there wasn't any, or at least not in the weather. Nobody else gave the rain any notice, other than to pull up the hoods on their wool cloaks.

"I can't believe we're heading back to Caer Dathyl," Hywel said.

They turned onto the road and picked up the pace, able to move more quickly even though the road had become a slough and their boots were coated with mud.

"Hopefully, Siawn's in charge now." Rhiann skirted an enormous puddle by moving to the edge of the road where it met the grassy rim of the forest and Cade followed suit. "He left the cavern just before Arawn fell and I'd like to know for sure what's become of him."

"And Teregad," Hywel said.

"And Mabon," said Rhun. "He has my knife."

Goronwy snorted laughter. "As you left it in his throat, you can hardly blame him for not giving it back."

"It was his knife initially," Cade said. "Do you really want to keep something of his?"

"I suppose not," Rhun said.

"Unless a weapon from the world of the *sidhe* is the only way to harm him, just as with Arawn," Goronwy said.

Taliesin grunted assent and everyone turned to look at him. "I suspect that is true." And then he elaborated further, "I find it likely."

"How about a good punch to the nose?" Dafydd said. "He certainly deserves one."

Even Taliesin laughed at that. "That I could not say. You'll have to try it next time you see him."

"Be that as it may," Cade said, "Arianrhod told me that Mabon *has been returned to her.*"

"What?" Taliesin halted in the middle of the road, down which he'd continued to move boldly, ignoring the puddles, even though his cloak was now six inches deep in mud. "What did you say?" The rain dripped off the end of his pointy nose, which he directed at Cade.

Cade shrugged. "That's all I know. The conversation was rather one-sided and I didn't dare ask what she meant by it."

"My lord!" Ahead of them, Dafydd broke into a run. "Men call to one another ahead of us!"

Taliesin shot Cade another look—a despairing one—which was an expression Cade had never before seen on Taliesin's face.

The other companions ran after Dafydd, but Cade caught Taliesin's arm before he could follow. "You fear the demons?"

"The demons?" Taliesin said. "Why would I fear them?"

"But—"

"It's Mabon," Taliesin said. "Arianrhod may have given you gifts, for which we can't help but be grateful—and which I hope we won't come to regret—but that Mabon is with his mother instead of banished to the Underworld with his father is the worst news possible."

Another shout came from ahead of them as their friends disappeared into the woods to the west of the road. "We must hurry," Cade said. He wished he could question Taliesin more, but they had no time. "We'll talk later."

"We've dragons everywhere we look, my friend," Taliesin said, now jogging beside Cade. "And I suspect that I'm not the only one who is having trouble with his *sight*."

"You can't mean Arianrhod?" Cade said. "Her plan worked out just as she intended, don't you think?"

"I think she left a great deal to chance. I suspect that she would have found several possible outcomes acceptable," Taliesin said.

"I don't like the sound of that," Cade said.

"The gods are taking sides in our world. That can't be good for any of us." Taliesin reached out a hand to Cade and caught his arm. "I cannot *see*, and because the gift has deserted me, I cannot help you. I have lost my bearings."

And though Cade had never understood Taliesin's reliance on his *sight,* he could see the dread in his friend's face. And share it.

2

Rhiann

Dafydd's long strides outpaced Rhiann's smaller, quicker ones, but after his initial head start, she hadn't fallen further behind. She wasn't sure she was ready for another battle but at least this time, she and Dafydd wouldn't be defending helpless women and children on a lonely path all by themselves. They'd fight among the other men, in the thick of things with everyone else. On second thought, maybe that wasn't better after all.

They'd run no more than a quarter of a mile before shapes of men showed through the trees. Rhiann had feared that it might be hard to tell in the dark which side was theirs, but it took only a moment to make that determination: these men had Cade's Dragon Banner waving above their heads and that was the only side she wanted to be on. Dozens of torches lit up the forest and the hillside ahead of them, even as the rain continued to pour down. Cade's men had established their position to take advantage of their strengths. Unlike the demons, they had archers and a significant number of men on horseback.

Just in front of her, Dafydd skidded to a halt. "Wait!" He held out a hand to stop her headlong rush. "We have time. The demons aren't upon them yet."

Now that she'd stopped running, she saw that Dafydd was right. No arrows had yet been loosed. The shouts Dafydd had heard must have been the warning calls that the demons were coming, rather than cries of men in the midst of battle. They'd come upon the scene from the north, with Geraint's forces taking up the hill to the east of their position and the demons marching through the valley to the west, their own torches sputtering and guttering in the falling rain, but still lighting up the night and showing their progress for all to see.

"Better for them to march in the dark so we couldn't guess their numbers," Dafydd said. "Did they think we would quake before them?"

"Mabon probably thought it, he's that arrogant," Rhiann said. Rain plunked on her hood and she brushed her wet hair from her face with her fingers. The humidity in the air pressed on her, heavy with the scent of moist earth and foliage. "I'm not sure these demons do any thinking on their own."

"Geraint couldn't have set this up better if he'd planned it." Goronwy came to stand beside the other two. "He owns the high ground. The demons march along a narrow valley and will be within arrow range for two hundred yards before they reach Geraint's position on the heights."

"What I don't understand is why the demons didn't get here earlier," Rhiann said. "It was after midnight when we entered Caer Dathyl and ages before we reached Arawn's cavern."

"We're some ten miles from Caer Dathyl, give or take," Dafydd said. "It's far, but not so far that I wouldn't have to agree with Rhiann."

"They could have ransacked a village or two on the way," Goronwy said. "That would have slowed them some and isn't outside their capacity."

"Remember what I said about time," Taliesin said, as he and Cade caught up with the others. "It passes differently in the world of the *sidhe* than in this one."

"Of course," Cade said. "Why didn't I think of that before?"

Rhiann moved closer to Cade, comforted by his presence. "You mean just like when we went into Caer Ddu, time passed differently when we were inside Caer Dathyl?"

"That's exactly what I mean," said Taliesin.

"No wonder the moon never moved in the sky," Cade said. "If you hadn't woken me so forcefully, I would have thought myself dreaming still."

Rhiann flashed back to the horrible feeling of Cade's lifeless body beneath her hands. If that was what sleep was to him, she much preferred having him out and about in the middle of the night, even if it sometimes got him into trouble. Because he had no breath or heartbeat, it was as if he had been truly dead.

Two years before, Arianrhod, the goddess of time and fate, had appeared to Cade in the form of a beautiful woman. With no warning, no query or discussion on her part, she had changed him into a *sidhe* of a sort. He'd become a god among men, except that in exchange for power, she'd taken his breath and heartbeat, and maybe even his soul. Arianrhod was a triple goddess—manifesting at different times and circumstances as mother, maiden, or crone.

Cade had lamented to Rhiann more than once that her coming had made him only one thing: a demon. Rhiann had consoled him with the notion that every man feared the beast inside himself, but Cade had countered that in him it became tangible, and each time he released the power of the *sidhe*, it became harder for him to hide.

And it was only when he took a man's life that he felt truly alive.

That was the part of him Rhiann didn't know; didn't ever want to know, though she'd seen it more than once. Yet if they were truly to be together, she would have to come to terms with it. Somehow.

"And then once we left the clearing and the clouds moved in, it was impossible to tell the time at all," Hywel said.

"But surely it hasn't been three days since we entered Caer Dathyl?" Dafydd said.

"No," Taliesin said. "I believe the magic has worked in the opposite fashion this time. By my estimation, it's been only three hours. We've many hours still until dawn."

"Look!" Hywel pointed towards the southern ridge across from the one on which they were standing. "A rider comes!"

"That's Bedwyr," Rhiann said. "I can tell from his bulky shape."

"Let's go." Cade grasped Rhiann's hand and tugged her forward.

"*He's* going to be surprised," Rhun said.

To the companions' amusement, they arrived at Geraint's command post simultaneously with Bedwyr, who dismounted from his horse in front of the pickets.

"What took you so long?" Cade said.

"How—" Bedwyr's mouth opened in astonishment, but then snapped shut. "Don't tell me, I don't want to know."

"It's a long story and worth the hearing." Goronwy clapped Bedwyr on the back in greeting. "Glad to see you made it too, and in one piece."

"I take it by the fact that you stand in front of me that all went well inside Caer Dathyl?" Bedwyr said. "Did you find Arawn?"

"We did," Dafydd said.

"Suffice to say, Teregad has been deposed, Arawn banished to the Underworld where he belongs, and the black cauldron closed," Cade said. "For now."

"There's more, but first, we've some demons to kill," Rhun said.

"Right." Bedwyr blinked. "Glad that's straightened out."

Geraint and Tudur hurried over. "My lords!" Geraint said. "You've come just in time." His eyes scanned the companions and Rhiann could see him counting them to make sure none were missing. His brows furrowed as he got to eight and realized they were one short, but he didn't ask about Siawn. "I trust everyone is well?"

"Very well," Cade said. "What's our situation?"

Geraint nodded at Tudur, who stepped forward to speak. "We've archers arrayed in a half-circle at the crest of the hill. They'll do their work first and we'll see how many demons they can bring down. After that, it will be hand-to-hand, I'm afraid. We don't have enough arrows to take care of all of them."

"We brought you a few more," Dafydd said.

Rhiann glanced at the quiver he wore and the bow in his hand, noting them for the first time. "Where did—"

"It was to hand when I awoke." Dafydd shrugged. "I put it on. Your quiver has more arrows in it than it did too, you know."

Rhiann had been so occupied with Cade that she hadn't noticed that either. Shameful, really, because the first obligation of a warrior was to his weapons. Or hers.

Hywel moved to stand beside Dafydd. "I've arrows as well." He held up a bow and twisted to show the quiver on his back. "It seemed petty to question the gift."

"I know what you mean," Cade said. "Not that any of us would have benefitted from turning the goddess down."

"It's time to move, Cade," Rhun said.

"Right. You three go with Taliesin." Cade stabbed a finger at Dafydd, Rhiann, and Hywel. "And no putting yourselves at undue risk! It would be a shame to have survived Caer Dathyl only to fall to an errant demon axe."

"We'll protect her," Hywel said, taking this as what Cade really meant. Dafydd nodded vigorously beside him.

"Just as likely to be the other way around." Taliesin turned on one heel. "But no matter. Young ones, with me." He set off along the top of the bowl on which they were perched.

Cade called after Rhiann, imitating Bedwyr's growl. "Rhiann—"

"I know. I know." She flapped a hand at him over her shoulder. "I'll be careful."

"You'd better, *cariad*!"

Rhiann waved again and then focused on the task at hand. She walked steadily behind the others until Taliesin came to a halt by a group of archers from Aberffraw. They stood in a row, gazing west towards the relentlessly advancing lines of demons. Rhiann read fear in the set of their shoulders—and perhaps a bit of misery, given the weather conditions. Nobody had yet strung a bow, as the rain would harm the bowstrings. But that meant nobody was really ready for this fight either.

"Lady Rhiannon!" It was Llywelyn, the captain of the Aberffraw garrison. "You're safe and whole!"

"Quite safe," Rhiann said. "I expect you to let me know if my draw isn't as precise as you expect."

"Always, my lady," Llywelyn said, to general laughter. The tension she'd felt in the men on the ridge eased for a moment. Then it ratcheted up again as Dafydd, Hywel, Taliesin, and she took their places alongside them—not *because* of them, but because the demons were approaching arrow range, though they still had a little bit of time.

Taliesin had positioned the four of them on the left flank so they'd be among the first to shoot at the demons. Hopefully, the archers on the other side of the valley, some three hundred yards away, would do the same and together they'd catch the demons in a pincer movement.

"We're going to be all right, Rhiann," Dafydd said. "These demons aren't so tough. We've fought them before."

Rhiann choked on a laugh. In truth, the demons were tougher than humans, as Dafydd knew well. But maybe not as smart. That had to help.

"What's the worst thing that can happen?" Hywel said.

Rhiann wrinkled her nose at his irreverent tone. The worst thing that could happen was when the arrows started flying, the demons would charge at them, thinking to break through their lines, rather than flee the other way. If that happened, if the foot soldiers who stood on the slopes below them couldn't stop them, the archers would be unable to defend themselves adequately. More lightly armed than the rest of the army, they might all die. At least as full-fledged knights, Hywel and Dafydd had swords at their waists. Rhiann had only a knife.

"We planted stakes twenty yards ahead, on the uphill slope," Llywelyn said, reading her thoughts. "If they try to get through them, the stakes will give us time to regroup."

"Or run away," Hywel said. "That means you, Lady Rhiannon."

"At the very least, the stakes will slow the demons down," Dafydd said.

"How did you know the demons were coming?" Rhiann said. "King Cadwaladr sent Bedwyr to warn you of their numbers, but he arrived when we did."

The little light at the end of Taliesin's staff gave off enough illumination to reveal Llywelyn's offended expression. "Scouts, of course. We've been ready for over an hour."

"And what is the hour?" Hywel said.

Taliesin glanced at him and nodded his approval at the question. All of them had wanted to know the answer to that since they'd woken in the clearing.

"Four hours after midnight, I reckon," Llywelyn said. "Less than three until the sun rises."

"Dawn will not save us from the demons this time," Taliesin said. "It will be over by then, come what may."

Now that the demons were closer, the archers settled into whatever stance they found most comfortable. Their joviality and humor, which had been false to begin with, was gone. The leafless branches above their heads continued to drip onto their heads in an offbeat rhythm which Rhiann couldn't help counting out in time to the marching of the demons.

Dafydd slipped a knife from his belt. Like the sword at his waist, the join between the blade and the hilt formed a cross and he kissed it. Hywel, for his part, pulled his sword from its sheath, stabbed it into the ground in front of him, and knelt. Rhiann didn't follow suit, but said her own prayer, perhaps a mirror of his: *Dear*

God, keep me safe. Let all those here return to their homes in one piece, both in body and mind.

Rhiann closed her eyes. As she'd been trained by the captain and friend who taught her to shoot, long ago at Aberffraw, she forced herself to stuff all emotion into a box in her mind and put it away, as if placing it on a shelf out of reach. Cade had told her that some men fought angry and it gave them power. For her, it was better to feel nothing—no anger, hatred, love—for it would distract her from the task at hand and she couldn't afford that. *For now, there is no love for Cade; no fear for my friends; no regret for a life half-lived. There is only the bow in my hand and the arrows in my quiver, with death a widening abyss beneath our feet.*

3

Cade

"The truth now," Cade said, once Rhiann and the others had disappeared up the trail. "What do we face?"

"Two thousand demons," Geraint said.

"That's my count too," Bedwyr said. "I caught up to them an hour out of Caer Dathyl. It was lucky I had a horse to ride because I could never have kept up with them on foot."

Cade looked beyond his companions to the oncoming march of the opposing force. He might be a *sidhe*—changed by Arianrhod into a creature out of legend—but these demons were no legend. He'd fought them for two years on his own, and recently with friends, and knew their strength. Arawn and Mabon would have had confidence that such an army could overpower twice that number of men, and Cade had a paltry eight hundred foot at his disposal. Cade gritted his teeth. He was just going to have to prove Arawn wrong. *Again.*

"The archers are well situated," Geraint said. "Each have a dozen arrows to hand. I have confidence they can bring down a great number of the beasts."

"From what I could see," said Bedwyr, "the demons are not well armored."

"It's too bad we couldn't have delayed them somehow," Tudur said. "The dawn is too far off to count on its aid."

"The dawn might slow them down some, but not as much as it will me," Cade said. "Besides, it's raining. There won't be a sun today. The clouds will protect everyone."

"Right." Rhun rubbed his hands together. "Archers around the sides, foot soldiers to the front as the demons come on, and cavalry to flank them. It's the old way, but the best way."

"One thing they haven't done is send out scouts," Geraint said. "I don't understand it. It's almost as if they knew exactly where we'd be."

"They were being aided by Arawn and who knows what other gods," Cade said. "Arawn may have been banished to the Underworld, but that doesn't mean he's impotent; that doesn't mean we still can't lose everything."

"Or, if Arawn is otherwise occupied, we have Mabon to deal with again," Goronwy said. "He's not in the Underworld with his father, right? Arianrhod was quite clear on that?"

Cade gave Goronwy a curt nod. His stomach roiled at the thought of what Mabon had done and could still do, loose in the world. Arawn hadn't been able to control him, so Cade didn't have much hope that Arianrhod could either.

"It doesn't matter," Rhun said. "Whoever it is, whomever we face, we have no more time."

The companions' horses had come to Arfon with Geraint. Cade was glad to see Cadfan again. The stallion whickered as Cade rubbed his nose. As one, the companions mounted and led the other horsed knights and men-at-arms away from the camp, circling into the trees to the north of the valley through which the demons marched. When the archers had expended their arrows and the foot soldiers had drawn the demons fully into the valley, Cade would lead his cavalry to slam the door behind them.

As they waited for that first flight of arrows, a hush descended on the human watchers, broken only by the muffled march of the demons' feet. Cade had one hundred and fifty men on horseback. How could that be enough? They'd survive only if the archers were able to reduce the numbers of their opponents—and Cade's men were able to catch them unawares.

"Half." Goronwy leaned in to speak to Cade. "If the archers can reduce their numbers by half, that will make us nearly even."

Cade nodded, although he wasn't going to hope for such a positive outcome. Still, the demons had strength but no brains. Maybe that too could tip the balance in their favor.

Then the archers released the first rush of arrows, their passage sounding as much like a flight of birds as wooden shafts, except for the moment they hit. Demons didn't scream their pain. Cade wasn't sure they felt pain, but they felt something and the calls among them were guttural and wrenched the ear.

Goronwy stood in his stirrups, straining his eyes to see through the water-logged air. "What can you see, my lord? My eyes aren't what they used to be."

Cade didn't like the sound of that. Didn't like the idea that any of his companions were growing older with increasing frailties. Not that Goronwy would be frail for a long time, but it highlighted the fact that they didn't yet know if Cade would age alongside Rhiann. Perhaps that was the next gift Arianrhod could give him.

"Second flight ... third flight ... fourth flight ..." Cade counted as the shafts flew past them. "The arrows are finding targets. They're hitting and demons are going down, but they're not turning. They haven't lost enough of their numbers yet."

"That's a side effect of not having a coherent thought," Rhun said. "They don't know when to run because they lack a sense of self-preservation."

"I hoped for a while that returning Arawn to the Underworld would affect them," Cade said. "That they'd lose their motivation to fight."

"I guess not," Goronwy said.

The demons continued to march up the valley, pushing through the flights of arrows and climbing over the fallen bodies of their companions. At one point, Cade thought he heard Rhiann's cry *aim for the neck or heart!* over the rush of battle. He hoped he'd heard it, anyway.

He peered through the darkness, trying to make out what was happening. "They're getting closer now. It's almost time." The barrage of arrows decreased in volume. Still, the demons came on.

"The archers don't have enough arrows." Rhun urged his horse to the edge of the trees. "The demons' numbers are still too great and the arrows they have left they'll need to save for the end."

"I know." Cade met Goronwy's eyes, and then Rhun's.

Rhun nodded and straightened in his seat. What more was there to say?

Cade unsheathed his sword. He'd waited until this moment because as he raised it above his head, Caledfwlch shot light into the sky. The air glittered around it and the light shot into the trees above their heads, reflected off the raindrops, the branches, the burgeoning leaves, the water in the air, and onto the men. Even demons couldn't fail to notice.

Cade stood in his stirrups. "We ride!"

The knights and men-at-arms burst from the trees and rode down the slope in a rush, death a roar on their lips. They came out ten yards from the rear of the demon force and catapulted into it.

One demon after another fell before Cade. It took only a few heartbeats, which neither the demons nor Cade had of course, for the demons to realize that they faced a greater enemy from behind them than from the front. Rhun kept to Cade's left and Goronwy to his right, each chopping and hacking with him.

"By the Saints, they stink!" That was Rhun.

Cade glanced at him, noting the greenish blood coating him and his shield, even as the rain washed it from his face. None of it was red. None of it was his.

Glad for Rhun's dark humor, Cade returned his attention to the creatures in front of him. Horned, furred, bear-like, antlered, from brown to green, even some who looked more human than not. Cade met each one's eyes as they fought, looking for some sign of humanity—some notion of what they were doing beyond mindless killing. He didn't see it and Cade should have known that he never would. Cade himself wanted to hold onto his own humanity as long as possible, but as he hacked and slashed at his foes, he admitted, yet again, that he would do better as a *sidhe,* that it was sheer stubbornness that kept him from releasing the demon that lived inside him. Still, he hesitated.

Cade blocked the axe of a demon who was trying to behead Goronwy. His friend had been a hairs-breadth from going down because of the creature and Cade cursed himself for his stupidity. What was pride when his men's lives were at stake? He needed that *sidhe* within him. It was why Arianrhod had changed him in the first place—not because he was evil like the demons, but because she knew that in order to defeat them, he needed the strength that the world of the *sidhe* gave him.

In the time it took to lift his sword and let it fall, he released his power. It flooded him as if he were standing under a waterfall in full spate, or drawing a deep breath after swimming underwater for too long. Except Cade hadn't drawn breath in two years.

Goronwy spoke from beside Cade. "Mary, Mother of God!"

"What?" Cade plunged his sword into the mass of demons again while half-listening for Goronwy's response.

"You—" Goronwy said.

"Leave it," said Bedwyr from beyond them. "It doesn't matter."

The friends fought on, cutting a swath through the demon line. After the first rush of battle, Cade had led his men up the valley, heading around the perimeter of the demon force, before turning into the central mass of bodies. He'd tried to cut off the bulk of the demons from the foot soldiers, hoping to alleviate the pressure on them and divide the demon force. In that, they'd been successful, to the point that some of the demons at the western end of the valley had finally turned to run away.

At the same time, a few had gathered on the far side of the field for a counter-attack. Once he saw the danger, Cade called to his men. "To me! To me!"

A dozen formed up and charged with him. Again, Cade's arm rose and fell in a deadly monotony until he came out the other side and turned Cadfan, looking to renew the fight. Bedwyr pulled up in front of him, however, blocking his path back, and the red cleared from Cade's vision.

"You've done enough, my lord," Bedwyr said "By the grace of the gods and your power, the demons are almost done."

With that, Cade came completely to himself. Bedwyr was right. Cade pointed with his sword to the demons who'd begun to flee and Goronwy understood without him speaking.

"I'll take them, my lord." Goronwy stood in his stirrups and raised his voice. "After them!"

"Go with him, Bedwyr," Cade said. "I'll clean up here." His friends spurred their horses away, leaving only Rhun beside him.

Cade let them go in favor of killing a few more demons. He urged his horse back across the field. But as he and Rhun rode forward, the remaining demons scrambled to get out of their way, tripping over each other in their haste and desperation. It was as if Cade had dropped boiling oil on an anthill. The demons streamed away in all directions, too quickly for Cade or Rhun to keep up, even on horseback—not with the piles of dead surrounding them on every side. His shoulders sagging in relief, Cade pulled up in the center of the field and turned again to Rhun.

"Do you know what Goronwy was talking about earlier?"

Rhun rested his sword in his shoulder and a smile hovered around his lips. "I couldn't say."

That clearly wasn't the whole truth. "It isn't as if Goronwy hasn't seen me fight before—he's seen what I become," Cade said. "You all have."

Now, Rhun laughed, and it was an incongruous sound given the rain and the battle. He lifted his sword and gestured to the fleeing demons with it. "This time, even I have to admit that you look different. You can't tell yourself?"

"Tell what—?" Cade said and then stopped, finally taking a good look at himself and seeing what everyone else couldn't help but notice. In the past, when he'd allowed the power to flow through him, he'd looked different from his normal self, he knew.

His eyes shimmered green and he emitted an aura that was just short of tangible—at least according to Rhiann. Now, however, he *glowed* with a white light. He glanced at Rhun. "How—"

Rhun shrugged. "Arianrhod's doing, I imagine. I'm sure Taliesin will have something compelling to say about it. But for now, it seems you've driven the demons mad."

And it was true. The demons who remained were running in circles, falling either upon their own blades or that of Cade's men, whom they'd ceased trying to avoid or even fight. Watching them, Cade held the door to his power open even further. It flooded him and through him. He was light itself, fire itself, and like Caledfwlch, shot sparks and diamonds in every direction.

Rhun smirked and urged his horse towards their own lines. Once he was sure no demon remained alive within two hundred yards, Cade moved to follow. Although he couldn't help those who'd already died, of which there would be far too many, Caledfwlch could heal the injured.

Next would come the part of battle that men usually didn't talk about. After a fight, it wasn't horror or fear or revulsion that a man felt, but utter joy at having survived another day: *I am alive! And my enemy is not! Against all odds, I will live to see another sunrise!* At the same time, he couldn't help but acknowledge that he'd known from the start that the fight was going to go his way. It always had. He believed it always would. That probably wasn't something he should share with Rhiann. Cade almost smirked too, mocking himself for his pretensions to grandeur.

This post-battle optimistic and joyful feeling was generally followed, in Cade's case, by chills—purely emotional now, for his physical body no longer reflected what went on inside his mind. In the past, too, the final stage was exhaustion. Even though he no longer felt it, it was important to remember that his men did and make allowances. Cade lifted his eyes to the heavens. The fat drops of rain hadn't let up for a single heartbeat during the battle. Now, they washed the grime from his face, a loathsome mix of mud and demon blood.

And that was when he saw it. At first the demon didn't register as a demon: it was a boar, and far bigger than any he'd seen in all the years of hunting and stalking the woods of his land at night. It was far larger than the hounds they'd defeated outside the walls of Caer Dathyl. The boar's red eyes glowed as they stared at each other—and then the creature coiled itself like a cat and leapt at Cade.

His first thought was: *boars don't leap!*

And then Cade brought up his shield to block the attack. But the boar had moved so quickly, even Cade's reflexes couldn't deflect him. He barreled into Cade and brought him off Cadfan. It was a move Cade had used many times himself because it was an effective means of disabling an opponent. Cade shouldn't have been surprised. Just last night, Dafydd had brought down one of the humans at Caer Dathyl with the same technique—it was just the timing, force, and speed that he'd failed to predict.

Cade fell to the ground, the boar on top of him. If Cade had breath, it would have been knocked from him. As it was, the back of his head snapped into the ground and with a tangible *whoosh*, the power that had fed him over the last half hour sucked back into his center as if a whirlpool had replaced the flame. The boar's front hooves rested on Cade's chest and it brought its snout and horns to within inches of Cade's flesh. Cade stared at the demon and tried to gather his wits. "Who are you?"

The boar grunted, but then spoke as no boar could. "Silence! Do not bother me with trivialities."

"My men—"

The beast barked what could only have been a laugh. "Only you can see me."

"But—"

The boar snarled again. "I have a message for you. You may have spoiled Mabon's plans; you may have closed the black cauldron, but he is still among us; Mabon walks the earth and I with him. I will always be here. Give me what I seek and I may let your friends live."

"What is it you seek?" Cade spoke clearly now that he didn't have to force the words through a constricted throat. He understood that the boar wouldn't kill him, and perhaps didn't have the power to kill him.

"Someone will come," the boar said. "Be ready."

Then he vanished.

Cade tried to lift his head to rise, but his body wouldn't respond. He lay back, confused and exhausted.

"My lord!" Rhun's uncharacteristic use of his title scared Cade almost more than the boar had. Rhun's concerned face appeared above him. He leaned down from the saddle, his face a mask of worry.

Cade blinked again and the battlefield came into focus. All was as he'd left it. "Did you see it?"

Rhun dismounted and fell to his knees beside Cade. "See what? Are you all right?" He patted Cade down, looking for wounds.

Cade brushed his hands away. "I'm fine. But I've had another visit from the *sidhe*."

4

Rhiann

"Cade!"

Rhiann screamed his name. She'd not seen what had pushed him off his horse, but there was no mistaking the moment he fell from Cadfan and his power collapsed. When he'd first released the *sidhe* within himself, white light had flashed throughout the field. It had blinded Rhiann and because of it, she'd released an arrow accidently and wasted it. It had sailed off over the trees to the south. She hoped if it hit anyone, it was a fleeing demon. After that, Cade had shone like a beacon on a rocky point, guiding his people to him and scattering their enemies before him.

She'd stood beside her friends, pressing and loosing arrow after arrow. The demons had never reached the stakes that Llywelyn had ordered set, and when she'd released her last arrow and stepped back, she'd found herself calmer than she ever would have expected during a battle. Even along the trail by Llanllugan, it hadn't been fear of dying that had overwhelmed her, but fear of failure: that she and Dafydd might not be able to protect all the women and children who depended on them, and only them, for their survival. That had been a test unlike any she'd ever imagined. This had been target practice by comparison.

She'd made her arrows count and had killed over a dozen demons by herself. Combined with her friends, they'd killed a hundred, and among the full compliment of archers in both companies, had killed nearly a thousand before they'd run out of arrows. It hadn't been enough to turn the tide, but it had winnowed them more than a little. Enough to give Cade what he'd needed.

Now, she gazed towards the center of the battlefield, peering through the pre-dawn murk for sign of Cade, who must have killed a hundred all by himself. She'd kept watch on his form out of the corner of her eye as she'd fired the last of her arrows.

"Wait—I see him," Dafydd said. "He's all right. Rhun's with him."

"What could have happened?" she said. "One instant he was fine and then he was on the ground. Nobody came close to him. Perhaps he's ill. Could it have been something Arianrhod did to him?" She strained to stop her voice from going high in her anxiety.

"We'll know soon enough," Hywel said.

Rhiann didn't intend to wait. She ran for the path that led down from the ridge. With the demons scattered and no arrows left in her quiver, she couldn't do any more good here anyway. Once she made sure Cade was really all right, she would help the wounded. Hopefully, with Cade's healing sword, they could save many who might otherwise have died.

She hadn't taken more than ten steps, however, before Taliesin appeared in front of her, blocking her way. He stood unmoving and unseeing. Although her heart told her to hurry and she was worried about Cade, she didn't go around him. Instead, she pulled up short and touched his arm. "Taliesin?"

He blinked and focused on her face. "I must go."

"What?"

As she gazed into the depths of his eyes, a pool of sorrow welled up inside her—whether for him, from him, because of what she saw there, she didn't know. She'd never seen such a look of sorrow in another person's face, not even in Alcfrith, Cade's mother.

"Tell King Cadwaladr that I will meet him at Deganwy Castle for your wedding, but I have business to the east," he said.

"Wedding—what? Taliesin!" Rhiann reached for his arm but he'd already melted into the woods. She gazed after him, uncertain whether to follow him. He obviously didn't want her near him or he would have asked her to come with him, but would Cade want him to go off on his own, especially with stray demons about?

Dafydd had been conferring with Tudur and now hurried over. "What was that about? Where's Taliesin?"

"Gone," she said, still stunned by his sudden departure. "He said he'd meet us at Deganwy."

"What are you talking about? When?"

"I-I-I don't know," she said. "I don't know any of that. He's just gone." She didn't want to tell Dafydd that Taliesin said he would meet Cade at their wedding, not without talking to Cade first. *I need to see him!*

Rhiann fled down the hill, running hard towards the spot where Cade had fallen. She leapt over the bodies of men and demons, ignoring everything but the bulky shadow of Cadfan who stood where Cade had left him, his head up and his ears pricked forward.

"Rhiannon, he's fi—!" Rhun tried to stop her headlong rush but she barreled past him.

Rhiann fell to her knees beside Cade who lay just as he had that morning, for all intents and purposes, dead. "Why is this happening again!" She put a hand on either side of Cade's face and pressed her lips to his. She released him and to her relief, he opened his eyes.

"It is as Rhun said." Cade brought up his hands and grasped each of hers.

"Sorry." Rhiann glanced at Rhun.

Rhun shrugged. "I thought he had perished too, at first."

"What happened?" Rhiann glared at Rhun. "I thought you were supposed to protect him!"

"Rhiann, please." Cade ran a hand over his eyes. "My limbs feel heavy still."

Rhun held a hand out to Cade. "Let me help you up." Cade grasped his hand and pulled to a sitting position and then unsteadily to his feet.

Rhiann gazed up at him, unexpected tears tracking down her cheeks. Cade looked down at her, and then put his hand under her chin. "Come here."

Rhiann allowed him to pull her up too and fold her into his arms until she sighed and relaxed. "I'm sorry again, Rhun," she said. "I know how impossible it is to protect Cade if he doesn't want protection."

"I heard your love for him," Rhun said. "But the truth is, I didn't see anything amiss until Cade was on the ground."

"Nobody but I did," Cade said. "Nobody but I could. Rhun couldn't have protected me in this case, even were he standing beside me."

"Tell me," Rhiann said.

"If you could pardon the wait, I'd like to tell the story only once," Cade said. "Taliesin must hear it too. Where is he?" He scanned the ridge above the field.

"I don't know how to tell you this," Rhiann said, "so I'm just going to say it—Taliesin's gone. He said he had business to the east and he would meet you at Deganwy for our wedding."

Cade's arms tightened around her. "I feared he'd leave us. I could see the compulsion in his eyes the moment he confessed that he could no longer *see*, way back on the road to Bryn y Castell. That knowledge has haunted both of us every day since." Cade barked a laugh that didn't sound amused at all. "I guess we know where we'll be getting married though, don't we, *cariad*?"

Rhiann choked on a laugh that his cloak muffled. "I guess." It wasn't quite the proposal she'd imagined, but then, he was holding her as if he would never let her go and that was far more than enough.

"It was a demon in the shape of a boar," Cade said. At Rhun's exclamation of dismay he added, "... a manifestation that only I could see and that could only affect me, or so it said and so it appears."

"Not a regular demon, then," Rhun said.

"No," Cade said. "He told me he wanted something from me and that he would send an emissary soon to ask for it."

"Did he say what?" Rhiann said.

"Or who he was?" Rhun said.

"No."

"Besides, who manifests as a boar?" Rhiann said. "I can't think of any gods off the top of my head—."

Cade made one of his forceful sighs. He loosened his arms around Rhiann enough to tuck her under his shoulder and then tipped his head back to look up at the clouds above him and let the rain pit-patter onto his face. "I can think of one, but it isn't going to make anyone very happy."

"Are you telling me that it was Mabon?" Rhiann said.

"No," Cade said. "It wasn't, which is precisely what concerns me. Taliesin said that the gods were taking sides in the world of the *sidhe* and it meant they would among us as well."

"So who do you think it was?" Rhun said.

"The only god who manifests as a boar that I've heard of is Camulos, a god of war," Cade said.

Rhun nodded, grudgingly. "That would make sense."

"So Mabon has other allies now, besides Arawn," Rhiann said. "That's what you're telling me?"

"It looks like it," Cade said.

"Yet Mabon is with Arianrhod now," Rhun said, "and she appears to think he's on her side."

Rhiann pressed the back of her hand to her forehead, trying to ease the stabbing ache that had formed behind her eyes. "If it was really Camulos who attacked you, it sounds to me as if Mabon is still playing the same game he was playing when he was with Arawn. He's just enlisted some otherworldly help."

Cade nodded. "Unfortunately for us, I think you're right."

"And if that's the case," Rhun said. "Does Arianrhod have allies too? Or is it just you on whom she depends?"

Now Cade shook his head and gave a half-defeated shrug. "I don't know. But if I'm all she's got, it's hardly going to be a fair fight."

5

Cade

To have an emissary from Mabon approach him like this just when Taliesin took it upon himself to disappear was more than irksome. *Just when I needed him.* And then Cade chastised himself for that kind of thinking. As it was, it was likely that Taliesin *was* thinking of Cade, he'd seen what had happened to him, known something about it, and run off because the answers lay somewhere else. That Taliesin didn't *see* anymore only made it that much worse.

"We've wounded, Cade," Rhun said as they left the battlefield.

Cade shook off his dazedness. He checked the sky. A few moments remained before sunrise—long enough to see to a few men who were too hurt to move to the trees. "Organize some stretchers," Cade said. "I'll help here while I can."

"Over here, Cade." Rhiann had dismounted and begun moving among the fallen men and demons. There were plenty of both. The man she chose to succor first was a foot soldier who had a gash along his upper thigh. The wound was similar to many Cade had seen. Soldiers were taught to aim at an opponent's neck or limbs because armor that was difficult to penetrate without forceful pressure protected the rest of the body. A slash wouldn't do it. Head wounds too, were common.

Cade crouched and lifted the man's hand to touch the hilt of Caledfwlch. "What's your name?"

"Llelo, my lord. The demons—" The man broke off, seemingly unable to articulate further.

"They're frightening, aren't they?" Rhiann said. "Everyone's frightened of them."

"You have it right, my lady." Llelo sighed and closed his eyes.

Cade watched the healing of the man's wound. Another few heartbeats and it disappeared altogether without leaving even a slight scar. Cade snorted a laugh. A man might regret its total absence. It was well known that a strategically-placed scar might aid in courtship of a lady. Cade pressed a hand to the man's shoulder. "Wait a moment while you get your breath."

The man opened his eyes and pushed himself onto his elbows. He stared at the smooth skin where a moment before he'd been bleeding out. "Wait, you—"

Cade turned away, not wanting to hear the man's horrified protest, even if Cade had saved his life. When it didn't come, Rhiann spoke instead, "King Cadwaladr must seek the shelter of the trees now. If you could help bring the wounded to him, he might be able to save most of them. He hopes to aid them as he has aided you."

"Of course, my lady! Anything!" Cade glanced back to see Llelo rub his leg one more time and then pop to his feet. "It's a miracle!" Llelo held out his arms, twisting his hands back and forth as if he'd just discovered them, and then gazed past Rhiann to Cade. "Thank you, my lord!"

Cade gave him a small smile and turned away, more content with his so-called gift than perhaps he'd ever been before. He looked towards the trees at the top of the ridge. Rhun stood above him, waving a hand to get his attention. Cade lifted his own hand in acknowledgement and picked up his pace. His head had begun to pound. With the rain lessening in conjunction with the rising sun, he needed to get himself safe.

"Over here, Cade," Rhun said.

While Cade had been working, so had others: collecting armaments, clearing the demons from the grass and tossing them onto an ever-growing pile, and preparing food and drink for the survivors, of which, Cade was glad to see, there were many. He'd feared, in the first moments of battle, that none at all would survive the onslaught.

"Do you need ...?" Rhun gestured towards a roped pig, one of many that the army had brought with them as food. The pig gazed placidly at Cade, unaware of its lack of a future.

Cade checked himself internally. "Not now. Not unless the cooks were going to butcher him anyway."

Rhun peered at Cade curiously. "Are you sure? It's been a long night, and it was an even longer day before that."

Cade probed his insides, at that well of power that now lay quiescent. "I'm sure."

*   *   *   *   *

Many hours later, covered in blood but with a light heart, Cade gestured to Rhun to bring him the last wounded man. As with all the others over the course of the long morning of labor, Cade reached for the man's hand, intending to put it on Caledfwlch's hilt.

But instead of acquiescing, the man tried to throw himself off the stretcher. "Stay away from me, demon!" His motion only succeeded in opening wider the wound that gaped in his belly. "I've been watching! I know what you are!"

Cade brought back his hand. "I've made no secret of it from the start. If you don't want to live…"

"I'm sorry, my lord." Tudur had his hands on the man's shoulders, holding him down. "We thought he'd changed his mind."

Cade sat back on his heels. This man should have been one of the first to come to him. As it was, Cade was glad he was the last. This was the response he'd expected from Llelo, but as each of the wounded had come to him and left healed and grateful, he'd put his trepidation from his mind. The man was correct that no gift from the world of the *sidhe* came without a price, but in this matter, it was Cade who paid it, not those he helped.

Rhiann stepped in and leaned over the wounded man. She put her hand to his forehead. "King Cadwaladr can help you."

"Jesus save me!"

Cade got to his feet. "I'm not Jesus. I have no jurisdiction over your soul, but I could save your life if you'd let me." The words came out more dry and detached than he expected. After a canter around his emotions, Cade realized that was how he really felt. He could let this man die if that was what he wanted. He'd saved too many today to allow one man's opinions to bring him low.

"No!" The man grew more agitated.

Rhiann tried again. "We know that death is not evil. But those demons weren't of this world. You don't need to die because of them."

The man gargled at her, still protesting despite the blood filling his mouth, and fell back.

"Let him go." Rhun stepped in to block the man from Cade's view.

Cade tugged on the edge of Rhiann's cloak to get her to look at him. "It's all right."

"No it's not!" Rhiann's voice was full of anguish.

"If this is what he wants, I can't argue with him," Cade said. "I'm exactly what he thinks I am."

"He has a wife and three children who might wish he'd made a different choice," Rhun said.

"He's so wrong about you." Rhiann reached up and brushed back a strand of hair that had come lose from the tie at the base of Cade's neck.

Cade clasped her hand. "Thank you. Until I met you, I feared that I was like those demons. You've helped me understand that I'm not."

"If he would just open his eyes, he would know it too." Rhiann craned her neck to look around Rhun at the man, tears in her eyes at his pain and their impotence.

Her profession of staunch support reminded Cade ... he pulled her back to him. "Taliesin spoke of a wedding," he said.

"He did." Rhiann's bright eyes flashed at him.

"Out in the field I didn't do the comment justice," Cade said. "I haven't asked you to marry me yet. We've never actually spoken of it."

Rhiann waited, not giving him any help at all, just gazing at him with those bottomless brown eyes.

He brought his forehead down to hers. "Rhiannon ferch Cadfael, will you do me the honor of becoming my wife?"

"Trust you to ask me on the edge of a battlefield," she said. "But at least it was a battle we won."

"I can't promise you anything but my love," he said. "We might not have a roof over our heads tomorrow; we might not survive the war against the Saxons we know is coming. And then we might. You might even become Queen of Wales."

Rhiann laughed at that. "Are you trying to get me to say no?"

"I'm giving you the truth." He lowered his voice further. "I can't even promise you children." Those last words caught in his throat. He'd overheard Rhiann talking to Bronwen about how much she wanted children and what it might mean to her never to have them.

"I know." Rhiann tightened her arms around his neck. "But I'll marry you despite, and because of all that."

Cade wrapped his arms around her waist and kissed her until she ran out of breath.

Rhun spoke from behind Rhiann. "Doesn't anyone do any work around here besides me?"

Cade reluctantly released Rhiann and smiled at his friend. "Rhiann has consented to become my wife."

"That, alone, is an excellent outcome for the day." Rhun rubbed his hands together. "She's a much better choice than that last girl. Far more reliable."

"What—?" Cade said.

Rhun laughed. "Arianrhod. Isn't she the only other woman you've ever kissed? I just meant her."

Cade smiled at his friend. That wasn't quite the truth, as Rhun well knew, but Cade didn't even remember that boy he'd been, who'd sought attention from maids and other lord's daughters.

Rhiann threw up her hands. "I don't even want to know."

Cade tucked her arms back around his neck. "There will never be another woman for me but you." And kissed her again.

* * * * *

With no wounded to carry or care for, and the dead buried, within the hour the army was ready to march again. But they would not travel all together this time either.

"I will head east," Tudur said.

"To Porthmadog?" Cade said. It was the seat of Pod, king of Dunoding, who'd married Tudur's sister. He'd been an ally of Cadfael, albeit not a very enthusiastic one.

"I will speak to him of the error of his ways," Tudur said. "That he did not come to Aberffraw is permissible, in that he is not as young as he once was. But that he didn't send his sons, and was thus unable to give you support when you needed it is unacceptable. If I have any say in the matter, his men will be with you against the Saxons when the time comes."

"Thank you." Cade held out his hand to Tudur, who clasped it firmly. "Until then."

"Send me word," Tudur said. "I don't relish battle any more than the next man, but to return home with only thirty dead and no wounded after facing an army twice our size is unprecedented. We will sing of this for generations."

Geraint too declined the opportunity to see Caer Dathyl. "From what you've told me, I don't relish a visit. Dafydd, here"—he clapped the young knight on the shoulder—"can tell me all about it later. Our men will be wanting to see their families anyway and the sooner we start back north, the sooner we'll be home."

Cade allowed it, thinking that this was perhaps for the best, as it saved unnecessary explanations of what had gone on at the fort the night before. The men of Gwynedd who'd fought the demons would have enough unbelievable tales to tell that wouldn't be believed, without the additional stories from Caer Dathyl.

"I, however, will come," Bedwyr said. "I refuse to let you out of my sight again. The most strange and unprecedented things happen when I'm not among those who protect you."

So it was a much reduced company that remained behind, waiting for the sun to set so Cade could travel south to Caer Dathyl. Cade sat on a log with his arm around Rhiann who closed her eyes and leaned into him. He studied his friends one by one, their faces illumined by the light of the fire as the sun faded from the sky. The atmosphere was subdued, as was Cade himself, thinking what they'd each gone through with him and for him.

How could so much have happened in one night? What with the shipwreck, the events in Caer Dathyl, and the defeat of the demons, how are any of them still upright?

The thought brought Cade up short. *And how is it that I feel as strong as ever, when I haven't*—he stopped, feeling a hollowness inside himself that he hadn't known in over two years.

"Does anyone have anything to eat?" he said.

Hywel had been worrying at a hole in the dirt with a stick and now tossed it into the fire. Flames shot up, crackling anew. "I've some bread that's not too dry and an apple in my bags. Why?"

"I'm hungry," Cade said.

"You're what?" Rhun said. He turned to Rhiann. "Did he say he was hungry? He doesn't have a heartbeat, does he?"

Rhiann looked into Cade's face, reached out a hand to put a palm to his cheek, and then her head to his chest. "No. Are you feeling all right, Cade?"

Laughter tickled his throat and he couldn't contain it. The sheer joy of being hungry had his spirits soaring. "Can't a man want a good meal every now and then?" Cade's stomach growled loud enough for everyone to hear, punctuating his request.

Hywel got to his feet. "I'll get what I have, my lord." He walked to his horse, a grin a mile wide on his face.

"Every man but you!" Rhun said. "You ate more than any of us as a youth, when you used to eat."

"I recollect your mother making a similar comment once, but she was speaking of you at the time, not me," Cade said. "She said she had to feed you every two hours, just like an infant, or you'd get grumpy."

Rhun laughed. "You can tell yourself that all you like, but it isn't true." He rummaged in his own pack and tossed an apple to Cade who caught it, rubbed it on his shirt, and took a bite. He closed his eyes as the tang of it hit him. Juice ran down his chin.

Rhiann was staring at him, wide-eyed. "You can taste it too, can't you?"

Another wave of laughter bubbled up within Cade, filling him so that he almost choked on a piece of apple. "I can. Is there more?"

"Here's my contribution." Hywel dropped an apple and a small loaf of bread into Cade's lap.

"Why didn't you eat when we did an hour ago?" Goronwy said.

"I wasn't hungry then," Cade said.

Soon, Cade had a small pile of food in front of him: dried meat, a bit of bread, a carrot Dafydd had been saving for his horse. Then it was gone and nobody had any more to offer him. Cade licked his fingers and wiped them on his breeches.

"I can't believe I've agreed to marry such a barbarian," Rhiann said.

"I can't seem to help it." Cade glanced up at his friends, each of whom gazed at him with expressions ranging from amusement to concern. "What has Arianrhod done to me?"

"Surely enough by now?" Rhiann said.

"We'd better get him to Caer Dathyl," Rhun said, still enjoying the knowledge that Cade wanted to eat. "They'll have more food for him. You'll see that what I say is true."

And so they did. Two hours later, with full dark cloaking their movements, they approached the fort. It appeared exactly as Cade thought it should—that is to say, small, plain, and with a wooden palisade rather than walls of black stone. Bedwyr and Rhun lit torches once they reached the pathway leading to the fort, so watchers on the ramparts spotted them—and Cade's banner— from some distance away. Siawn himself came out to meet them, his horse flying down the pathway. A dozen retainers followed him.

Siawn pulled up in front of Cade, dismounted, and bowed. "Sire. It is my honor to welcome you to Caer Dathyl."

"Thank you, Siawn," Cade said. "What a difference a day makes."

"Is—are—" Siawn looked past Cade to the others clustered behind him. He swallowed whatever first question he'd thought to ask. "All is well?"

"The demons are destroyed," Cade said.

Siawn's expression cleared. "I am very pleased to hear it. I apologize for not being with you at the end." Siawn's face indicated he wanted to say something else—to ask more questions but thought better of it with so many witnesses.

"We missed you," Cade said, "but understand that you had business to attend to at home."

"Teregad has fled," Siawn said. "He will never trouble us again."

Cade nodded his acceptance while at the same time studying Siawn's face. Siawn met Cade's eyes, but still, Cade wasn't sure if that was the whole truth, or if Siawn's interpretation of 'fled' meant that Teregad's body had ended up in the Irish Sea. "You, then, are King of Caer Dathyl—if you will accept the challenge."

"If it means that I still serve you," Siawn said, "then yes."

"With you on the throne here, I don't have to worry about this region of Gwynedd and am content," Cade said. "I will not pretend, however, that I won't be calling upon you and your men in the near future."

Siawn took a moment to reflect on that. "More demons?"

"Perhaps," Cade said. "I wouldn't bet against it, even with the black cauldron closed. I'm referring, however, to the Saxons. It isn't as if we've yet dealt with the aftermath of Cadfael's death. Cadfael had many Saxon allies, including Penda—my mother's brother—and Peada, Penda's son and my cousin, who not long ago planned to seal his alliance to Gwynedd by marrying Rhiann. They will find that I'm not quite as willing a pawn as Cadfael, for all that I can call Penda 'uncle'."

"We will be ready, my lord," Siawn said. "For now, please accept the hospitality of Caer Dathyl."

"Thank you," Cade said, and then added, unable to contain his news. "Penda might also object to the fact that Rhiann has consented to become my wife."

Siawn gave Cade his first genuine smile. "Congratulations, my lord." He fell in beside Rhiann, a pace behind Cade as they finished their journey to Caer Dathyl.

"It looks so different," Rhiann said. "I can hardly credit that so much could have changed in less than a day."

"Remember that Mabon's greatest power is that of illusion," Cade said. "He turned Caer Dathyl's wooden walls into black stone overnight and convinced everyone here that all was as it should be. That does not mean, however, that the walls were ever stone—only that we perceived them thus."

"Taliesin said as much when he led us into Caer Ddu, though I didn't understand what his words meant at the time," Rhiann said.

"The gods belong to a different realm," Cade said. "Even I don't understand them, not even a little, for all that I carry a small part of the *sidhe* inside me."

Dafydd spoke from behind them. "You mean—" He gestured broadly, which Cade interpreted as referring to Caer Dathyl, his companions, and the world in general. "We can't trust our senses at all anymore?"

Cade glanced back at him. "The gods put on a *glamour* that is impossible for humans to penetrate, myself and Taliesin included, though he might see more than he lets on."

"Or did." Rhun muttered the words under his breath.

"Camulos could have thrown a snowball at me, were it snowing, made the ball appear as a boar, and I would still have felt it hit my chest. I would have fallen over just as easily."

"That would have been just like Mabon to trick you that way and amuse himself with the memory of it afterwards," Rhiann said.

Similarly, back in Arawn's cavern, Cade's companions had seen doors that weren't there, until demons came through them. Only Cade hadn't been fooled. Cade had prided himself on his ability to stand as one of the *sidhe* when he needed to, and see through their deceptions. The notion that in this case he hadn't, or that Mabon had some new power over him, was disconcerting to say the least.

"What else have we witnessed that wasn't real?" Dafydd said.

"The golden throne in Arawn's cavern could have been a rickety wooden chair," Goronwy said, "or the golden ship at Caer Ddu a rowboat."

"Do you think—" and now it was Rhiann's turn to swallow her words. Cade looked at her, concerned, because her face had paled. "What about my father? Is he really dead?"

Cade swallowed hard himself at that thought. The body of Cadfael, which they'd been unable to remove from the wall at Caer Ddu, could have been nothing more than a rat, put there in Cadfael's form for Mabon's amusement. Admittedly, Teregad had been certain that Cadfael was dead, and claimed to have had something to do with it. Cade decided to take that, of all the strange incidents leading up to this point, at face value.

"He's dead, Rhiann," Cade said. "It doesn't pay to second guess ourselves too much. For all that Camulos was on that battlefield, or Arawn in his cavern—"

"—Or Arianrhod in the clearing," Rhun said.

"They don't bother with us most of the time," Cade said.

He didn't mention that were Taliesin with them, he might have said something to the effect that humans couldn't be sure *anything* was real—whether or not a god bothered to play games with a man's mind. How often did a man's senses lie to him? At night, he could turn a cloak on a hook into an intruder, a whisper through the shutters into a ghost, and a windstorm into an angry god. Cade pressed his hand to Caer Dathyl's wooden gate as he passed through it, feeling the grains in the wood. If only he could ensure that he always saw so clearly.

6

Rhiann

Just as when she'd arrived at Aberffraw as 'a king's friend', Rhiann was somewhat discomfited by her reception at Caer Dathyl. True, she was the only woman among the companions and was dressed in boys' clothes, but the subservience of the occupants of the fort set her teeth on edge.

"It wasn't very long ago that I was one of them," she said to Cade that evening at dinner after yet another servant had bowed deeply as he poured her mead. And then some for Cade, who so far had consumed four entire trenchers of food and a gallon of drink. Rhiann had looked closely in his eyes several times. He was neither sated nor—more importantly—drunk.

"It isn't just that you are my betrothed, *cariad*," Cade said, taking another sip from his cup. "I believe Siawn has been talking."

"About me?" Rhiann said. "What could he have said about me?"

"That you are a true heroine," Cade said.

"Cade—"

"Eighteen hours ago, this hall was full of men who'd drunk from Mabon's barrels and slept the night away. They'd lived among demons for heaven knows how long. This morning, they awoke to find Mabon gone and their fort back to the way it was a month ago. It was as if they'd gone on a drunken binge with only vague memories of their lives, even if the men we spoke to were coherent at the time."

"I guess I can see that," she said. "But I did no more than any of you."

Cade canted his head at her and smiled, not responding to her assertion. Instead, he said, "That dress becomes you, by the way."

Rhiann blushed, but then recovered to glare at Cade. "I'm not giving up my other clothes, just because I'll be the Queen of Gwynedd."

"I haven't asked you to, have I?"

"But you've thought it," Rhiann said. "I can see it in your eyes. Marriage isn't going to give you an excuse to leave me behind at home, minding—" Rhiann caught herself before she let *the children* escape her lips. "—the fort," she finished lamely.

She hoped Cade didn't realize what she might have said.

Cade actually had the nerve to look sheepish. "Of course not."

Rhiann poked his arm with one finger. "After all we've been through, you think you could get away with that?"

"The people will expect—"

"The people!" And then Rhiann couldn't keep back her thoughts, much as she didn't want to burden Cade with them. She leaned in until their foreheads were almost touching and lowered her voice. "They'll expect a son within a year too, and that's not going to happen either."

Cade licked his lips. "I know, Rhiann. I'm sorry. If I could be other than I am—"

Rhiann put a finger to his lips. "Don't say any more. I couldn't stop myself from speaking of it, but I won't dwell on it, I promise. I love you—"

Rhiann didn't get any more words out because Cade had clasped her hand in his, leaned in, and stopped her mouth with a kiss, to general applause from tables high and low alike. He released her and she sat back, breathless as usual.

Cade brushed his lips on the back of her hand. "I don't want to risk you ever again. I can't promise that you will come with me to every battle or even the threat of one. But I will not banish you to the solar either. How about we take it one day at a time?"

Rhiann allowed him to study her and met his eyes once again. They were as clear and intent as always, blue and bottomless. "All right. One day at a time. Now..." She rubbed her hands together. "I have some questions for you."

The blue eyes brightened. "Do you?"

"We're engaged, soon to be married, and you owe me some answers."

Cade rested his elbows on the table, obviously amused. "Anything, *cariad*."

"First," Rhiann said, "do you ever get tired?"

Cade blinked and then his mouth twitched as if he was about to laugh. He opened it to say something and then closed it again.

"What's wrong?" Rhiann said. "I'm serious."

"I know you're serious," Cade said. "I just don't know how to answer. Do I get tired ... of what?"

"I mean your body—does it ever get tired? You slept in the clearing. Was that because you were sleepy tired, emotionally tired, physically tired, or none of the above."

Cade barked a laugh. "Of all the things you could have asked me..." He sat back in his chair, still laughing until Rhiann wasn't sure he was actually going to give her an answer. Finally, he wiped at the corners of his eyes with the tips of his fingers and got himself together. "The short answer is *No, I don't get tired.* The longer answer is that when I slept, back there in the clearing, my mind truly rested for the first time in over two years. So, then yes, emotionally tired is the only *tired* I get. Anything else?"

"That first day at Aberffraw when we met, why didn't you escape earlier? You could have killed everyone in the fort, particularly those two guards who brought you in. You didn't need me at all."

"Ah," Cade said. "In that you are potentially correct. I could have. But swords do hurt me and can kill me if a blade separates my head from my body. So even if I'd killed the initial two guards, another—or seven—would have run me through before I'd gotten two steps. At the time, I thought it better to wait. I intended to jump from my window. I would have if you hadn't appeared."

"You left it a bit late," Rhiann said. "It would have been dawn soon."

"In truth, I was lost in my thoughts," Cade said. "My mistake. In my defense, however, I was thinking of you."

Rhiann ducked her head, foolishly pleased to have him say that. "So you did need me."

"That's what this is about?" Cade said. "Whether or not I need you?" He leaned in and put a finger to Rhiann's lips before she could reply. "Don't answer that. Did I need you to help me escape? I might have managed it on my own without you, but it was far better and more easily accomplished with you. Do I need you in my life? Now, that is a different story. I admit that I could live as I have lived without you. But was that really living? And do I want to return to that kind of life? No."

"Cade—"

"You are far more independent and resilient than I am," Cade said. "You could live without me far more easily than I could live without you."

"That's not true—"

"Ah—" he said again, hushing her. "Don't deny it. You honor me with the knowledge that you don't want to."

"I love you," Rhiann said.

"I know that too," Cade said.

* * * * *

The fort of Deganwy sat on and between two hills overlooking the eastern bank of the Conwy River. The great Maelgwyn Gwynedd first made it his seat, and the Kings of Gwynedd had maintained it ever since. Rhiann was glad that she and Cade would marry here instead of at Aberffraw. While Aberffraw was an ancient fort, built over the top of even older ruins, memories of her life there haunted her.

She and Cade had traveled to Aberffraw before, when Cade assumed the throne. They'd found the hall much improved from when her father had ruled it—but in her mind it would always be Cadfael's, not Cade's, and her childhood had not been a happy one. Perhaps Taliesin had understood that, although knowing him, he could have chosen Deganwy for their wedding for reasons that had nothing to do with her.

Rhiann had spent the day in a most unusual manner for her: with other women fussing over the style of her wedding dress. Even she had to admit that it was beautiful, a dark green with white at the wrists and neck—and that she might look beautiful in it. Their wedding, however, would otherwise be unlike any she'd ever attended, and not just because the groom was the King of Gwynedd and a *sidhe*.

Usually weddings involved fathers and signed contracts, distribution of property and the arrangement of dowry. Rhiann came to Cade with nothing but her bow and the quiver on her back. His mother, Alcfrith, was the only mother she'd ever known, and she hadn't been much of one at that. Usually, too, the guests invited to the wedding wanted to be there.

In this case, Cade was using their wedding as an opportunity to gather the Kings of Gwynedd and Powys to him, those that would come. Some hadn't attended the ceremony at Aberffraw and would need to pay homage to him or risk his wrath. He was their liege lord, after all, even if the gods had touched him. Over the last three days, more than one lord's eyes had shown trepidation as he entered the great hall and greeted his new king.

From the heights above the river and the Irish sea, which lay just to the north of the spit of land on which Deganwy Castle was built, Rhiann and Hywel watched another group of travelers peer up at the fort. The sun shone into Rhiann's face and she shielded her eyes against it. Then she smiled, recognizing the man at the head of the company. This time, as he'd promised, Tudur had brought his brother-in-law.

Rhiann waved down to him before checking Hywel's profile beside her. "Have you spoken to Dafydd?"

Hywel glanced at her, but otherwise continued to gaze studiously at the river below them and the men crossing it. "You should talk to him yourself."

"I can't," she said. "We've been such good friends and I trust him completely, but ..."

"It isn't as if your wedding to King Cadwaladr is a surprise to him," Hywel said.

"Her wedding is a surprise to someone?" Dafydd had mounted the stairs to the battlements without them noticing and now came to stand on the other side of Hywel. His words had been for Hywel and although an outsider might note that they stood in close proximity, Dafydd hadn't looked at Rhiann.

Well, this is awkward. In the long pause that followed, all three gazed over the ramparts at the influx of new guests. Finally, Hywel took a step back. "King Cadwaladr asked me to … check on our supply of arrows. I'd best be off." He turned on his heel and trotted down the stairs to the courtyard.

Rhiann watched him go, not knowing if she had the fortitude for this. She took in a breath and turned to Dafydd. "Can you forgive me?"

"You've done nothing that needs forgiveness, Rhiann," Dafydd said, not pretending to misunderstand. "You loved the King long before you were my friend. I've cherished that friendship, but today is the last day I will call you by your given name."

"Dafydd—" Rhiann touched his arm and then drew her hand back. From his expression, her sympathy would only make this worse.

"I've asked the King for an assignment," Dafydd said, "away from here." He gestured with one hand, indicating the castle, her, Gwynedd—maybe all of it. "He says after the wedding, he will send me south, if I wish it. I will be his emissary to the rulers of Ceredigion."

"Cade told me that he'd been thinking about what needs doing," Rhiann said. "It's a long way to travel, and maybe dangerous."

"I need to go," Dafydd said. "And the King needs allies. Despite what happened at Caer Dathyl, he's not as immediately concerned about Mabon and his plans as he is about the Saxons and theirs."

"He can't predict what Mabon will do," Rhiann said. "He knows the Saxons are not our friends and never will be, even if they allied with his birth father and Cadfael after him."

"The lords of Ceredigion have always focused their trade and ties in the direction of the western sea, towards our cousins in Ireland," Dafydd said. "They don't fear the Saxons yet. The mountains protect them. But if we fall, or Powys falls, Ceredigion will be as exposed as we are now."

"It is your task to explain that to them?"

Dafydd glanced at Rhiann. "You doubt that I can?"

"Of course not, Dafydd," Rhiann said. She'd hurt him, and now he saw criticism in the most innocuous of comments. That hurt her, but his was a pain that wasn't going to heal in a day, not even with the help of Caledfwlch—or especially not with the help of Caledfwlch. "You're the son of a king; you lived for a year in the kitchens of Caer Dathyl to see what kind of man you were; you've held Dyrnwyn and lived. I was merely clarifying so I could fully understand."

Some of the tension in Dafydd's shoulders eased. "I have your blessing, then?"

"You are my friend, Dafydd," she said, "my staunch companion and a hero in your own right. I look forward to shooting with you again."

"I wish you the best, Queen Rhiannon." Dafydd bowed and left her.

As she watched him go, tears pricked at the corners of her eyes. Marrying Cade was what she wanted—what she needed—but she hadn't wanted to hurt Dafydd along the way. She replayed something Alcfrith had said to her when she arrived, the joy shining through her but coming out as sorrow as well. *You've taken the reins of your life in both hands and held on. No matter what happens, don't let go.*

Dafydd, too, had left home and followed his own path. She had faith he'd make his way through this trial too.

7

Cade

"You have the ring, right?" Cade said.

"Of course." Rhun held up his left fist. "Right here."

Cade's throat closed so he couldn't speak. He nodded instead.

"You're not nervous, are you?" Goronwy said. "No second thoughts?"

"Have you lost your mind? That's not it at all," Cade said. "I didn't want anything to go wrong and already it has, because Taliesin isn't here, though he sent word ahead—"

The entrance to Deganwy's great hall flew open, cutting Cade's sentence short. And it was Taliesin himself strolling across the threshold as if nothing were amiss. Rain poured outside and he shed water from his cloak on all and sundry as he passed among the many guests, grinning a mischievous grin all the while. A path cleared before him and with a nod to individual dignitaries, peasants, and warriors he singled out especially, he made his way to where Cade waited.

"I see I'm just in time," Taliesin said.

"That you are," Cade said. "I thought I was going to have to do this without you."

"Not possible," Taliesin said. "Even if Father Siawn might be adequate to the task, I couldn't countenance such a thing. Where's Rhiannon?"

"Coming," Rhun said. "Bronwen and Alcfrith are getting her ready."

"Excellent," Taliesin said.

Cade observed his friend. He hadn't really looked at him since Arawn's cavern, when Arawn had broken Taliesin's staff. Whether through Arianrhod's magic or his own, Taliesin had held it again in the clearing and while they fought the demons in the field, and now carried it as he always had. Cade couldn't even discern a crack where Arawn had split it. Taliesin's shock of white-blonde hair was slightly more kempt than usual, and he appeared to have made some effort to clean himself for Cade's big day. Instead of his usual tattered black cloak, he wore the green one Cade had acquired from the man he'd killed outside the entrance to Arawn's cavern. Cade didn't remember giving it to him.

"You're in a good mood," Cade said. "Why? I know it isn't for my wedding."

"I am very pleased for you and Rhiannon, of course," Taliesin said. "But you're right. I finally have conceived a stratagem that will put us back on the path to solving some of these problems that face us."

"You have a plan to defeat the Saxons?" Cade said.

Taliesin flapped his hand in a dismissive gesture. "We'll deal with them in due course—I've much to report that you will not yet have heard. No, my plan is how to get my *sight* back."

Cade stared at Taliesin. "And that's why you're happy?"

"Yes," Taliesin said. "It's far better than not having a plan."

"I thought you had it back," Cade said. "After the demon presence attacked me on the battlefield, you told Rhiann that you would meet us here, at Deganwy, for the wedding, so..." Cade trailed off at Taliesin's puzzled look.

"I didn't need the sight to know that you were going to marry Rhiannon soon, nor to know that you'd choose Deganwy over Aberffraw for the event," he said. "Aberffraw has too many memories for either of you to be content marrying there. And now, the gods have smiled on us further. It's raining and rain is lucky for a wedding."

"That's because it always rains in Wales," Goronwy said.

"No matter," said Taliesin, still smiling happily. "Rain makes it easier for our lord, here, to travel."

"There's some place you want me to go—with you?" Cade said.

"You and I—and your lovely bride of course—mustn't separate you two so soon—will ride to Dinas Bran. I need to complete a task there before the High Council meets."

"You do have a plan." Cade looked at Taliesin suspiciously, not trusting his uncharacteristic cheerfulness.

"Will it be dangerous?" Rhun said.

"Of course." Taliesin's brow furrowed. "Why would you even ask such a question?"

Cade smiled, despite his apprehensions. He'd missed Taliesin. Regardless of the reason, he was pleased to see his friend in such a mood. He was about to ask more questions when he sensed movement in the side doorway to the hall. Because it was raining, Alcfrith had scrapped the notion of having Rhiann arrive through the main door as Taliesin had.

At Rhiann's entrance, the room silenced.

"Close your mouth, Hywel," Goronwy said from beside Cade. "And don't drool. It's unbecoming in a knight."

"She's beautiful," Hywel said.

Rhiann's dress perfectly set off her deep brown hair that the other women had swept up from the base of her neck. She wore no jewelry. Her only adornment was a just-blossomed sprig she carried. Even Siawn hadn't objected to their choice of the spring equinox as the date of their wedding. *A rebirth for Wales* he'd said, *as well as the Christ.*

Rhiann moved towards Cade, her eyes fixed on his, and Cade had eyes only for her. He couldn't begrudge Hywel his admiration, since Rhiann was *his*. She'd told him that it was wrong to think that he needed her above everything else, and he'd accepted that when she said it, not telling her the absolute truth—because what she'd said wasn't true. He would gladly give up everything he valued if only she would stay with him. That she'd pledged to do exactly that brought him to his knees every time he thought about it. He loved her so completely he thought he would come apart at the joints sometimes with wanting her. He might be the King of Gwynedd, but she'd never valued his station. He might be *sidhe*, but she loved him despite his affliction.

She loved *him*—that part of him that was just Cade; that part of him that Arianrhod couldn't touch—and it humbled him. It was pure and rare and was only matched by the love he felt for her. As she came towards him, he wanted to sweep her into his arms and kiss her until she ran out of breath, but it wasn't quite time for that. He didn't bother to hide the thoughts behind his eyes. The time was past for keeping secrets.

They clasped hands and their friends who stood up with them made way for Taliesin and Siawn to come forth together, one on each side of Cade and Rhiann. In unison, the two priests—sometimes rivals, sometimes friends—raised their hands to the heavens and called down the blessing together. For all the world, it looked as if they'd practiced it, which Cade knew they hadn't.

Then it was Cade's turn, and he brought Rhiann to stand at the edge of the crowd of onlookers in the hall. Rhun handed him the ring, while Rhiann passed the sprig to Bronwen. Cade took Rhiann's hand and recited by heart—and from his heart:

> *There are three fountains*
> *In the mountain of roses,*
> *Each, I pledge to you.*

One of love, to drink deeply together,
The second of desire, to trail our hands in its heated flow,
The third of fidelity, that quenches our thirst
When all other waters fail.

And before I set my eyes on the end of existence,
And before the broken foam shall come upon my lips,
And before I become connected to wooden boards,
May there be festivals to my soul,
With you beside me.

We are young; we are old.
In heaven, in earth, at the end,
In straits, in expanse, in form,

In body, in soul, in habit,
In the valleys and mountains, under the stars.
Thou art always, wife.

Rhiann responded. "Thou art always, husband."

His heart lighter than it had ever been, Cade slipped the ring on Rhiann's finger and leaned down to kiss her. The room exploded with applause and laughter. Cade laughed himself and wrapped his arms around Rhiann. He looked over her shoulder at his friends, and then past them just in time to see two demons slither into the room from the same side passage Rhiann had used.

Heedless of the revelry, they snapped out their arms as if laying a tablecloth, and with a *flash,* cast the room into frozen silence.

8

Rhiann

Cade's grip on Rhiann tightened.

"What's happening?" Rhiann's voice came out a whisper, muffled by Cade's cloak.

"Hold still," Cade said. "I'm going to need your help and I don't want them to know you aren't unconscious."

That didn't sound good.

Carefully, as if she was a large doll, Cade carried Rhiann off the dais where they'd said their vows. She caught a glimpse of their friends, each frozen in a grotesquery of their usual selves, so she kept her legs stiff to keep up the façade that she was affected too. Cade forced her to bend at the waist and sat her on a bench near the dais, with her back against a table, conveniently located next to Hywel's bow and quiver, which he'd taken off for the ceremony.

Since Llanllugan, she, Hywel, and Dafydd never went anywhere without their bows. Today, however, for the first time in a month, Rhiann herself wore no weapons at all, not even a knife strapped to her calf or at her waist. When she'd gone to buckle on her old belt and sheath over her gown, Alcfrith had laughed, pried it from her fingers, and taken it away. Her friends still had their swords, but everyone except she and Cade was frozen solid and the only reason that she could think of that she wasn't was because she'd been holding onto Cade.

Once Cade settled Rhiann, he straightened and stepped closer to the demons, half-blocking Rhiann from their view. Rhiann was sure he was standing in that position on purpose, but she scootched incrementally to the left so that she could see around him to the demon's faces, even if she didn't dare give the game away by looking at them head on and glaring like she wanted to.

They wore black cloaks and had tucked their hands inside their sleeves. Their faces were the only part of their bodies that weren't completely covered, though they wore deep hoods. Each was a mirror image of the other, with pinched mouths, black and narrowed eyes, and deep lines carved into what passed for skin. Rough leather was more like. These demons weren't projecting a *glamour* like Mabon did—perhaps that wasn't part of their powers—and didn't appear to be warriors, but they frightened Rhiann all the more because of it. They didn't need to threaten with weapons. Their appearance was enough.

"What do you want?" Cade said.

"Such hostility." Oil and the ice dripped from the demon's voice and Rhiann shivered. Fortunately, the owner of the voice didn't notice the movement. It probably hadn't occurred to them that their spell hadn't been universally effective.

"We are here because you have something our lord wants," the second demon said.

Cade was focused entirely on whomever this was and Rhiann didn't want to disturb him, even though she longed to leap to her feet and scream *They're dangerous! Don't get any closer!* She didn't dare move at all, either to ask if Cade knew who they were or to scoop up Hywel's bow and an arrow to fire it off in their direction. In truth, she didn't really want to know who they were. She just wanted them gone.

Despite her fear of being caught, tiny movement by tiny movement, she shifted to bring herself closer to Hywel's weapons.

"How many of my people have you killed?" Cade said.

Like the other men, he'd come to the wedding armed—not because he feared that anything might go wrong, but because knights wore swords as a matter of course and as a symbol of their station. Now, Cade pulled Caledfwlch from its sheath and held it out, pointing it at the two demons. It shone as brightly as ever, reflecting the light of the torches, spitting it back out as when oil is thrown on a fire, and casting diamonds across the ceiling. Both demons blinked at the light and one of them lifted a hand to shield his eyes.

"That was not our charge," the first demon said.

His face took on a look as sinister as Rhiann could imagine, the features sharp and unnatural. A scream choked her throat but she swallowed it down, refusing to give in to the fear. She needed to stay calm if she was to help Cade and her friends.

"However, Lord Mabon didn't restrict us to mere conversation if the opportunity for amusement presented itself and you were accommodating," the demon continued. "I'm sure you, of all humankind, understand our needs."

"Mabon," Cade said.

"We'd appreciate the gift of one or two women who wouldn't be missed," the second demon said. He pulled his hood down further to leave his face in shadow.

Rhiann catalogued the women in the fort. Whether wife, companion, or servant, she knew them all. Alcfrith and Bronwen had stood up with her as she married Cade so were safe for now, if anyone was. Her chest tightened and a cold settled in her belly at what havoc these demons might have wreaked before they'd entered the hall. But not so much so that she couldn't think. She began to unroll the bowstring that Hywel had wound around the tip of his bow.

"You have something our master requires," the first demon said. "Where is it?"

"I wouldn't know what you are talking about," Cade said. "You'll have to explain."

Rhiann flicked her gaze to Cade and back down to the bow. His clipped intonation and the tension in his shoulders indicated an extreme anger he was struggling to control.

If it made sense that a demon could scoff, this one did. "We want the sword. Give it to us."

"Do you mean this sword?" Cade raised Caledfwlch higher.

The demon took an involuntary step backwards.

"Never," Cade said.

"Although you stole Caledfwlch from Caer Ddu, my master has said you can keep it." The demon said these words as if Mabon had truly bestowed on Cade a favor. "It's Dyrnwyn we want, the sword of the white hilt. You took it from Caer Dathyl when Arawn fell. Our lord has had word that you house it here, at Deganwy."

"No," Cade said.

All three paused. Cade stood with his sword still pointed at the demons while the two demons appeared to be struggling to find the right words to counter him. Rhiann was still trying encompass the demons' request. *Dyrnwyn? Here? Why would Mabon think Cade has it?*

Rhiann clenched her teeth as she tried to affix the string to the bow without calling attention to herself. She shot a quick glance at her husband. The power within him was growing, although the demons appeared completely unaware of what was happening.

Then Cade released his power.

Rhiann would tell herself in those between times that she was used to it—or as used to it as it was possible to become—but the truth was, she hadn't ever gotten used to what happened to him.

It took less than a heartbeat for Cade to fill the room. This power was the same as he'd displayed on the battlefield. He *became* light. Rhiann swallowed hard and looked away. Cade took a step forward. He had himself in hand.

Now it was her turn.

The demon quailed before Cade, holding one hand out to keep him at bay. "It is as the prophecies foretold."

That had Rhiann swallowing hard again.

Then the demon pointed at someone in the audience who Rhiann couldn't see from where she sat. "Another step and that man loses his life."

Cade froze. He glanced at Rhiann, just one flash of those iridescent eyes, before turning back to the demons. "Harm one of my people, and I will send you to a place from which you could never return."

Rhiann couldn't tell if the demon believed him. Then again, Rhiann didn't know if she did either. If it were possible, however, she had no doubt Cade would do it.

"Let's try this again," the demon said. "No, I do not possess Dyrnwyn or 'no' I don't know where it is."

"Just 'no'," Cade said. "Your threats are meaningless; tell your master that he will get nothing from me."

"Mabon predicted you'd say that but thought it worth the effort to ask." The demon hesitated, his eyes flicking from Cade to the man he'd threatened.

"Don't do it," Cade said. "The consequences will be more severe than you can imagine."

"I act only by my lord's will," the demon said. "Lord Mabon can kill any one of your people merely with the thought that it should happen. Only his hope that that you would join forces with him has stayed his hand up until now."

The demon's words hung in the air. Neither they nor Cade moved and Rhiann tried to still her own breathing so it didn't seem so much like it was echoing in the hall.

"You tell Mabon that the next time he wants to talk to me, he comes himself. I don't negotiate with intermediaries, whether you or one of his allies in the world of the *sidhe*. I am tired of his games."

"You dare threaten Mabon, son of Arawn?"

"I do not threaten," Cade said.

Another pause. "So be it. " The demon surprised Rhiann by bowing stiffly. Then, with a jerk of his head to his companion, he swept his cloak around himself.

The other followed suit and said, "You would have done better to aid my master."

Then with a snarl, both demons threw off their cloaks, revealing bared teeth and gleaming swords. The first demon released a high cackle. The sound raised the hair on the back of Rhiann's neck as it filled the hall. "Perhaps we can make you reconsider our master's offer!"

"Now, Rhiann," Cade said.

Rhiann had hoped it wouldn't come to this, but since it had, she was ready. She pulled two arrows from Hywel's quiver and rose to her feet in the same motion. She ripped the fletching down one side of each arrow with her teeth and spit out the feathers. Then she pressed the arrows into the bow, one on each side of the bowstring.

Cade moved out of the way to give her a clear shot. *"I am a sword, a staff, the tear of an arrow through the air."*

Rhiann loosed the missiles. They flashed across the hall, catching both demons unaware. One arrow hit the first demon straight in the chest, punching through his cloak with a sickening thud. The second arrow failed to penetrate as fully and hit the other demon in the right shoulder, injuring him, but not enough to kill him. The demon shrieked—whether in anger or pain, Rhiann didn't know, since she still didn't know if demons felt pain.

Cade had started moving the moment she released the arrows. He raised Caledfwlch high. By the time Cade had crossed half the distance to him in the blink of an eye, the second demon spun around to face him, his sword out and ready.

"Cade!"

Rhiann called her husband's name, as if that single word might save him from an unexpected thrust. As it was, Cade severed the demon's hand at the wrist in one blinding slash and then drove back the other way at the demon's neck. The creature fell to the floor, headless.

With equal suddenness, the lights in the hall came up. The torches ceased to sputter in their sconces and the fire in the central hearth flamed yellow. A man groaned. Cade leaned down to clean Caledfwlch with the edge of one demon's cloak and then slid the sword back into the sheath at his waist. He strode back towards Rhiann. The set of his shoulders and the narrowing of his eyes told her that his earlier anger was a small thing compared to what he was feeling now.

Cade spoke through clenched teeth, his jaw bulging with the effort of containing his emotions. "He seeks to strike at me in my own home? At our wedding? The one day that should have been sacred ..." He reached Rhiann, wrapped his arms around her shoulders, and pulled her to him. "You should not have had to do what you did. You should not have had to face them."

Rhiann had begun to shake as the tension of the last half an hour left her, but his words settled her a bit. "We've agreed I'm not a delicate flower, Cade. You can count on me, just as much as you count on Rhun or Goronwy."

"I know that," he said. "And I did count on you. I just don't want to have to."

9

Cade

Hywel moaned and staggered to the nearby table at which Rhiann had sat earlier, nearly falling twice before he reached it. He rested both hands on the flat surface, his head hanging. Then he scrubbed at his hair with one hand, still supporting his weight with the other. "I don't feel so good."

"That wouldn't come as a surprise to anyone." Cade rested a hand on Hywel's shoulder and squeezed once, before moving around him to catch his mother as she fell into a faint in his arms. He cradled Alcfrith like an infant and carried her to where Rhiann waited beside Hywel.

"It's all right." Rhiann smoothed the hair back from Alcfrith's face.

"What happened?" Alcfrith opened her eyes and gazed blearily at Rhiann.

"Nothing Cade couldn't handle," Rhiann said.

She sat with one arm around Alcfrith and the other massaging the back of Hywel's neck. Hywel held his head in his hands, having seated himself beside her, since his legs were too wobbly to support him. Still on the dais, Rhun stirred and swung his arm in a reflexive movement, knocking over a half-full goblet of wine which Siawn had used as part of the ceremony to bless the fruitfulness of their marriage. Cade pushed away the fruitlessness of that hope. Rhiann had promised not to dwell on it. It wouldn't do for him to, either.

Even Taliesin, only now blinking his eyes, had not been immune to Mabon's spell, and to Cade's mind, that was perhaps the most disturbing thing of all.

"I feel as if I've eaten something unclean." Hywel managed to straighten his back, and then fell forward again, retching, his fingers clenching his hair as if pressing hard could contain his pain.

"You're not far off," Cade said. "We've been visited by Mabon—or least his emissaries. They wanted Dyrnwyn and thought to ask us for it."

"Mabon thinks we have Dyrnwyn?" Rhun had collapsed on the edge of the dais with Bronwen in his arms, fortunately awake and blinking if not yet articulate. Cade and he shared a look, more of speculation than concern.

"I wonder why he would think we have it?" Taliesin said.

"I would have preferred it if you already knew," Cade said.

"My gifts have deserted me." Taliesin looked down at his feet, hiding his face from Cade's scrutiny. It was a pose so unlike

Taliesin that Cade stepped closer, thinking to speak. Taliesin glanced up again and Cade read that same something in his face—something that looked to him like real fear—but then his expression smoothed and his eyes hid the thoughts behind them.

Cade nodded to show his acceptance—for now—of Taliesin's privacy. He turned back to his mother, who'd recovered enough to sip at a glass of wine. Rhiann still held Alcfrith's hand, but Cade's exchange with Taliesin had caught her attention. Rhiann's gaze tracked from one to the other.

"I thought—" she stopped.

"Leave it, *cariad*," Cade said. "We'll talk later."

"You!"

Cade turned at the shout to see King Morgan of Powys and his son, Rhys, push their way towards the dais through the crowd of people, all of whom were in various stages of semi-consciousness. Morgan and Rhys had been the most outspoken opponents of Welsh unity at the council meeting Cade had attempted to hold before the wedding, even as they ardently promoted their own personal authority. This they maintained despite the fact that it was Morgan who'd asked for Cade's help when the combined Saxon and demon force had swept through his lands earlier in the year. He was in favor of combining forces to fight off his enemies, just as long as *he* didn't have to be responsible for the defense of other men's lands.

Cade closed his eyes in a brief prayer for strength and then opened them to study Morgan as he approached the front of the hall. It was just like him to point an accusing finger at Cade, no matter what the situation or the fault. Cade found his anger dissipating instead of increasing as Morgan got closer, even turning to amusement. He had to swallow hard to contain it. If he could deal with two demons, he could speak to a recalcitrant lord.

And then he did laugh when Morgan and Rhys stumbled over the prone figure of one of Cade's men-at-arms as they scampered to get away from the two demons on the floor.

Christianity had made its greatest inroads among the nobility of Wales, more than among the common folk, and Morgan and Rhys were no exception. They ascribed to the new religion, viewed themselves as superior for holding with it, and believed the ancient traditions of the Welsh were a thing of the past. To them, the sidhe had lost themselves in their misty world and no longer had any influence over the world of men. More than that, they were sure—or had been right up to that moment—of their place in that world and their knowledge of it. Cade damped down his amusement and chose, again, to follow the high road in his dealings with them.

"I apologize, my lords, for the refuse on the floor," he said. "As you can see, the entire fort was taken unawares by powers over which not even I have control."

While Rhys and Morgan gaped at the demons, Taliesin sidled up to Cade, half-turning his body so the men from Powys could neither hear him nor read his lips. "Congratulations. That was just about perfect. You disarm their anger with your apology, while at the same time implying that your strengths are superior to anyone who is not a god. Excellent."

Rhys pointed his finger at Cade. "You promised us we would be safe here."

"I appreciate that you accord me the ability to control demons," Cade said, "but I'm afraid in this you give me too much credit. I have killed every demon I have come across, but these were sent by Mabon, son of Arawn, who does as he pleases, even in my castle. In truth, we should all be frightened of that power. It is more than an inconvenience."

Morgan's eyes narrowed. If Cade had breath, he would have held it, knowing that his words, although spoken mildly, might have pushed Morgan too far. The last thing Morgan wanted to do was acknowledge Cade's authority.

"If the demons have harmed anyone from Powys, I will hold you personally responsible," Morgan said. "None of the rest of the kings of Wales treat with them, yet the songs that bard of yours creates say you meet them at every turn. I find it disconcerting that demons would make themselves known to the King of Gwynedd."

"Sometimes a man finds battle thrust upon him," Cade said. "In those instances, there is little he can do but stand and fight."

"My lords." Rhiann glided forward, brushing off this catastrophic ending to her wedding as if it meant nothing to her. "I'm sure you are concerned about your ladies. Perhaps it's best if we see to their safety and comfort."

Rhys appeared to want to continue posturing and sputtered his protest, but his father nodded at Rhiann, the movement curt but approving. With Rhiann at their side, they made their way back to where their wives huddled, only just beginning to recover from Mabon's spell.

"First Arawn at Caer Dathyl, then Camulos on the battlefield, and now demons at Deganwy." Rhun helped Bronwen to her feet and moved nearer to the other companions. "Striking you at the times you feel strongest shows an audacity and cunning with which I hadn't credited him."

Cade looked at Taliesin who was leaning on his staff, studying Rhun. "Do you think this is really all Mabon's idea?" Cade said. "Could he not only be working with other gods, but for one more powerful than he is?"

Taliesin didn't answer, didn't even acknowledge that Cade had asked a question. Hywel, meanwhile, had recovered a bit more. He walked to where the two demons lay and crouched beside the first. He fingered one of the arrows, surely noting that it was his, and then straightened before poking the body with his toe.

Cade tucked a foot under the hip of the demon Rhiann had killed and flipped him onto his back. He recoiled at the creature's grotesque features.

"*Black thy horse and thy cape and thy heart, Mabon, the messenger of death.*" Taliesin spoke in a deep voice that almost didn't sound like his own.

Cade hadn't heard him speak those words before and glanced at the bard.

Taliesin gave an uncharacteristic shrug. "It has come to me that we sail in uncharted waters—more and more so every day.

The brotherhood of seers, of which I am the last, did not foresee what has come to pass, either at Caer Dathyl or here. We are outside the old prophecies now."

Cade looked at Taliesin, who, perhaps was already regretting his frankness and had turned his face from him to gaze at the demons' bodies. "I know you fear it, Taliesin," Cade said, "but to my mind, that is a good thing. It is time we left their world and made our own."

* * * * *

Rhiann's breathing quieted, becoming slower and more even. It was the moment for which Cade had been waiting—but now that it came to it, he didn't want to leave her and a part of him didn't see why he should. This was their first night together after all. He'd held her, and loved her, and been loved in return. Since Arianrhod had changed him, he'd assumed that such a love wouldn't be possible for him. Arianrhod might have given him gifts of *sidhe:* immortality, strength, a fire within him beyond all imagining. But Rhiann had given him the gift of herself. Nothing could be more powerful than that.

Rhiann had fallen asleep in his arms, curled onto her side and facing away from him, her hands tucked under her chin. Cade brushed his lips over her hair and ran his hand along her hip, but she didn't waken. He would have stayed if she had, but he forced himself to ease away from her, sit up, and swing his legs over the side of the bed. Rhiann had told him that even on her wedding night, she would rather wake with him gone, than find herself lying beside his still body. It would be like waking beside a dead man.

Even though he *was* that dead man, he could appreciate how awkward that might feel. The panic in her face when she'd shaken him in the clearing before the battle with the demons had stayed with him. Besides, sleeping left him far more vulnerable than he wanted. It was difficult for him to believe, even though he used to be human, that men could sleep and lose themselves to dreams every night.

He hadn't remembered worrying about it particularly as a youth. What if disaster struck while everyone was asleep? While it gave greater urgency to the importance of setting a watch, it was he, among all the residents of the fort, who had the best chance against what came against them now.

Cade sketched a path through the sleeping fort, more shadow than man when he chose to be, and exited through a side door to the keep. Rhun stepped out of the entrance to the stables. The afternoon's rain had stopped and the moon had come out. It shown brightly, illuminating Rhun's face.

"I didn't know if the lure of sleep would draw you in again," Rhun said.

"Not tonight." Cade walked to where Rhun waited.

"Are you ready?"

"Always." Cade turned and led the way to the postern gate.

Rhun greeted the sentry. "Evening, Aeron."

"My lords." Aeron leaped to his feet. Fortunately for him, he didn't have a doxy on his lap and had no need to fear Cade's wrath. One might think that the postern gate watch would be the most despised of all watches at Deganwy, seeing how the guard stood alone, isolated from his companions, other than perhaps a sleepy stable boy. Cade knew from boyhood, however, that it was coveted for just that reason. It was the perfect spot for a man to tryst, should he be of that mind.

"We'll knock as usual when we want back in," Cade said as he slipped through the gate. Rhun followed close behind. Cade felt his friend breathe deeply and relish the night air outside the fort. It shouldn't have been any different than the air inside, but Cade and Rhun had looked forward to their evening sojourns throughout the years.

Rhun's marriage to Bronwen, coupled with Cade's conversion to *sidhe*, had put a stop to them for a while. After the debacle at Bryn y Castell last winter, when Cade had gone out on his own and encountered a band of hostile men and demons, Cade had promised not to travel alone anymore unless he couldn't help it. He didn't need Rhun to remind him what kind of trouble he'd gotten into.

Rhun was thinking along similar lines. "Do you remember the first time we left Bryn y Castell like this?"

Cade's lips twitched. "We were what? Seven? We imagined ourselves bold knights, sneaking past the guard while he was distracted by a maid. We didn't realize it wasn't yet ten in the evening, for all that the fort was quiet."

"We lasted all of a dozen heartbeats before we were scrambling to get back inside." Rhun grinned. "The guard swore he'd never tell, but that we weren't to go out on our own again. He ran to Father instantly, of course."

The two men laughed together, recalling the subsequent summons to Cynyr's study and his stern visage. He'd not reprimanded them as they'd feared he would, however. Instead, he'd confessed that he was short two guards. He'd asked that they take their turn at watch duty along with the other men-at-arms, in order to prevent those who didn't have permission to leave the fort, like Rhun and Cade had done, from finding themselves in trouble. The boys had been excited to do real work, staying up far past their previous bedtimes, and relieved to have escaped punishment—or even detection. Or so they thought.

"How long was it before we realized that it was all a scheme to keep us within the gates?" Rhun said. "Three years?"

"At least." Cade smiled at the memory. "We were much loved."

Then he shifted, scenting the air. After the hubbub in the hall had subsided, Cade had sent men to find out how the demons had gotten into the fort. As it turned out, they'd taken out the guard who had been watching the postern gate, although they hadn't killed him. For that, Cade had to be thankful, and it made him wonder even more what Mabon was up to. The guard, naturally, didn't remember a thing.

Cade crouched low to the ground. Despite their varied and unusual qualities, demons couldn't fly. Just like humans, they would have left traces of their passage at the base of the wall, along with a smell that hadn't dispersed so much that Cade couldn't detect it. Cade led Rhun away from the fort, following the clear footprints the demons had left.

"Could they have come through the village?" Rhun said.

Cade glanced back at his friend. Rhun strolled unconcernedly behind Cade, acting as if he hadn't a care in the world. Of course, he possessed neither the sight nor smell to aid Cade in his work. He was there as bodyguard and to rein Cade in if he became reckless. Cade had overheard Rhiann's admonition to Rhun and his subsequent promise to protect him. Cade resolved not to do anything foolish, at least not tonight.

"I hope not. I think we would have heard." Cade returned his eyes to the ground. "Many of the villagers were invited to our wedding feast. None of them knew of our strange visitors in advance, nor were missing family members, despite what the demons threatened."

"Perhaps Mabon is both powerful, and powerless," Rhun said. "Perhaps he can only work through demons or humans to harm us—as with the murder of Cadfael by Teregad."

"That's an interesting thought," Cade said. "Even Camulos, though he did knock me from my horse, didn't rip out my throat."

"Perhaps the gods only have the power we give them," Rhun said.

Which was a more philosophical statement than Cade had ever heard from Rhun. Still, Mabon had done damage, if only by releasing the demons that preyed on human flesh. It did seem, however, that his great strength lay in influencing others to do his dirty work for him. Something to think on.

They left the defenses of the fort and entered the rugged terrain that restricted any secretive approach to Deganwy. Many stunted trees and bushes had found a home on the slopes of the mountain. After following the precipitous slope for a hundred feet, they reached the bottom and slipped together under the trees that formed a ring around the fort.

Once inside the woods, Cade pulled up short. Silence descended on them and it was one that Cade recognized as unnatural. The small sounds of the forest were never quiet unless they were frightened into it. A slight breeze lifted the leaves on the trees and the lock of hair across Cade's forehead. Cade turned into it, still trying to catch the scent of the demons, but it had dissipated. Something else had disturbed the creatures here.

Cade glanced back at Rhun who gazed west towards the fort, listening. "Do you wish for a torch?" Cade said. It was dark under the trees, but they weren't so close together that some light from the moon and stars didn't penetrate.

"No." Rhun appeared to shake himself out of a reverie. "I can see my feet."

Cade led Rhun eastward, deeper into the forest, always following the footprints. Then Rhun pulled up short. "See here." He gestured to the ground, to footprints that intersected the ones they'd been following. "These also belong to our two demons."

Cade crouched to inspect them. "You're right. It looks like they circled the fort before entering it."

"We should foll—"

A sudden shaking interrupted Rhun's words. The two men froze, uncertain what they were feeling, but when a branch above their heads cracked and fell, missing Rhun by inches, Cade pushed at his friend.

"Back!"

They fled towards Deganwy, dodging dead trees and branches that seemed to leap out at them as they passed.

"This could shake the fort right off its mountain!" Rhun jumped over a tree that had fallen in the path.

Cade had Caledfwlch in his hand and hacked at a tangle of bracken than blocked his way. Every time he put a foot down, it felt as if his knees would buckle and bring him to the ground. Part of him wanted to stop and just hang on to the nearest tree, but he was compelled to keep running. He felt he was only safe in the brief moments he was airborne.

Gradually, as they got closer to the fort, the shaking slowed and then subsided. Cade's heart, if he'd had one, would have been pounding right out of his chest. They'd returned home ten times faster than they'd gone out. From the edge of the woods, he gazed up at the fort, relieved to see it still stood and looked the same as it had an hour earlier.

"It's been some time since I felt such fear as that." Rhun stumbled to a halt, one hand on a the smooth surface of a tree trunk and the other at his ribs.

Cade snorted under his breath. "I shouted like a wounded cow. I let every animal, human, or demon within a mile of Deganwy know we were here."

"It was the unexpected nature of it," Rhun said. "I've heard of rumblings in the earth but never felt one. Is this Mabon's doing too?"

"Let's pray it isn't. For Mabon to have the power to control the surface of the earth would make him even more daunting—and erratic—than we'd already thought him."

"Your conclusion pleases me as well."

The voice echoed on all sides. The two men twisted around nearly full circle looking for its source, before they saw the shimmering of light and smoke. As they watched, the light took the shape of a woman, coalescing out of mist into solid flesh. She stood in the cleared space between the base of the mountain and the trees, as unexpected and unlooked for as after the events at Caer Dathyl.

"Madame." Cade bowed low. Hastily, Rhun followed suit.

"Noble servants," Arianrhod said, "I am looking for my son. I heard his name fall from your lips this night. Have you heard from him?"

Cade blinked, uncertain how to respond to Arianrhod's request and undone by the fact that here was something Arianrhod didn't know or couldn't control. "Mabon is not here." Cade straightened and forced himself to look into Arianrhod's face. "We do have word of him, however. This evening, two demons entered Deganwy at your son's behest. Or so they said."

Arianrhod fixed her eyes on Cade's. The force of her will burrowed into his mind and he couldn't look away or move. He couldn't have breathed even if he were capable of it. He hoped that Rhun, who was also frozen, wasn't finding it equally impossible.

"Did these demons, as you call them, say what they wanted?" Arianrhod said.

"They claimed Mabon sent them to collect Dyrnwyn, the Sword of the White Hilt, from me. Mabon believes that I have it," Cade said.

"Does he?" Arianrhod sounded very much like Taliesin. Cade couldn't read her any more than he could his friend.

"Yes, Madame. I know no more than that," Cade said.

"But my son did not come himself."

"No." Cade warred with himself as to whether he should mention the incident with the boar after the battle against the demons, but while he was deliberating, Arianrhod spoke again.

"Very well." She snapped out of existence with hardly a blink or heartbeat between the instant she was there and then not. In her place stood a doe. Her soft eyes gazed at the two men with guileless innocence. The three creatures stared at each other, and then with a twitch of her tail, the deer bounded into the woods.

At her departure, Rhun collapsed onto his hands and knees in the grass, gasping for breath. "Is that what it's like every time?"

"Yes, and no," Cade said. "Every time is exactly the same, and yet unique."

"Where do you think the doe's gone?" Rhun said. "A foolish man might harm it."

"I will send word to the people of the village not to touch her. None of them want to be indebted to Arianrhod," Cade said.

Rhun nodded. "Better to starve than that."

Cade knelt next to him, one arm across his shoulders. "She didn't hurt you, did she?" The sudden fear of it burned in his chest. "Tell me you don't feel any different than an hour ago!"

"Her very essence bored into me," Rhun said. "From the moment she stood in front of us, I couldn't move; couldn't think. As far as I could tell, even my heart ceased to beat. She sucked all life and breath from me."

Cade could appreciate how Rhun felt. Cade's first encounter with Arianrhod had left him a *sidhe*. He couldn't blame Rhun for being overwhelmed by her presence, even if she'd ignored him and focused, as usual, on Cade. Cade helped Rhun to his feet and turned him so he could study his face. Rhun's eyes were bloodshot, but still his own.

"I am well," Rhun said. "She came to see you, as she always does, although as always she leaves us with more questions than answers."

"She's searching for Mabon," Cade said. "Why can't she find him?"

"Maybe because he doesn't want to be found," Rhun said. "Not a pleasant thought."

Cade returned his gaze to the spot where Arianrhod had stood. "The gods meddle in the lives of men," he said. "I fear that when they do that, the result is never what we'd hope."

"Come," Rhun said, more in control of himself. "You and I should return to the fort. I know you hoped we could linger at Deganwy, but Arianrhod's visit puts a new urgency to the coming fight with the Saxons. We can't face Mabon and the Saxons at the same time, and the Saxons are pressing. I will go with Siawn to muster his men and mine. Where shall we meet you?"

"Caer Fawr, in Powys." Cade fell into step beside Rhun, thinking hard. "I wish Taliesin had been with us tonight. This is something he should have been able to foresee."

"He doesn't see at all anymore, does he?" Rhun said.

"No," Cade said.

"Even had he foreseen the events of this night, would you have been well served by him telling you of them in advance? Would we have done differently than we did?"

Cade thought about that for a moment. "Perhaps not." Again, Taliesin's first words of advice came to him: *Without the prophecy, would the man still act? Or does the prophecy determine the action? Only one who knows himself can answer that.*

Did he know himself? He used to think he did. Now... maybe he should ask Rhiann.

10

Rhiann

Cade and Rhiann left Deganwy for Dinas Bran at sunset two days later. They were doing as Taliesin had asked, as a precursor to facing the Saxons. Taliesin thought they had a week or two of breathing space before an actual assault would come. But no more than that.

"Are you sure you're all right with leaving so soon after the wedding?" Cade said as they set out along the Conwy River, heading south towards the old Roman road that would take them to Dinas Bran. Their men carried a dozen torches to light up the night and for once it wasn't raining. They weren't moving particularly quickly either, and Rhiann hadn't even changed into her male garments, but wore a dress with a voluminous skirt designed for riding.

"I'm with you," Rhiann said. It hadn't exactly been the wedding she'd planned and hoped for, but she'd ended up married to Cade and that was all that mattered in the end. "Besides, Taliesin is sure that this is the right course."

"The Saxons gather in Shrewsbury," Cade said, "near the old Roman fort of Viroconium. We must prepare to counter them."

"Going to Dinas Bran now is the first step towards doing that," Taliesin said from Rhiann's other side.

"What I don't understand is the Saxons' purpose," Rhiann said. "Why do they confront us now?"

"Cerdic of Wessex wants Morgan of Powys' rich farmland, even if Morgan doesn't want to face the magnitude of the threat," Cade said. "The Mercian alliance with Gwynedd which my father made and Cadfael confirmed, only bought us time. The Saxons still want what we have. With Cadfael dead, they know I won't be as easy a mark and they seek to strike before I've fully consolidated my power."

"Are you sure they even know that my father is dead?" Rhiann said.

"Of course they d—" Cade began to speak and then broke off. He turned to look at Taliesin. "Don't they?"

"Did you send them word?" Taliesin said.

"No," Cade said.

"It isn't like he hasn't been a little busy," Rhiann said.

"It would be more normal than not to have sent him a message, however," Taliesin said, "at least to tell Penda that you claimed the throne of Gwynedd. Didn't you think to inform him of the severance of the treaty?"

Cade blinked and Rhiann knew what was going through his mind: There was a lot more to governing than winning battles and you would have thought that *someone* would have mentioned diplomacy a little sooner.

"Penda wouldn't have heard from Cadfael since February," Rhiann said. "Surely he must realize that something is amiss?"

Cade laughed. "That was the day you refused to marry Peada and we killed his warriors while escaping. That would be reason enough for Penda to assume Cadfael has turned against him."

"So Penda might attack us out of revenge for that?" Rhiann's heart leaped to her throat.

Cade put a hand on her arm. "Do you regret refusing him?"

"Of course not!" Rhiann said. "But if that's true, this is my fault!"

"If we meet Penda's army in Powys, it will be Penda's doing," Cade said. "You are not responsible for another's actions."

"But—" Rhiann still felt sick.

"Wasn't the purpose of your escape from Aberffraw to save your husband's life?" Taliesin said.

That brought Rhiann back to her senses. "This isn't going to be easy. Penda knows his ground and has fought over it before. I was only seven at the time, but I remember what an important victory it was for Penda and my father, in defeating King Oswin of Northumbria. Cadfael thought he'd be crowned High King after that."

"Even then, the kings of Wales didn't trust him enough to grant it to him," Cade said. "For good reason."

"Who holds Dinas Bran now?" Rhiann had never seen the lonely fortress that her father's men had described to her, squatting on its mountain a thousand feet above the valley floor.

"Last I heard, it was abandoned," Taliesin said.

Rhiann stared at him. "Abandoned? It's the seat of the High King!"

"And how long has it been since we've had a High King, Rhiannon?" Cade said.

"Since your father died, I know," Rhiann said. "But I hadn't realized things had decayed so far in twenty years."

"The alliance with the Saxons—by both my father and Cadfael—allowed the Welsh to become more comfortable with their lives and lands than was wise," Cade said. "We became complacent."

"So why won't you ally with Penda too?" Rhiann said. "It would be a logical course of action. He is your uncle."

"You can't seriously be asking me that, Rhiann," Cade said.

"It would give you breathing room to strengthen your position as King of Gwynedd," Rhiann said. "And give you time to convince all these Welsh kings to band together instead of taking on the Saxons separately because they don't see the need to work with one another."

"Peada was going to marry you by force," Cade said. "How can you suggest that I ally with any Saxon?"

"It isn't I who's doing the asking, Cade," Rhiann said. "You are half-Saxon yourself. Penda is your uncle! Your men, your allies—all will wonder why the change in policy. You need to have an answer. *Before* we find ourselves attacked by an overwhelming Saxon force that refuses to talk peace."

"Isn't it enough that Cadfael and Penda—or his emissaries—find it convenient to ally themselves with demons?" Cade said.

Rhiann laughed. "I suppose that's a compelling argument."

Taliesin rubbed the stubby blonde hairs on his chin that refused to grow to a man's length. "To my mind, it's time the Welsh stopped dying in Saxon lands. It would be one thing if the alliance was a treaty of non-aggression. It's quite another to march our people east and north to die for Penda, when the Saxons have never died for us."

"My father was still trying to win back the lands that Vortigern had lost," Cade said. "He thought an alliance with Penda might help him gain territory from other Saxon regions. I have no such hope. The Saxons are too many now and we understand them too little."

"And it's only Penda who increased his reach, not your father—not mine," Rhiann said. "I wonder if it wasn't more of a devil's bargain Penda offered rather than a promise to work together in mutual trust and agreement: ally with me or I'll attack you."

Cade smiled. "Can you imagine Cadfael experiencing mutual trust with anyone? It's horrifying to think on."

Rhiann couldn't help but agree with that. Cadfael may have been her father, but he was a tyrant and a bully. The ambush and murder of all of Cade's men, including his foster father, was just the last in a long list of atrocities Cadfael had ordered. That Cade had any companions left was due more to chance and good fortune than planning. Back in February, he'd left Rhun and a handful of his men at Dinas Emrys to guard the fort—and that was the only reason they were still alive.

And now those companions were scattered: Rhun had left for western Gwynedd with Siawn, as had Tudur, each to marshal men under their jurisdiction. Cade had sent Dafydd, Bedwyr, Hywel, and Goronwy south as Dafydd had wanted. Dafydd was for Ceredigion, in southwest Wales, and the other three had gone to Powys and Gwent, in hopes of gathering an alliance of kings. They would meet again at Caer Fawr, in Powys, in ten days' time.

Although Dinas Bran was the seat of the High King, in these dangerous times it was too far for the southern and western kings to travel. Not that they couldn't have made the journey north as easily as Cade could come south, but it would leave their lands unguarded for too long. Asking them to come all the way to Gwynedd to meet him—perhaps even to crown him High King— would be one request too many.

Caer Fawr was a fortified outpost near the road from the old Roman fort of Caersws and within striking distance of Shrewsbury, where the Saxons gathered. The other kings who'd attended the wedding had sworn their allegiance to Cade, some more out of fear than loyalty, given the appalling events of that day. The question that remained unanswered was whether or not they were willing to give Cade fighting men as well. That was always the question.

Other than Taliesin, Geraint was the only close companion to accompany them. He rode at the rear, taking what was usually Rhun's place and allowing Cade to lead the three dozen men-at-arms and knights. The company reached the Roman road at the Conwy River crossing and turned east. Soon, the land became more difficult and forested and they could no longer see the sea. They skirted hills and mountains that enclosed them on all sides.

"How long do we have to ride?" Rhiann said.

"Denbigh is just a few miles further on. I hope to reach it by morning and we'll spend the day there." Cade glanced at her. "I would hope you could sleep today."

Rhiann pulled her cloak closer around her shoulders and gripped the reins more tightly. The wind whipped her face and the branches above their heads swayed with it. She glanced towards the woods to her left and thought she saw something move among the trees. She peered closer, but could make out nothing more than the shadows of the trees themselves, eerie in the half light of their torches. A chill ran down Rhiann's spine.

"What is it?" Cade said.

"I don't know." Rhiann focused again on the trees. For the next mile, she watched and waited, splitting her attention between the road and the woods surrounding them. Then she saw it again—or rather, sensed it. She put out a hand to Cade and he slowed.

Geraint trotted his horse along the side of the column to the front. "There's something there. Taliesin?"

But the bard merely hunched his shoulders and didn't answer.

"Rhiann has sensed it too," Cade said. "It isn't overtly hostile, at least not yet. We should just keep moving. The sooner we get to Denbigh the better."

They rode on. It reminded Rhiann of that endless journey in the dark from Bryn y Castell to Caersws a month before. She'd been fighting her love for Cade then, not married to him, and certainly that made a difference in her heart. But it still beat fast. Her fear, that night, had been about what was up ahead, not what was behind or beside her. "Can you see it?" she said.

"No," Cade said. "No more than you. But it races beside us."

"Like ... a boar?"

"I wouldn't say so," Taliesin said. "This is something different. More ominous."

"So you can sense it," Cade said.

"Of course," Taliesin said. "But its intent is not clear to me. I suggest we ride faster."

Boar or not, the menace rode at Rhiann's shoulder, though whenever she looked into the woods, she saw nothing but endless trees. There was something about the darkness that pressed on her. She wished they could have traveled during the day. In daylight, this *thing* wouldn't have menaced them, she was sure, and the trees would have waved in the breeze as if nothing stalked underneath the branches. But that would have been impossible for Cade. The forest was just leafing out in spring, normally her favorite time of year. Tonight, the trees appeared black and menacing, glistening damply in the moonlight from the shower that had just passed.

Taliesin sat completely silent, beyond that one comment. Both Rhiann and Cade kept glancing at him, hoping for insight or at the very least an appropriate poem, chant, or incantation that might drive it away.

Finally, Taliesin spoke, and the words when they came were obviously reluctant. "I've told you. I no longer see—I am no longer of any help to you whatever. For now, I remain a dead weight around your neck."

"Even were you in your dotage, you would never hinder or hang on me in any way," Cade said. "You are still wise, even if your knowledge is no longer augmented by the *sight*."

The murkiness of the night was drifting towards morning when they finally approached the outskirts of Denbigh. This fort was situated on a rocky height, with the ridgeline of mountains behind it.

"You should travel on without me," Cade said as they pulled to a halt under the gatehouse of the fort. "This creature, whatever it is, won't harm you in daylight."

That was close to what Rhiann had thought herself, though she wouldn't consider riding without her husband. Fortunately, instead of leaving it to her, Taliesin told him he was ridiculous.

"You claim to respect my wisdom, so listen to it now," Taliesin said. "That is a foolish idea. No good would come of it."

Cade pursed his lips but didn't contradict him, for which Rhiann was glad. As much as she feared this shadow, it hadn't harmed them so far, and leaving Cade to travel on his own or with a smaller escort, would have been far worse than living with the fear.

Or so it seemed while they were within the safety of the fort. But when Rhiann tried to sleep, the light in the room and the memory of the shadow under the trees kept her awake. By evening, she felt as if she had sand under her eyelids.

They'd survived one night, but they had two more before they would reach Dinas Bran. Cade tried again, just before they left the fort, to change the plan. "I will ride ahead. It will follow me."

"Are you sure of that?" Taliesin said.

Rhiann sensed that he meant to sound witty, but she heard fear in his voice and a possible truth hit her: this could be something that stalked Taliesin, not Cade. "No," she said. "We ride together or not at all."

Taliesin shot her a glance that told her he'd heard her thoughts. She didn't care. It seemed to her that Taliesin was torn between admitting his need for Cade's protection, and fearing that he was putting them all in danger. In truth, if he needed help, he had only to ask. He should know better than to be so stubborn, but then, her husband was equally recalcitrant. Fortunately, in this case, Cade didn't need more persuading.

The shadow haunted them as they rode.

"Let's just go in and get it," Geraint said, finally, his patience stretched too thin.

"No," Taliesin. "That is what it wants. If you were to enter the woods, it would lead you on and we would lose you."

"It," Cade said. "You mean Mabon? Or Camulos?"

Talisein shook his head. "I'm not sure this is Mabon's doing."

"Then who?" Rhiann said.

Taliesin shook his head again. "I can't—" He stopped and tried again. "I don't know."

Another night passed, and then another day. Three hours out of Dinas Bran, it happened.

A man in the middle of the company was first to call a warning. "Watch out!"

Rhiann, whose head had been sinking to her chin, jerked awake just in time to find Cade's arms wrapped around her. He dragged her from her horse and she sprawled across his lap, her face in his chest.

"Don't look."

She didn't even think to struggle, so commanding was his voice. "What's happening!" Her voice went high in fear, but Cade answered, as calm as ever.

"Something you don't need to see." But then he raised his chin. "Hold! Hold I say!"

All around her men shouted and swords clashed, not obeying Cade, which was almost more horrible than the fear of what surrounded them that he refused to let her see. From somewhere to her left, Taliesin chanted words in a language she didn't understand, and all the while, Cade hugged her to him. She wished she could feel the beating of his heart and the rise and fall of his chest, but it was like being pressed against a pillar, though one that was more secure than any support she'd ever known.

After a short while, the noise of fighting faded and Cade eased his hold on Rhiann. She kept her face in his chest, however, afraid to look at what had happened to her friends and companions. "Is Geraint—"

"Taliesin protected him, but he couldn't save everyone."

Rhiann raised her head to look into Cade's face, and he shifted with her so she could see Taliesin and Geraint. She didn't know what Taliesin had done to their friend, but it couldn't have been pleasant since Geraint lay on the ground beneath him, unmoving, if not unconscious, with Taliesin straddling him. Taliesin held his staff out in front of him with both hands clenched around the middle, as if he planned to spar with it. Perhaps he had. All around them, their men moaned in pain, some with bleeding wounds, others with hands to heads that had suffered heavy blows. One man threw up beside the road. There was no sign of any enemy who might have attacked them.

"What happened?" Rhiann said.

"A malevolent force." Cade nodded at Taliesin, who lowered his staff and crouched beside Geraint.

"Up," he said.

Geraint put a hand to his head. "What did you do to me?"

"Stressed your throat until you passed out," Taliesin said. "Better that than allow you to run one of your own men through."

And as Rhiann looked around at the fallen men, she realized that was exactly what had happened. "Do you mean to say they did this to each other?"

Cade forced out a breath. "Yes. When the shadow overcame us, it drove them mad. They fell upon each other until Taliesin was able to drive it back, into the woods."

"But you were immune?" Rhiann said.

"Of course," Cade said.

"As was I," Taliesin said, "but only because I could see through it and could name its core."

"And what was it?" Rhiann said. "Its name, I mean?"

"Evil," Taliesin said. "More than that, I will not say as yet."

Cade lowered Rhiann to the ground and she went to her saddle bags where she kept her cloths and bandages. She didn't need them often, what with Cade's healing sword, and as she turned to ask Cade whom she should tend first, he'd already crouched beside one of the wounded men. A sword had slashed the man's belly and he scrabbled to close the wound. Gently, Cade pushed one of his hands away and laid the other on the hilt of Caledfwlch. The wound began to heal and the man fell back. "Thank you, my lord."

Rhiann met Cade's eyes. One of this man's own companions had done this to him, and perhaps he'd done worse in return. This shadow was a menace beyond reason or reckoning. Perhaps that was what Taliesin had been trying to tell them.

11

Cade

How many times had he done this? Left his bed when everyone else was asleep? He'd long since lost count of the nights he'd walked; of the men he'd killed. He liked to think he never killed anyone he didn't have to, but the words with which Arawn had mocked him still rang in his ears: *You think yourself so noble, Cadwaladr son of Cadwallon, even as you lie to yourself. You're still trying to fill your father's shoes, aren't you? And failing, I might add.*

Cade honestly didn't know if his father had been a particularly wise man or simply a battle leader, born in the right place at the right time to make a difference. Cade had always thought that his father had been what his people needed: a good king, uniting his people and ruling over them with a strong hand. But recently, he'd begun to doubt that this was true. He'd heard stories, things that people said in passing when they didn't know he could overhear, about his father's temper, or his ruthlessness, or his neglect of his country while he was away, fighting for Penda.

Cade had always thought his father had been fighting *with* Penda, who after all was his wife's brother, but given the demands of kingship, Cade had a new perspective on why his people might not think that was the case.

It seemed to Cade that if he couldn't unite the warring lords of Wales, he would be remembered as little more than a battle leader himself. Perhaps that was enough. Perhaps that was what his people needed most, but he was too close to his own life to tell. Cade wished that he could have known his father and have had his guidance. He wanted, somehow, to be *more* than he was— more than just a battle leader—and to find the words to bring all the Welsh to his side.

Cade *was* grateful that Taliesin had come to him. Without his advice, Cade might have made more mistakes than he had, and fallen into another trap such as the one that took the lives of Cynyr and his men. Still, a father's hand—a father's presence—was invaluable. He and Rhun had needed Cynyr and regretted his loss every day of their lives.

Tonight, it was Taliesin who needed him. The darkness that had attacked them on the road could upend all Cade's plans if they didn't deal with it. Taliesin refused to explain or to name the force, other than to say that Mabon's power was fleeting in comparison. Regardless, it was keeping Taliesin from contact with his patron, Gwydion. And without his help, Taliesin would never *see* again.

Once outside his chamber, Cade headed down the hall to what passed for a receiving room at Dinas Bran. Taliesin was there already, just shrugging into his worn cloak. Cade smiled at the ancient garment. Taliesin didn't have to wear it. He had the new one—the one that was a deep green color and brought out the green in his tawny eyes—that he'd worn to their wedding.

But Cade wasn't surprised this particular evening to see the faded, black cloth Taliesin had always worn wrapped around his shoulders. It may have been the same cloak worn by the man he'd been when he'd taken the infant Cade from his mother. There was comfort in the long legacy of mysticism from which Taliesin arose, and which the cloak represented. They might need that comfort before the night was over.

"Are you ready?" Taliesin said.

"If you are," Cade said.

"Given the menace that surrounds this fort," Taliesin said, "I have thought better of your assistance."

"You've been seeking this on your own for far too long," Cade said. "You have even gone to Anglesey, where the old groves used to grow before the Romans cut them down. Your visions have not returned to you and with the trouble on the road last night, we can no longer delay."

"There are places I haven't been," Taliesin said. "Questions I haven't asked."

"We have both avoided this day ever since you came to me," Cade said. "I can help you. Let me help you. Let me do for you what only I can."

Taliesin studied his friend, and then nodded. Together the two men walked quietly down the stairs to the great hall, and then took the second stairway into the kitchen. A pigeon hooted in its cage, ready for tomorrow's meal. Cade moved his hand to touch it as he passed and then drew it back. For whatever reason, whether Arianrhod's gifts or some new strength of his own, he no longer needed it.

Taliesin was already through the pantry door and as Cade trotted down the cellar steps after him, Taliesin lifted his staff so the light he'd conjured at the end of it could fill the room, illuminating the stones on the floor.

"Do you know under which stone lies the passage we seek?" Taliesin said.

"I checked for it earlier." Cade crouched, slipped a knife from the sheath at his waist, and slotted it between two stones. One slid out easily and Cade hefted it and set it aside. "I can slide it back into place once we're through. It will be easy enough for me to find it again from the other side."

"My apologies, Cade, for what may come next."

Cade looked up at the bard, who was observing him gravely. Taliesin had used Cade's nickname—something Cade never remembered him doing before. "You and I both know there is need. And, in truth, we've been in far worse places."

"That we have, friend," Taliesin said.

"And I, in turn, might ask why you continually seek such places out?"

Cade laughed at Geraint's dry tone, and turned to see him descending the stairs, his sword in his hand. Cade smiled apologetically and got to his feet.

"When the King of Gwynedd sneaks about in his own castle," Geraint said. "What can I do but follow and try to dissuade him from embarking on whatever potentially disastrous adventure he's contemplating? You know this isn't a good idea if you opted not to tell me of it in advance."

Cade laughed again. "I thought, when I first learned of my inheritance and that one day I should be High King of Wales, that when I ordered a man to jump, like as not he'd say, 'Yes, my lord, how high?'"

"And now," Geraint said, "you wonder why those around you are far more likely to tell you that whatever you intend is the god-damned-stupidest plan they've ever heard."

"That does seem to be the case, more often than not," Cade said.

Geraint met Cade's eyes, held them for a moment, and then smiled himself. "But then, as you well know, we still jump."

Cade relaxed and held out his hand in greeting. "Thank you for coming, although, as you say, I did not ask for it."

Geraint reached for him and they grasped forearms. "I heard you pass in the hall and was worried about more intruders." He gestured with his head towards the hole in the floor. "Am I allowed to ask what you're doing?"

Taliesin stared down into the gap. It was impossible to see anything beyond the rim of the hole.

"Could be we don't really know," Cade said.

"Nice," Geraint said.

Cade sat on the edge of the opening and dropped to the rough stones that formed the floor of the cave below. He reached for Taliesin's staff, and then caught the bard himself as he released his handhold to drop into Cade's arms. Taliesin was sweating slightly. Cade checked his face. The sweat wasn't from exertion but from fear of heights.

"That wasn't as bad as last time," Cade said, remembering the fifteen foot drop Taliesin had needed to navigate in Arawn's cavern under Caer Dathyl.

"It's always bad," Taliesin said. "But seeing as how we're here now, we might as well keep going."

Cade glanced up to Geraint, who leaned into the opening Taliesin had just vacated. "I could come with you," Geraint said.

"I would feel better knowing you were guarding the fort and our backs," Cade said.

Geraint nodded, mollified, and took his head from the hole. Taliesin had already turned away. The light at the end of Taliesin's staff lit the small space, about fifteen feet on a side. It bore little resemblance to the caves under Caer Dathyl, with their high ceilings and arched corridors. This was less than an anteroom, compared to those. Cade pulled Caledfwlch from its sheath. The familiar colors that bounced and shimmered off the crystals in the stone walls comforted him.

Taliesin led Cade a few paces to a tunnel that led north from the fort and down at a sharp angle. The walls glistened with moisture and Cade was aware of the tons of rock that pressed down on them from above. After forty-seven steps, Cade counting them out in his head in case things went horribly wrong and he had to come back in the dark, the path forked and Taliesin took the right-hand choice. Unspeaking, they descended further into the mountain. If they hadn't brought light with them, they would have been surrounded by suffocating blackness. Cade gripped the hilt of Caledfwlch more tightly.

After another twenty yards of careful navigation on the rough stone pathway, Taliesin halted. "So it *is* here."

Cade peered over Taliesin's shoulder and contemplated what had brought Taliesin up short. Stairs, surely ancient beyond reckoning, had been cut into the path just in front of them. Instinctively, Cade moved in front of Taliesin, who gave way. Even more carefully now, feeling with his feet for any obstacles that might hinder them, Cade walked down the stairs. He gained confidence as the treads held and the edges didn't crumble away to spill them onto their backsides, or forwards onto their outstretched hands.

"How much further, do you think?" Cade said.

He didn't need to look behind him to register Taliesin's smirk. "You're asking me? The seer who no longer sees? I imagine we will reach the place when we get there."

"You will *see* again." Cade put all the assurance in his heart into the words.

"That is my hope," Taliesin said. "I would give up almost anything, excepting my life itself, to have that gift returned."

"And that is why we have come," Cade said.

A hundred of Taliesin's heartbeats later, the pair came to a halt, their path barred by a wooden door.

"How old do you think this place is?" Cade said.

"Ancient," Taliesin said, "but I'm not sure that we're quite there yet. I would not have expected to find a door where we are going."

"And yet, here it is," Cade said. The door had been once been connected to the frame by leather ties, but they'd disintegrated, leaving only holes where the hinges had been.

"Can you move the door?" Taliesin said.

There was room enough for only one of them in the narrow space, so Cade handed Caledfwlch to Taliesin, who stepped back to give Cade room. With a grunt, for the door was solidly made, Cade lifted it from its rest and turned it against the rock that made up the side wall of the tunnel. Blackness, even deeper than in the staircase they'd just come down, gaped at them.

Cade was still adjusting the door to ensure that he'd properly braced it on the uneven stones when Taliesin passed through the doorway. He stopped short and released a sigh of surprise.

Cade looked past him into the room. The two men stood on the threshold of a room lined from floor to ceiling with shelves. Instead of books or implements, however, as Cade might have expected—were he to expect to find anything down here—the spaces were filled with bones. Hundreds of them.

There were so many that Cade supposed they were looking upon a resting place for many generations of Britons. What's more, the bones were organized by type: long bones on this shelf, skulls in that corner, hands on a shelf above feet. At some point after death, once the flesh had dried off the bones, someone had sorted and separated them and brought them to this spot.

A creeping sensation raised the hair on the back of Cade's neck at the notion that a man might inter a body, only to dig it up again once the flesh was gone.

"Have no fear," Taliesin said, "these are dry bones, nothing more." Absently, Taliesin handed Cade his sword and raised his staff high, then crossed the floor towards a table in the center of the room.

A man's body rested on it, the skeleton complete, unlike the rest of the dead in the room. His desiccated remains, still fully clothed, lay on its back, the flesh dried and yellowed with scraps of hair clinging to his scalp and face and his hands folded across his chest.

"He must have been a great man," Cade said.

"With loyal followers whose loyalty continued after death," Taliesin said. "Why else would they have gone to such effort?"

At the same time, the dead man had no weapons or armor, as any lord or battle leader would have wanted at his burial. His only possession appeared to be a plain wooden box, perhaps a foot long and half that wide, resting at his feet on the end of the table.

Cade took a step closer. "Who buries their dead this way?"

"Early Christians," Taliesin said.

"Why do you say that?" Cade said. "We came looking for a pagan site. Perhaps we've found it."

"No," Taliesin said. "As was the lot of my spiritual ancestors, the Roman legions hounded the Christians all across their territories before becoming Christian themselves. The early believers were forced underground in order to preserve their dead without interference and to save their bones from desecration." He glanced at Cade. "If you recall your history, the Romans cremated their dead."

"I do remember," Cade said. "And I have heard of tombs like this, but I thought them limited to the place of Jesus' birth."

"The early Christians appear to have brought the tradition to Britain, along with their religion," Taliesin said.

Cade detected a bitter tone in Taliesin's voice. They rarely discussed their respective faiths, and Cade had taken to ignoring their differences, because they meant so little to him. Perhaps that had been a mistake.

"Come," Taliesin said. "The place I want is older and further on."

Cade moved to follow Taliesin out of the room. He stopped, however, at the foot of the table on which the man lay. The wooden box was closed and something Cade couldn't express in words drew him to it. He propped Caledfwlch against the table beside the man's feet, and with gentle hands, lifted the lid of the box. Lying nestled within a nearly disintegrated piece of deep blue cloth was a clay cup, crafted no differently from any of the cups from which mead had been drunk that evening at Dinas Bran. Looking closely, however, Cade saw that someone had taken care to etch the image of a fish into the side of the bowl. Any colors, however, had long since faded, along with the sheen of firing.

Noting Cade's attention, Taliesin returned to his side and looked over Cade's shoulder. "It's just a cup."

Cade allowed himself a small smile. "Yes. You're right. It's just a cup."

He closed the lid and recaptured his sword. With Taliesin in the lead again, they continued their journey, exiting the room through a rear doorway and then following a path which descended deeper into the mountain.

Eighty paces on, with the tunnel curving in on itself so it seemed to take them directly below the Christian cavern, they found what Taliesin sought. Many tons of rock pressed down on them and Cade's thoughts shied away from the immensity of what lay above them. He focused instead on this new cave they'd found. Much grander than the room above, the ceiling stretched twenty feet above their heads. A wall on the other side of the room was so far away, Cade could just make it out in the dim light. Arawn could have found a home here.

"I thought the druids worshipped in the forests." Cade's voice boomed around the room, bouncing off the walls. He bit his lip, wishing he'd modulated his tone.

"They did," Taliesin said. "But they also found caves to their liking. Our power comes from the earth and the deeper within it we go, the greater the power we can wield."

Taliesin had once explained to Cade how he drew his strength from the natural world. The magic flowed like a waterfall through him, though rising upward, not down. Much of Taliesin's youth had been spent learning to control it, rather than let random acts of magic burst from his fingertips, or even from the top of his head. Cade thought about that for a moment, wondering if it gave him some insight into what had happened in Arawn's cavern, or about the source of the shadow's power, and then dismissed it as something he wasn't ever going to understand.

Taliesin continued speaking. "And as with your Christians after them, the druids found themselves forced underground at times when the Romans got too close." Taliesin shot Cade a look, then, and it *was* one of resentment, before his face cleared and the gentle expression he usually wore reappeared. "And unlike your Christians, my kind has all but disappeared."

"I can see why if the only place you can worship is this difficult to find," Cade said, trying to lighten the mood. Taliesin obliged with a smile, but it didn't rise to his eyes, and Cade resolved to keep to the business at hand.

Faded paintings adorned the walls, depicting scenes with trees and men—perhaps the sacred groves on Anglesey which the Romans had destroyed. Water gurgled from a spring in the distance, close to the far wall. The last druids to come here had set five sconces in the walls, with torches already prepared to light the room, and had etched a star with five points in the smooth stone of the floor. An altar sat in the precise center of the star. And in its center, in the place of honor, rested a nearly flat wooden bowl.

"What do you need from me?" Cade said.

"If you would light the torches first, and then fill this with water from the spring, I will prepare myself." Taliesin pulled a small wooden bowl from his satchel and handed it to Cade.

With a last glance at Taliesin, Cade set to work. He had the torches flaming with a few strikes of flint, and was able to slide Caledfwlch into its sheath as he no longer needed its light. Taliesin had already leaned his own staff against the wall beside the doorway through which they'd entered. In the furthest reaches of the cave, the spring welled up into a hole in the rocky floor. It bubbled merrily, a counterpoint to the intense and ominous atmosphere bearing down on Cade. Despite his growing concerns about this entire endeavor, Cade brought the full bowl back to Taliesin and set it carefully on the table in front of him.

Taliesin waved Cade away and focused on the bowl. "You are here to rescue me if I can't save myself. If all goes well, a way to defeat what we face will appear to me from within the sacred vessel and renew my *sight* at the same time. This might take some time, or if the gods have forgiven me, my vision might return to me in a powerful rush. Regardless, do not let me touch the water."

"All right," Cade said, not understanding, but deciding he didn't need to in this instance, and perhaps didn't want to. He moved to lean against the wall next to Taliesin's staff.

Taliesin poured the water from the small bowl into the larger one before stowing the smaller one again in his pack. Then he pulled his belt knife from his sheath, held up both hands as if in prayer, and sliced through the fat portion of his left hand below his thumb with the knife. He began to speak out loud, but in words

Cade didn't understand. The drops of blood dripped *one, two, three, four, five* into the water in front of him. After stuffing a cloth into his fist to stop the flow, Taliesin leaned forward to stare over the bowl, still chanting in that unknown tongue.

Cade watched him for a while, and then shifted his position. He loosened his shoulders. He crossed and re-crossed his ankles. It had never occurred to him that this would take so long or that Taliesin's magic could be so boring. Still, Taliesin continued to chant. Then, Cade realized that Taliesin's voice was growing louder, echoing with a growing cacophony off the walls. The volume increased moment by moment until Cade wanted to clap his hands over his ears to shut out the sound.

The fire in the torches dimmed, flared, and then dimmed again. A wind began to blow, circling around Taliesin, who only leaned ever more forward over the bowl. Cade was trying to pay attention to everything at once: the wind, the torches, the horrible, overwhelming sound, and then a growing darkness that seemed to rise out of the stones at their feet like a fog rolling onto the beach from the sea or over a mountain meadow. It welled up so quickly, Cade feared it would obscure Taliesin from his sight and he took a step forward, afraid for his friend.

Taliesin had closed his eyes and his pointy nose was within a hairsbreadth of the water. Cade took another step towards him, watching him intently. He was holding still, however, and Cade was loath to disrupt him before he'd finished his work. Cade stood, feet spread and braced against the screaming wind, while

Taliesin's chanting continued to fill the room. Cade could barely stay on his feet.

"Boom!" The torches exploded in their sconces, throwing flames in all directions and the walls themselves caught fire, for all that they were made of stone. Cade knew it wasn't possible, but he'd seen the impossible before and had been forced to accept it. He could accept this, and ignore it, because it was a small matter compared to saving Taliesin. Cade leapt toward the center of the room, grasped Taliesin around the waist, and pulled him away from the bowl.

Cade feared Taliesin might fight him, but instead, he collapsed the instant his connection to the water was broken. The bard was so tall, Cade nearly overbalanced at the sudden shift in weight. As Cade straightened, adjusting Taliesin in his arms, a dark shape, thicker than the fog on the floor, rose from the water in the bowl. It had no more form than a cloud or trail of smoke, but as Cade watched, transfixed, it took the form of a man, hooded and cloaked.

The being grew larger, rising to the ceiling of the room, and then the wind of before began whirling around the creature instead of Taliesin, accompanied by a rumbling and shaking that cascaded a pile of stones at the far end of the room to the floor. The water from the little brook shot upwards in a geyser, soaking the stone around the hole.

If he'd had breath, it would have been coming fast and hard. As it was, Cade staggered backwards with his burden, and then because he feared he wouldn't be able to flee the shadow in time, bent and threw Taliesin over his left shoulder. The bard hung boneless. The shaking continued, along with the wind which had become a piercing shriek. Cade grabbed Taliesin's staff and held it out, as if that might help ward off the evil force. Then, as the shadow loomed larger above him, he fled.

As soon as he crossed the threshold into the tunnel, the fire behind him went out, as if extinguished in one mighty breath. But who—or what—had done the breathing, Cade didn't know and didn't want to know. Cade ran up the passageway. Trying not to stumble in the total darkness, Cade mumbled the words to conjure the light at the end of Taliesin's staff, words that he'd heard Taliesin say so many times: *caith solas ar*. Cade didn't expect it to work, but despite his lack of faith, the staff lit.

The shadow dogged his heels. Only the little light on the end of Taliesin's staff kept Cade from being consumed by it. The journey upwards seemed to take four times longer than the one down to the cavern, but just when Cade thought he must have turned the wrong way in that initial darkness, he reached the chamber that held the Christian bones. Once he entered that room, the mountain began to shake even harder.

Cade's legs trembled with every step, not because he was afraid (though he was), but because the stones were giving way beneath his feet. The earth's motion catapulted the bones out of their resting places one by one. A skull hit Cade in the head and he raised the arm that held Taliesin's staff, prepared to defend himself and Taliesin against all the forces that might come against them, even the bones. Meanwhile, the man who lay on the table in the center of the room remained as he had been, undisturbed. But as Cade passed the table at a wobbling run, a tremor shook the wooden box and it fell to the floor.

Terrified that its contents had broken, Cade swung around in time to see the precious cup roll out of its protective cloth and right itself in the center of the room. The shaking grew stronger still and the cup rocked on its base, but didn't tip. Even though Cade didn't want to leave the room and its unattended cup, he retreated, backing through the far doorway and into the passage beyond which would take them back up to Dinas Bran.

The instant his left foot sought for purchase on the uneven stones in the entryway, the black shadow filled the far doorway opposite him. It surged forward. Cade opened his mouth in a silent scream, knowing that he needed to turn and run but unable to move. But when the shadow reached the spot where the cup rested, it drew up short. The shrieking wind grew louder and the blackness loomed from floor to ceiling in the back half of the room, yet it was as if an invisible wall prevented it from continuing.

The being fell backwards, like a wave crashing against a cliff wall and then retreating. It disappeared from the room. Thinking the threat had ended, Cade took a step towards the cup on the floor. He wanted to return it to its box. Before he could take another step, however, the blackness filled the doorway again and thrust towards him. Fear shaped in darkness and threat filled his ears in a wild shriek, but another appeal pushed it away.

Run!

Cade fled, Taliesin bobbing on his back like a sack of turnips. Cade took the stairs three at a time. When he was a step from the top, a great crashing of rock sounded behind him. He allowed himself one glance back. A mountain of stone that even he might have trouble penetrating blocked the doorway.

The further he ran from the hidden chambers, the quieter the rumblings, until he reached the last cave, below the castle's cellar. He entered the chamber warily, but was met with silence.

"Geraint!" Cade tilted his head towards the opening in the cellar floor.

A heartbeat later, the familiar face appeared above him, reminding Cade of why he trusted Geraint with his life. Geraint didn't ask questions, just reached through the hole for Taliesin, then his staff, and finally Cade, who boosted himself onto his stomach in the opening, and rolled onto his back on cool stones of the cellar floor.

Geraint crouched over Taliesin, his ear to his chest. "He lives."

"I'd hoped as much," Cade said, not moving. It wasn't so much that he was tired, but mentally spent.

"He does live," Taliesin said. He remained on his back and his voice cracked over the words.

Cade sat up and crawled the few feet that separated him from Taliesin. For the first time since Cade had seen the fear in his eyes, Taliesin allowed Cade to see inside him. His eyes revealed an inwardness that marked him as someone who'd lived through what no man should ever have had to see.

"Can you tell us what you saw in the water?" Cade said.

"What supports the world that it lies not in waste around us?
And if the world should fail, on what would it fall?
Who will uphold it when it descends into decay?
Again the circle closes."

The words meant nothing to Cade, and Taliesin didn't explain them. Instead, he answered Cade's question. "I saw the long cloud of war. It's a black shadow that will cover the land from mountain to sea."

"I saw a shadow too." Cade studied Taliesin's face. *"The* shadow, I think. It rose up from the water and followed us as I fled with you."

Taliesin's jaw clenched. "What happened to it?"

"It never left the room with the Christian bones," Cade said, not ready to speak of all that he'd seen. Not just yet.

Taliesin closed his eyes and his muscles relaxed, the lines on his face smoothing to that of a youth. "I remember nothing of what happened, other than my visions. I suppose it isn't too much of a stretch to think that you saved my life?"

"You told me not to let you touch the water," Cade said. "So I didn't."

"I do remember wind and fire," Taliesin said.

"The mountain shook around me, much as it did when Rhun and I searched for traces of those demons at Deganwy," Cade said. "Rocks fell behind me as I ran. They collapsed in front of the ossuary door. They didn't stop until I reached the fort and found it calm."

"I felt no rumbling," Geraint said. "All was quiet here."

Taliesin pushed up onto one elbow. "Then perhaps we still have time. Whether the gods have blessed me with the renewed gift of foresight, or it is only a temporary thing, I feel the weight of my gift pressing on me, like a great ache behind my eyes." He took Cade's shoulder in one hand and shook him slightly, so urgent was his warning. "The gods themselves have taken sides in the coming battle."

"Mabon," Geraint said. "And Camulos."

"And Arianrhod, and Arawn, and Llyr, and Gofannon, and even my own patron, Gwydion," Taliesin said. "All are arrayed in the unseen world, with their ancient grudges and shifting allegiances. We face the Saxons, yes, but I fear more than they, we fight our own selves and contest the essence of what it means to be Welsh."

Cade scrubbed his face with his hands. "Let's get you up. We can continue this discussion after you've rested."

"I will never rest again," Taliesin said, "though I close my eyes in sleep."

"I will speak with the lords of Powys, Ceredigion and Gwent," Cade said. "I will force them to listen."

"And meanwhile, we'll find out what the Saxons are up to," Geraint said, doing a good imitation of Bedwyr's growl. "We will find them, and meet them, and let that be an end to it."

Part Two

12

Dafydd

Every fort Dafydd had ever encountered invariably claimed the highest ground of the region in which it sat, even if the only elevation available was a knee-high hill. The seat of King Clydog of Ceredigion, however, crouched in the bend of a meandering river. It was in the middle—as far as Dafydd could tell—of nowhere. The king did seem to have made an effort to protect his fort with a system of surrounding ditches and palisades. Still, an enemy could approach from every side, even the river, which was hardly more than a creek where Dafydd's horse, Llelo, splashed through it.

As ruler of Ceredigion for the last twenty-five years, Clydog would have known Cade's father. Dafydd hoped that meant he'd give Dafydd himself a positive reception. Rhiann's father, Cadfael, had been a usurper, which no king with sons could countenance. Perhaps it was that sentiment, expressed by men such as Clydog, that had prevented Cadfael from achieving the much coveted station of High King.

Thwt! An arrow appeared in the ground at Dafydd's feet and he reined in. For all that Dafydd didn't think much of Clydog's fortifications, his men were certainly on alert.

"Who goes there?"

Dafydd gazed up at the man-at-arms, a bit stunned since one man, even a knight such as he, could hardly be a threat to the castle. "I am Dafydd ap Cynin, from Ynys Manaw—the Isle of Man—and Gwynedd."

"Whom do you serve?"

The man who glared down at him couldn't have been any older than Dafydd himself, but was affecting a glare that would have done credit to a man thirty years older. Dafydd saw, too, that the man-at-arms sported a sparse beard that hardly deserved the name. Dafydd's own growth flourished and he smoothed it along his chin with one hand. "My lord is Cadwaladr ap Cadwallon, the King of Gwynedd."

The man canted his head in acknowledgement of the legitimacy of that allegiance. Or at least that was what Dafydd hoped.

"You may enter," the guard said.

A moment later, the great double doors to the fort opened outward and Dafydd urged his horse between them. He entered into a courtyard that was as unusual as the fort itself. For starters, a fountain bubbled in the center of it, splashing water into a large basin. It was the fort's water supply, evidenced by the serving wench who filled a bucket from it. Rather than packed earth, stone had been laid in pathways leading from the gatehouse to the fountain, circling it, and then to the great hall. Dafydd dismounted, wondering at the beauty of it. While a stable boy ran to take Llelo and lead him away, Dafydd followed the stones to the front door. The hall itself was built of local stone on cobble foundations though the upper storey was timber-framed and plastered.

"Welcome," King Clydog said, a few moments later, after his guards had done a quick count and inspection of Dafydd's weapons. They didn't take them from him, but they'd catalogued his bow, arrows, sword, and three knives: one at his belt, another in his boot, and a third one, much smaller, tucked into his left bracer.

Dafydd bowed. "I come to you from King Cadwaladr ap Cadwallon of Gwynedd. He is seeking your council and support."

"And the use of my men, no doubt." Clydog lifted his chin. "King, eh? What happened to Cadfael. Did Cadwaladr skewer the old bastard?"

"Uh ... no, my lord." Dafydd found himself stammering under Clydog's gaze. He also had an accent that Dafydd hadn't heard before and Dafydd was having trouble piecing together the man's sentences. "Gwynedd has experienced some...uh...treachery and upheaval of late."

"So how'd the old bastard die?"

"Teregad of Caer Dathyl killed Cadfael. King Cadwaladr heard it from the man's own lips. Teregad has since been deposed and his younger brother Siawn rules in Arfon."

"Old Iaen finally stepped aside, eh?" Clydog said.

Again Dafydd blinked. "I apologize, my lord, but again that isn't correct. I'm sorry to inform you that Teregad murdered his father, before he killed Cadfael."

"Never say it!" Clydog surged to his feet. "Iaen was my friend!"

Dafydd bowed, sorry to have been the one to tell him.

Clydog subsided, a finger to his chin, studying Dafydd. Dafydd kept his head slightly bent to the floor, though he still managed to peer at Clydog.

"You do bring momentous news," Clydog said. "We must have a long talk. But not this moment. You've had a long journey and I've been remiss in my hospitality." He snapped his fingers. "Angharad!"

A girl—or woman, rather—of Dafydd's own age approached from behind Clydog's chair. She kept her eyes on the floor, not looking at Dafydd as she spoke so it was hard to get a sense of her beyond the red curly hair that formed a halo around her head and cascaded down her back, hardly contained by her attempt to tame it with cloth band.

"Allow Angharad to assist you," Clydog said. "You may wash the dust from your feet and then join me in the hall for dinner."

"Thank you." Dafydd followed the girl from the hall, down a corridor to a room lined in stone.

Sunk into the floor was a square hole, four feet on a side, which was also lined with stone. The girl gestured towards it with one hand. Dafydd stared in astonishment as two servants poured bucket after bucket of hot water into it to make him a bath. He'd never seen a room quite like this before. But it seemed the girl thought nothing of it. Of course, for her it would be normal.

"Let me assist you with your armor," Angharad said.

"Again, thank you," Dafydd said. "I've been sleeping rough this last week for most of my journey from Deganwy." Off came the mail, sword, and shirt. Bare-chested, Dafydd sat on a stool near one corner of the bath while the girl worked at his boots. When they came off, he leaned back against the wall and sighed in relief to be able to wiggle his toes freely. There was a time when his mother refused to let him have a pair of boots at all because she said his feet were growing too fast. By the time the cobbler finished one pair, Dafydd needed a bigger size. Thankfully, those days appeared to be past him.

"The passes were blocked with snow all winter." Angharad dropped his second boot to the floor. "You are most welcome here. My father hasn't been able to get much in the way of news out of the east."

Dafydd stared at her. "Your—your—" He stopped and tried again. "King Clydog is your father?"

Angharad forehead wrinkled in puzzlement. "Of course."

Dafydd swallowed hard. Now that he looked at the girl more closely, he should have known she was no serving wench or slave. The cloth in her dress was woven close and dyed a deep green that set off her red hair. It was the hair that had distracted him from the first, and it showed her to have ancestry from Ireland. Here on the west coast of Wales, relations between the two lands were close. He'd assumed that she was a slave for that reason.

Angharad reached for the ties that held his breeches up at his waist and Dafydd found his face coloring. He grasped her hands before she could untie them. "No, no. Please. I appreciate your efforts but I can take care of the rest myself."

Angharad smiled in what Dafydd interpreted to be an amused and superior way, and nodded. "As you wish." With a slight curtsey, she turned on a heel and left the room.

Only after Dafydd was sure that she was truly gone did he remove the rest of his clothes and slide into the warm water. Closing his eyes, he acknowledged that it was probably a good thing that he would only be here for a few days. King Clydog might be amenable to Cade's overtures. But his daughter, with that overstated hair and knowing look, could be more than he could handle.

The hall had filled with Clydog's people by the time Dafydd returned to it.

"What did you think of your bath?" Clydog said.

"I've never seen anything like it," Dafydd said. "It must have been complicated to build. That and the fountain."

"It was the Romans, you know," Clydog said. "Amazing engineers, even if they proved unworthy of our lands."

"Most of our people are reluctant to occupy their ruins," Dafydd said.

Clydog waved a hand dismissively. "Superstitious nonsense. There's nothing here but stone and dirt. Besides, our people won in the end, didn't they? Butchered the owners most like. I've noticed faded splotches on some of the walls that look to me like blood once dyed the stones red. I'm not afraid of a few Roman ghosts."

Dafydd nodded. He supposed he wasn't either, not after spending the last month in the service of Cadwaladr ap Cadwallon. He didn't mention that to Clydog, however. Not yet.

Clydog had other guests and his table was full. Dafydd sat three down from the center of the table and was content with that, even if—as a king's son and knight—he might outrank every man here but Clydog himself and his son.

"I've been thinking about you." Angharad's voice came low in his ear.

Dafydd turned to look into her bright green eyes that flashed at him from underneath pale lashes. Did he see anger there? Why? "Excuse me? What did you say?"

"Ever since I saw you walk into this hall, you've seemed familiar," Angharad said. "I just remembered why. Last summer, I saw you chopping wood behind the stables at Caer Dathyl. You've deceived my father. You're not a knight. You're a kitchen boy."

Dafydd groaned inwardly. He didn't regret his sojourn in the kitchens of Caer Dathyl, but hardly would have thought that it would come back to haunt him here. Still, he didn't look away. "I was a kitchen boy for a time. But it was only ever meant to be temporary. I've not deceived your father. I do serve King Cadwaladr of Gwynedd and I am a king's son."

"Of Ynys Manaw? That's hardly much of a kingdom, is it?"

"Don't tell my father that." Dafydd was stunned at her rudeness but tried to maintain a façade of politeness.

"I suppose you have brothers?" Angharad said. "Surely it isn't you who will inherit?"

Dafydd gritted his teeth. "I tell you again. I am the son of a king and was knighted in the presence of King Cadwaladr himself."

Angharad pursed her lips. "You don't look like a knight. You look like a big oaf."

Dafydd's jaw dropped. And then he coughed a laugh. "As I mistook you for a slave when we first met, I suppose that's only fair."

Although her own words had been cruel, Dafydd was appalled to see tears glistening in Angharad's eyes at his insult. She opened her mouth to speak, then firmed her jaw. Wiping at her cheeks with the back of her hand, she stomped her foot. "I can't do it. I can't!" Without explaining, she turned and ran from the room.

"Some knight." Dafydd cursed his foolishness as he took a long drink from the cup that Angharad hadn't had time to refill.

"The first girl you come across in a week, and hardly a moment passes before she leaves the room in tears ..."

The man next to him leaned in closer. "All women talk like that. My sister used to be an exception, but recently she's changed."

"Angharad is your sister?"

The man hadn't spoken to Dafydd earlier, having been too busy conferring with men on his other side when Dafydd had sat down, but now he held out his hand. "Seisyll, son of Clydog."

Dafydd shook his hand and looked closely at him. Seisyll wore his red hair close-cropped and had a small scar along his left jaw-line. The worn sheen to his scabbard and the broadened shoulders of a fighting man indicated he might be well-worthy of his station as Clydog's heir.

"Seisyll!"

A woman bore down on them. By any standard, she was beautiful, with thick, honey-colored hair, elfin face, and a perfect figure. Seisyll leaned back in his chair as she approached, affecting an unconcerned air. "My wife, Lilwen," he said, with a careless wave of his hand.

Dafydd had the instant impression it was a less than happy marriage.

"Yes, my dear," Seisyll said.

"Where is Angharad?"

"I don't know. She was here a moment ago."

"That girl." Lilwen's hands were on her hips. Then she noticed Dafydd. "Are you that knight who arrived this afternoon that I told Angharad to wait on?"

"Uh—" Rudeness seemed to be the order of the day among the women of Clydog's household. "I am Dafydd ap Cynin. My father is the King of the Isle of Man. I serve in King Cadwaladr's *teulu*."

Lilwen nodded as if that was no more than she expected. She gazed around the room, her hands still on her hips. "That girl. Never where she's supposed to be when she's supposed to be there. I told her—"

"Lilwen ..." Seisyll's voice sounded a warning tone.

Lilwen pinched her lips and didn't turn to her husband, but she didn't say anything more either. Dafydd thought it likely Seisyll would hear about this later. He might exert control in public, but Dafydd guessed that their conversations in private might be another matter.

"I will see to Angharad," Lilwen said.

Lilwen stalked through the same door through which Angharad had disappeared.

Seisyll leaned in. "I apologize for the behavior of my wife and sister. There was a time when we had peace, but not recently." What he didn't say was *not since I married Lilwen*.

"Don't trouble yourself," Dafydd said.

And then Seisyll's attention was caught by the man to his right again and Dafydd decided it wouldn't make things worse to exercise his curiosity before any one else insulted him. He wasn't used to having such an unfortunate effect on women. Normally, girls liked him. Certainly Rhiann liked him, even if she loved Cade more.

He eased to his feet and when nobody, not even Seisyll, appeared to notice, stepped down from the dais, walked to the door, and poked his head into the hallway. With a last glance towards the high table to see if anyone was watching him (nobody was), Dafydd trotted up the stairs to an upper floor. He didn't try to disguise his movements, but allowed his feet to tread normally. When doing something mildly surreptitious, it was always better to pretend one knew what one was doing.

There was no one to stop him, however, and it wasn't difficult to find where Angharad and Lilwen had gone. All he had to do was follow the sobs.

"Angharad! Shut. Up." Lilwen's dulcet tones echoed in the hallway. Dafydd checked behind him a last time. Fortunately, nobody else was in evidence and the noise from the hall below was great enough to drown out the smack that followed.

"Ouch!" Angharad said. "That hurt."

"I'll smack you on more than your bottom if you don't stop that weeping! You have a husband to catch!"

"I can't do it your way, Lilwen," Angharad said. "Please don't make me!"

"*You* don't have a choice. Your way of finding a husband was not to attract one at all," Lilwen said. "What did you look like when we spied Sir Dafydd in the distance? Clothes in rags; hair a raging mess. It's no surprise your father didn't try to sell you sooner. He mistook you for a boy of twelve!"

"I won't do it! You can't make me."

"I can and you will," Lilwen said. "The time has come for you to find a home of your own and get out from under my feet. This will never be my house as long as you are in it."

"You took the keys to the cellars," Angharad said, and now her voice had a little more strength to it. "You already got what you wanted."

"What I want is you married or in a convent by midsummer," Lilwen said. "Or I will tell your father that you dallied with one of his men-at-arms and then he won't have a choice. He'll banish you to some place where you won't shame him anymore."

"You wouldn't!"

"Try me," Lilwen said. "Now, go chat up that knight from Gwynedd again."

With that, Dafydd started backing away from the door, worried Lilwen would catch him eavesdropping. He'd grown up with only brothers and had never heard a conversation quite like this before. He didn't know what to make of it. Marriage to anyone, much less Angharad, was the last thing that interested him right now. But then Angharad spoke again and he held back.

"I can't." Angharad moaned as she said the words. "He seemed nice at first, but now it's all ruined. You've ruined it. He thinks I'm a cow."

"No, he doesn't," Lilwen said. "You need to try again. Men like it when girls say mean things to them. It makes you more interesting."

Dafydd almost snorted but caught himself in time. Lilwen couldn't have been more wrong. Although, if this was the technique she'd used to ensnare Seisyll, perhaps it worked on some men.

"But—"

"No *buts*," Lilwen said. "By the breath of Saint Mary, wipe your eyes and get downstairs again!"

Angharad had been reduced to sniffles. The conflict appeared to be winding down. Dafydd slipped into a room with a half-open door just in time for Lilwen to stalk out of Angharad's room and back down the stairs without seeing him. A moment later, Angharad followed. After she'd gone, Dafydd leaned his head back against the wall and closed his eyes. He was never going to understand women.

13

Dafydd

The next two days brought success, at least in terms of Dafydd's mission, as Clydog felt himself up to the task of supporting Cade. On the personal front, however, things went from bad to worse.

At first, Seisyll tried to help Dafydd out. He leaned across the table at Dafydd's first breakfast, his voice low. "My wife is sometimes hard to—" But before he could say more, Lilwen dragged Angharad to the table to sit with them and forced her to make small talk. With every meal that followed, Lilwen appeared more and more triumphant and the only consolation to Dafydd was that Angharad seemed as miserable as he. At least Angharad had stopped insulting him and he knew that even the ones she'd thrown at him earlier had been for show.

"Sir Dafydd, tell me of the kitchens at Caer Dathyl." Lilwen's tone had a sickening sweetness to it, and she wore her usual sneer fixed firmly in place, belying her façade of amenability.

"I—I—" Dafydd didn't know what to say and studied Lilwen's profile. When she asked the question, she'd made sure he met her eyes, but he'd felt Seisyll kick her under the table. Now, she kept her head bent over her plate and didn't look at him. That was probably wise as her husband, who sat across the table from her, was glaring at her with daggered eyes. Beyond Lilwen, Angharad's chin had come up and she gazed at the opposite wall as if she couldn't quite believe she what she was witnessing.

"No, my lord, don't say another word to her. Lilwen doesn't really want to know about your time in the kitchens. She wants to put you at a disadvantage by reminding everyone of a period in your life you'd perhaps rather forget."

"Angharad—" Seisyll put out a hand, either to stop her from saying more or out of sympathy.

Now that Angharad had snapped, Dafydd didn't care what he told them. He'd lain awake last night, worrying that his first mission for Cade had already become a disaster because he didn't know how to handle a woman's tongue. And now... amusement bubbled up within him that all his worrying was for nothing. Angharad was defending him and finally speaking up for herself.

It was such a relief to have an authentic word come out of Angharad's mouth. Neither the venom, nor the tears, had seemed normal for her. Dafydd threw back his head and laughed.

"I don't mind at all. Your sister-in-law hasn't offended me." Dafydd put the back of his hand to his mouth, trying to contain the laughter that wouldn't be contained. While Seisyll stared at him, Dafydd got himself under control.

"I served in the kitchens and lived among the common people as one of them in order to learn about myself as a man."

Lilwen's head came up at that. "Really, I don't think—"

"No, you don't think, do you, Lilwen!" Angharad said.

Lilwen's hand flew back and she smacked Angharad across the cheek. She was bringing her arm up for another blow when Seisyll caught it. "Don't."

Dafydd rose to his feet to place himself between Lilwen's chair and Angharad's. Angharad had a handkerchief to her face but looked up at him as he loomed over her. He held out his arm. "Take a turn around the courtyard with me?"

Angharad brought down her hand and wadded the cloth in her fist. The red marks left by Lilwen's fingers were clear on her face, but she had her chin up and looked straight at him. "Of course, my lord. It would be my pleasure."

"I like you more and more, Angharad."

Angharad's eyes widened, but she took his arm and the two of them strolled behind the other diners on the dais. He looked over the top of Angharad's head towards the front doors of the hall. Carved and painted with outlandish, possibly Roman, designs, he wished they were closer so they wouldn't have to navigate the distance under everyone's gaze.

But as it turned out, they could have been invisible for all that anyone cared about what they were doing. It was Seisyll and Lilwen who'd caught everyone's attention. They'd risen to their feet opposite each other at the high table, and were glaring at each other. Everyone else in the hall gazed towards them with rapt expressions, ranging from astonishment to outright pleasure. An open fight between Clydog's heir and his wife—one that had been a long time coming—was worth staying around for.

But not to Dafydd. Angharad's hand felt comfortable on his arm and her stride matched his. She was taller than most women—easily taller than Rhiann—with the top of her head at his shoulder.

"Why are you being nice to me?" Angharad said as they stepped off the dais and headed towards the front door of the hall.

"Everyone at that table was a heartbeat away from saying something they've long felt but might later regret," he said. He and Angharad had reached the side doorway that led upstairs and he paused to look down into her upturned face. "Seisyll has the conversation in hand—at last, it appears—and I wanted to meet the real Angharad."

"The real—"

The front doors to hall flew open, cutting off Angharad in mid-sentence. In walked—

"Christ!" Dafydd didn't wait to confirm his first impression. He wrapped his arm around Angharad's waist, hauled her through the doorway into the side passage, and pressed her to the wall on the other side of the opening.

"What is it? What's wrong?"

"Ssshh," he said. "Wait."

Dafydd peeked around the doorframe. Mabon ap Arawn, dressed in unrelieved black, strode towards the king's dais. Clydog had noticed him—who wouldn't have?—but so far all he'd done was glance at him, allowing his retainers to move in to surround

Mabon and prevent him from accosting the king. Dafydd guessed none of the people in the hall but he knew the identity of this visitor.

Mabon halted, his chin up and eyes blazing. He glared at each of the guards in turn. They fell back under the force of his gaze.

"Where is it, Clydog!" Mabon said.

Clydog lifted his head and leaned back in his chair, his elbow resting on the arm and a finger to his lips. His posture was relaxed, but the tension in the room—already high due to the fight between Lilwen and Seisyll—ratcheted up another three notches. Clydog's guards moved to ready stances. Dafydd could have told them that they shouldn't have let Mabon in the fort in the first place.

"Who are you?" Clydog said. "Who are you to violate the sanctity of my hall by storming in here uninvited?"

Mabon pulled himself up to his full height, which was close to Dafydd's own. Mabon was also what Cade had called *unreasonably beautiful*. Perhaps unsurprisingly, Lilwen stared at him, enraptured.

Unlike Mabon, however, the dozen men who'd entered the hall with him didn't try to hide behind their looks and they began circling around the edges of the hall, eyes scanning hands and faces, their own hands on the hilts of their swords. It would take just one word from Mabon and his men could massacre Clydog's people. Cade had wondered if Mabon worked only through the actions of humans, and if he himself had little power in the human world other than to obscure the truth and create *glamour*. But with two dozen human men-at-arms at his command, it didn't really matter what power belonged to him and what he borrowed.

"Who is it?" Angharad poked at Dafydd to get his attention. When he didn't answer right away, she burrowed under his arm so she could see into the hall.

Dafydd still held her around the waist and now leaned down to whisper into her ear. "He is Mabon, son of Arawn. He is the *sidhe* who caused King Cadwaladr's troubles earlier this winter."

"A *sidhe*—"

"Don't look at him. Don't think of him. He deceives you with a beautiful face, with the same *glamour* all the gods use when they walk among humans. He is not as he seems at first. He's not even real."

"I don't think he's more handsome than you are." Angharad said this as if it wasn't the most obvious of untruths. "What might he want with us?"

"I don't know," Dafydd said, "but it can't be anything good."

"I am Mabon!" As Mabon spoke, his aura seemed to expand outward from his body in a ring of light. "You must give me what I want!"

Clydog had gotten to his feet and now backed off from the table, giving way before Mabon's intensity. "I don't—I don't—I don't have it. I don't have anything you'd want."

Mabon stepped onto the dais and placed his hands flat on the surface of the high table. He leaned on them and gazed directly into Clydog's eyes. "I know it is here. Give it to me."

Clydog shook his head, but it wasn't as forceful as it might have been and sweat poured from his temples. Overall, his posture was uncertain. It made Dafydd think that Clydog might truly have this thing that Mabon wanted, unlike Cade, who hadn't. And if Dafydd realized it, Mabon might too. Still, Clydog appeared determined to deny it to Mabon if he could.

Mabon straightened, pulled a sword from the sheath at his waist, and pointed it straight up in the air. It lit with a white fire from hilt to tip.

Dafydd reacted without thinking. He pulled Angharad toward the stairway. He didn't want even the slightest chance of being overheard. "Do you know what he's talking about? Do you know what Mabon wants?"

Angharad's eyes were too wide and she stared past Dafydd without seeing him. "Did I really see his sword flame? What's he going to do?" Her voice went high. She was panicking.

"Forget the sword." Dafydd caught Angharad's chin and forced her to look at him. "Do you know what Mabon wants?"

Angharad swallowed hard and her eyes focused on Dafydd's face. "Yes." She nodded her head rapidly. "My father gave it to me to protect."

"To you?" Dafydd's voice was hard and urgent. "Knowing that Mabon might want it—"

"It isn't like that," Angharad said.

"What is it like?" Dafydd said. "Is it a sword? A weapon of some kind?"

"It's a pillow," she said.

"A what?"

When Angharad simply nodded vigorously again, Dafydd barked a laugh and then shook his head. "I almost don't want to know." He turned to look through the open doorway to Clydog and Mabon, still in confrontation. Dafydd returned his attention to Angharad. "Get it and meet me at the postern gate. We can't let Mabon's men find it when they search the castle."

"It won't come to that, surely," Angharad said.

Dafydd put a finger to her lips and continued as if she hadn't spoken. "If I don't come in time, if I don't find you, hide it in the woods and then hide yourself."

"What are you going to do?"

"I might be the only one here who has seen Mabon before—knows him from an earlier confrontation—and knows what he's like," Dafydd said. "I will distract him and his men to give you time to get away."

"What? No!" Angharad said. "He might kill you!"

Dafydd had her by the shoulders. "He won't."

"You don't know tha—"

"Go!" Dafydd pushed Angharad towards the stairs and to his relief, she didn't question his decision again. After one last glance back, she went.

Dafydd watched her disappear and then turned back to the hall. He closed his eyes and breathed deeply. Then, throwing back his shoulders in a show of confidence, even if that was the last thing he was feeling just now, he strode into the room and pulled his sword from his sheath as he did so.

"Don't listen to him, Clydog," Dafydd said. "He is all *glamour* and no power."

Instantly, Dafydd had Mabon's attention. Mabon seemed to puff up even more, his light and beauty filling the room. "Who are you?" And then Mabon's eyes narrowed. "You're not *sidhe*."

Dafydd managed not to hesitate in his walk and show his surprise. He'd expected Mabon to remember him and tried not to be offended that he hadn't. But then Dafydd recalled the scene in Arawn's cavern: Mabon had snuck away at the beginning of Cade's battle with Arawn. He really didn't know that Dafydd had grasped the hilt of Dyrnwyn and drawn it from Cade's body.

"No, I am not," Dafydd said.

"And yet you dare challenge me?"

"You are not welcome here, no matter what it is you *want* or which sword you carry."

In response to Dafydd's challenge, Mabon pointed his sword at Dafydd. It still sparked, but less than before. Dafydd came closer, his sword relaxed in his grip. Mabon stepped away from the table and before Dafydd had any more time to think about the intelligence of this course, they were circling each other in a cleared space fifteen feet on a side.

"My son," Clydog said. "You don't have to do this"

"I do, in fact," Dafydd said.

"He is a god!" That came from Lilwen, whose eyes were bright and had a fixed smile on her face. She seemed completely bewitched.

Mabon laughed. "You have the right of it, miss. Fight me, boy, and you throw away your life."

"I don't think so," Dafydd said.

"You are that confident?" Again, Mabon swelled with light and power, though Dafydd still felt that it was a show, and not real power like Cade carried within him. Dafydd had seen both now, and knew the difference, or hoped he did.

"What kind of god are you to terrorize your people?" Dafydd said.

"I rule over whomever I choose, and all men must obey my commands."

Dafydd considered his words, and then a thought struck him. "Does your mother know where you are?"

Mabon's face twisted and the *glamour* wavered. Dafydd didn't know that he could describe what was revealed at Mabon's core, except its darkness. Then Mabon's shape steadied and Dyrnwyn flared anew.

Dafydd's right hand still burned from the memory of holding the magic sword back at the caverns at Caer Dathyl. To see it again in Mabon's hand disgusted him. He had to almost physically push away the feeling. Cade had told Dafydd that he was worthy of the sword, and the sword had agreed, but Dafydd himself still couldn't quite believe it. A month on, Dafydd was still a long way from forgetting what had happened there.

Lilwen rose to her feet and now the light in her face was beatific. "My lord! You bear Dyrnwyn."

"I do." Mabon gave her a wide smile. "You are a most perceptive woman. Believe me when I say that only one of worth and valor can wield it."

"I would not have thought those characteristics described you," Dafydd said.

"You doubt my ability to hold it?" Mabon was incredulous.

"There are few men who can." Clydog's voice had gained strength as Dafydd and Mabon had been sizing each other up. The shock of Mabon's appearance was wearing off. "This lad is one of them."

Mabon sneered. "You jest! Did you not learn in my father's cavern that unlike King Cadwaladr, a mortal man such as you cannot harm a god?"

Dafydd was mighty sick of seeing that expression on Mabon's face. "I can try," he said.

Mabon's face remained full of amusement. "So now you challenge me to single combat? Do you dare?"

Dafydd's eyes went reflexively to Dyrnwyn, sparking as it had once done in Arawn's hand. And Cade's.

Mabon noted the attention. "Fear it, child."

"I dare to challenge you," Dafydd said.

Mabon struck. With a grin plastered on his face and showing his teeth, he flew at Dafydd, moving so fast Dafydd barely had time to bring his own sword to bear. He wasn't in time to deflect Mabon's blow and Dyrnwyn slashed at Dafydd's upper arm, right through the leather coat.

Dafydd spun away, seeing stars, the pain in his arm unlike anything he'd ever felt before. He expected to see blood pouring from the wound—it felt as if Mabon had poured boiling oil on it—but there was only a gash in his tissue. Dyrnwyn had cauterized the wound as it had sliced him.

Mabon leaped towards Dafydd again but this time Dafydd managed to parry the blow. His wrist was tight with the effort. His left arm hung useless, so he wielded his sword with just his right hand.

Dafydd spun away and put one of the benches between him and Mabon to give himself time to recover. He worked to control his breathing, and the blackness that had risen before his eyes dissipated, now that he knew he wasn't going to bleed out.

Mabon attacked again, leaping onto the bench and pressing Dafydd back. Dafydd fought him off. And then again, Mabon catapulted towards him. By Mabon's fifth attempt to dominate him, Dafydd realized that he was holding his own, and Mabon's first blow had been a lucky one.

He'd caught Dafydd off-guard that time, but Mabon wasn't an experienced fighter. He was quick, but as the fight progressed, Dafydd was able to absorb what Mabon had to give him. Dafydd should have known: Mabon was a bully, used to frightening his opponents rather than defeating them in close combat. And that caused a new internal debate inside Dafydd. He wasn't a *sidhe*. He didn't have the blessing of Arianrhod. Would the gods punish him if he really did defeat Mabon?

Dafydd continued to parry Mabon's blows, praying Mabon's attention would stray. Mabon, unfortunately, didn't oblige. His strength wasn't waning as quickly as Dafydd's either. Of course, he was a god. And not injured. One couldn't expect it. Marshalling his failing strength, Dafydd began to press Mabon back. They circled each other, Dafydd countering every move Mabon made. More time passed. If he didn't finish this quickly, he wouldn't be able to lift his sword. The pain in Dafydd's arm was blinding him and he could only see Mabon through a sheen of sweat and tears.

Dafydd and Mabon exchanged *one, two, three, four* more blows before Dafydd finally managed to catch the guard protecting Dyrnwyn's hilt with the tip of his own sword. With a twist of his wrist, he flicked the sword from Mabon's hand and it flew across the room, landing with a clatter on the floor against the wall by the door through which Dafydd had pulled Angharad. None of the men standing nearby moved to pick it up. Mabon himself froze and then held out both hands, as if he was going to throw bolts of lightning at Dafydd, as his father had done at Cade.

But he didn't.

Mabon grimaced—and Dafydd discerned a touch of uncertainty, or even fear in his eyes. In two strides, Dafydd crossed the distance that separated them. He switched his sword to his left hand, forcing his lifeless fingers around the hilt and then drove his fisted and gauntleted right hand into Mabon's face.

Mabon staggered back, his hands to his nose. He tripped on the heel of his boot, stumbled, and fell ignominiously on his rear. As in the case of Dafydd's wound, no blood poured out, but he spit at Dafydd, who loomed over him.

"I will see you suffer for this day." Mabon's eyes went to Dyrnwyn, which lay thirty feet away.

Dafydd blocked the way to it. He met Mabon's gaze and allowed Mabon to see the challenge in them. And that he wasn't going to let Mabon have it again without more of a fight. Mabon pointed to his captain with a black-gloved hand. "I want that sword. Leave without it, and you die."

And then he vanished.

14

Dafydd

Every person in the hall gasped and stared at the place where Mabon had been. Dafydd stepped back involuntarily, and then glanced towards Mabon's captain, a thickset man, older than Goronwy, with the demeanor of a fighting man. Dafydd didn't relish taking him on, but Dafydd was going to let the captain remove Dyrnwyn from Castell Clydog only over Dafydd's dead body. Dafydd weaved on his feet and swallowed hard to gain control.

Mabon's captain stared at Dafydd through three heartbeats, his eyes hard, and then he fisted a hand high in the air. It was the signal Mabon's soldiers had been waiting for. They sprang upon Clydog's men—whose feet were frozen to the floor just long enough for them to lose any advantage they might have had by their greater numbers. Many barely had time to clear their swords from their sheaths before they were beset.

Mabon's captain and Dafydd moved at the same instant, though not to fight each other, but towards Dyrnwyn. The captain was blocked by the press of men between him and the sword, however, so Dafydd reached it first. Dyrnwyn had skittered closer to the dais—someone must have kicked it—and had come to rest under a chair. The sword lay quiet, its light extinguished. A quick check showed Mabon's captain still twenty paces away, set upon by two of Clydog's men and no immediate threat.

Dafydd still didn't understand why Mabon had just left, rather than fight for what he wanted. Grimacing in advance of the pain he feared to feel, Dafydd stooped to pick up the sword.

Nothing. The hilt felt cool to the touch. Dafydd couldn't explain it, but didn't have time to think on it further.

He turned towards King Clydog, looking to protect him, but he was safe for the moment, backed into a corner of the room by Seisyll whose sword was out. None of Mabon's men had yet approached him. Lilwen cowered under the table where Seisyll had shoved her during Dafydd's fight with Mabon.

One of Mabon's men approached Dafydd who flicked the tip of the sacred sword back and forth. Strangely, the pain in his arm and the tension of the last few moments caused laughter to bubble in his throat. "You're jesting, right?"

Fortunately, two of Clydog's men-at-arms appeared in front of him to relieve him of having to fight again. Head down, Dafydd braced his right hip against the high table. The pain was such that he could barely walk. He focused on breathing in a steady pattern so he wouldn't pass out.

"Where's Angharad?" Clydog said.

"Safe—for now." Dafydd gritted his teeth, stepped closer to Clydog, and lowered his voice, his words only for the king. "I told her to get *it* and get out—that I would meet her at the postern gate if I could."

"*Sweet Mary*! Then what are you doing here? Go!" Clydog said. "I need you with her more than I need you with me. I don't want to see you again until you can tell me that *it* is safe in the hands of King Cadwaladr."

"You want me to bring it to King Cad—"

"I should never have kept it here this long. From what you've told me of him, it is better for him to have it, and use it. He is the rightful High King and will know what to do with it." Clydog paused. "Or Taliesin will."

"My lord—" Dafydd tried again.

"You heard him," Seisyll said. "We can handle this. Protect Angharad. She's the best of us."

"I'll keep her safe." Marshalling his strength, Dafydd ran for the doorway, still holding a sword in each hand. He raced along a narrow passage to the kitchen. A dozen workers clustered around the doorway and gave way as Dafydd charged into their midst.

"Save yourselves." Dafydd plunged past them, through the kitchen, to the far door that led to the rear of the fort and the postern gate.

Although Clydog claimed his fort was sturdy and defensible, it was no more than a manor house with a palisade surrounding it and just as vulnerable as Dafydd had thought it when he first spied it from the far side of the river. Bright sunlight hit his face as he burst from the kitchen doorway into the garden. A low wall protected the garden from invading stock and he leapt it to enter the courtyard proper. The stables had been fitted awkwardly between the buttery and the barracks, skewed at a strange angle so people could get to the hidden gate behind it.

Angharad had been watching for him and stepped out from the stable door at his approach. Her eyes took him in from head to toe and settled on his left arm. "Are you all right?"

"No," Dafydd said. "But your family is, for now." He glanced back towards the kitchen door. Mabon's captain wasn't coming through it, but that wasn't to say he wouldn't in another few heartbeats. Every fiber in Dafydd's being told him to hurry but he swallowed and forced himself to slow down. Angharad depended on him and him alone, now. He needed her cooperation and it would be counterproductive to scare her.

Angharad peered at the gash in his upper arm. "Did Mabon do that to you? Why isn't it bleeding?"

Dafydd held out Dyrnwyn. He didn't quite know what to do with it.

"Is that—?" Angharad said.

"Dyrnwyn. Or at least I thought so," Dafydd said, "but now I'm not so sure. Its fire has gone out." He focused on her face. "Your father told me to get you away from here, along with … whatever it is you've got. Where is it?"

"In the bags, along with the bandages. I need to wrap your arm."

"We have no time," Dafydd said.

"You can't ride with a hole in your arm."

Angharad pulled a length of clean linen from a pouch on the back of the lively grey she'd led from the stables, and without a by-your-leave, wrapped it tightly around his arm. He gazed down at her, silent with gritted teeth, while she tied the ends. The wound still burned him, but she'd pressed the insides of the gash together and lessened the pain enough that Dafydd could unclench his left hand from the hilt of his sword and sheath it.

"I've saddled your horse too." She clicked her tongue. His horse, Llelo, whickered softly from the darkness within the stable.

One-handed, Dafydd pulled a blanket from his bags, wrapped Dyrnwyn in it, and tucked it under his saddle bags, with an assist from Angharad when he couldn't lift the bag and slide the sword under it at the same time. Then he pulled open the postern gate. "What happened to the guard?"

"I sent him to help my father in the hall," Angharad said.

Dafydd smiled inwardly. "I like you much better this way." He led Llelo through the gate and Angharad pushed it closed behind her.

"What do you mean—*you like me better this way*?"

Dafydd glanced at her, not sure if he should explain, but then decided that if he didn't tell her the truth, his dissembling would act as a barrier between them. "I overheard your argument with Lilwen, the first day I was at Castle Clydog."

"What?"

"I'm sorry." He shrugged. "It wasn't entirely by accident, but you had been so unkind ..." His voice trailed off as he realized she was glaring at him again.

"I can't decide whether to be angry, hurt, or embarrassed."

"How about none of those," Dafydd said. "How about we start now as we mean to go on—as friends."

Angharad looked away, worrying at her lip with her teeth, and then nodded. "I would like that. Where are we going?"

"Dinas Bran."

Angharad took the news with no more than a hard swallow, the same acceptance she'd showed with everything Dafydd had asked from her so far this morning. They mounted their horses and turned them to the Roman road which ran northeast from Clydog's fort. Their horse's hooves thudded on the ancient cobbles, which the years had filled in with moss and dirt.

"Where does this lead?" Dafydd said.

"Caersws," Angharad said, and then shrugged, "Eventually."

Dafydd glanced at her. "It goes all that way? You're not serious?"

"Yes, of course," Angharad said. "Why wouldn't I be?"

"I should have known that to reach Dinas Bran we'd have to go through Caersws on the way north, but I hadn't thought that far ahead," Dafydd said.

Angharad picked up on the hesitation in his voice. "What happened at Caersws?"

"Not so much there, but at Llanllugan, a few miles north of the crossroads," Dafydd said. "We fought a great battle. I'd just as soon not revisit it."

"Is it the place you fought the demons, before King Cadwaladr went to Caer Dathyl?" Angharad said.

"So you were listening when I talked to your father," Dafydd said.

"Of course."

Dafydd checked behind them for the twentieth time. He was beginning to think that they might have gotten away without detection, but almost didn't dare admit it to himself. Still, when facing Mabon, it was hard to say if it was possible to outrun him. He glanced at the sky.

"What are you looking for?" Angharad said. "You keep looking at the road behind us, and then at the sun."

"It's going down," Dafydd said.

"Why does that matter?"

"You haven't traveled far in your life, have you?"

Angharad looked affronted. Dafydd grimaced inwardly. He'd been sparring with Angharad for three days and had forgotten that they'd declared a truce.

"We went all the way to Caer Dathyl last summer, as I told you," Angharad said. "I'm not a child."

"I didn't say you were," Dafydd said. "It's just that it stays light so late in the summer you would never have worried about the dark. Believe me, today, we need to worry."

"Because of Mabon?"

"Him and other things I'm not going to tell you about just yet," Dafydd said. "Not until I have to."

"I hate it when men are cryptic, as if I couldn't understand the truth. As if I have no knowledge of the way the world works." She looked away from him and Dafydd hoped they weren't going to revert back to the Lilwen version of Angharad instead of the genuine one.

Dafydd studied her downturned head. "I would prefer it if you never need to understand. However, I will tell you when you need to know. Either that, or I will tell you when we have reached safety and it no longer matters. I promise."

Angharad nodded her head, though she still didn't look at him.

"All you need to do is look at *that*." Dafydd gestured towards the mountains looming ahead of them. The road bent and weaved around them, hardly the straight path for which the Romans usually strove. "If we're going to get through those, it isn't going to be tonight, as much as I'd like to continue in the dark."

"We're going to have to sleep outside?" Angharad clutched the reins more tightly. As for Dafydd, he knew well that tendril of fear curling inside at the thought of sleeping outside, unprotected by a company of soldiers.

Dafydd wanted to reassure her. "We've blankets and food. I'll build a fire and keep watch. It didn't even rain today so the ground won't be wet."

"Why don't we just go back?" Angharad said. "You said yourself that Mabon disappeared from the hall and didn't return. I want to know what's happened to my family."

"Your father told me to get you to safety—to get both you and this thing you carry that Mabon wants. I think your father knows that *it* is no longer safe at Castell Clydog." Dafydd paused. "I've never heard that a pillow could be so dangerous."

"It isn't really a pillow," Angharad said. "It's just wrapped up inside one."

"So what is it?"

"I don't know," she said.

Dafydd opened his mouth to speak—perhaps even to mock her—and then thought better of it. They were dancing around each other right now, trying to figure out how to talk to each other after their rocky start. He didn't want to raise her hackles if he didn't have to.

An hour later and a good fifteen miles from Castell Clydog, they sat together on a log, deep in the woods to the east of the road. Angharad had checked Dafydd's arm again. It oozed lymph now, which meant it was healing, but it burned like hot fat sprayed from a pan and his left arm and hand remained nearly useless. With some effort, Dafydd had managed to light a smokeless fire.

"All right. Let's see what your father has risked so much to keep safe," Dafydd said. "I don't want to travel any further without knowing what he's given you. If we can shed any light at all on why Mabon might want it and how it might serve him, I think that could only be a good thing."

Angharad opened her satchel and pulled out the pillow. "My father gave this to me three years ago. Even then he'd wrapped it in soft sacking, so I couldn't see what it was. He never told me and I didn't ask. He told me to hide it in plain sight."

"So you covered it in the richest fabric you could find." Dafydd rubbed a finger along the fine needlework. She'd embroidered the deep blue fabric with her family's crest.

Angharad set it in her lap and carefully removed the stitching along one side of the pillow with her belt knife. Then she handed the open pillow to Dafydd. "I'd prefer that you do it. Just pull it out."

With a wary look at her, he took the pillow, reached inside, and tugged the sacking into the open. Unfolding the top, he looked inside, looked at her, and then reached in. Out came a six foot length of black cloth. It cascaded through Dafydd's hands. They both stared at it and then Dafydd stood up and shook it out.

"It's a cloak." He held it higher. It was designed for a man of his stature and looked much like the cloaks the demons at the wedding had worn, with enveloping expanses of fabric and deep hoods.

"Put it on, my lord," Angharad said.

Shrugging his acceptance, even if the comparison to the demons' cloaks gave him a moment's pause, Dafydd swung it over his shoulders. He held out his arms and spun on one heel full circle until he faced Angharad again. "It's just a cloak. Why would Mabon want this one? He's got dozens probably."

Angharad sat with her hand to her mouth.

"What is it?" Dafydd said. "I haven't grown horns have I?"

"Take it off!" she said. The words came out strangled, as if her throat had closed over them. "Right now! Give it to me!"

Puzzled, Dafydd did as she asked. "What's wrong?" And then when Angharad began stuffing the cloak back into the sacking with frantic movements, "What are you afraid of?"

Angharad stopped. Visibly trying to gain control, she tipped her head back to look up at the leaves above her head and took a deep breath. "This isn't an ordinary cloak, Dafydd." She eased the cloth back out of the sacking, stood, and held it high so that it wouldn't drag on the ground. "When you put it on, you disappeared."

Dafydd stared at her. "Surely not."

"Watch." Angharad swung the cloak around herself, as Dafydd had earlier.

As soon as the fabric settled on her shoulders, she vanished. Dafydd's heart sank to see it. Or rather, not see it. Somehow, he wasn't even surprised. He studied the space where he'd last seen her and rubbed his jaw line with his good hand. "I hate magic," he said. "It upends too much of what I think I know."

"But it isn't all bad." Angharad reappeared, three feet away from where she'd been when she'd put the cloak on. It lay limp in her hand, looking like nothing more than a fine garment that any lord would be proud to wear. "Perhaps we need the use of it in order to face Mabon. We can hardly be expected to counter him if he has all the advantages and we have nothing to hand ourselves."

"Maybe you have something there," Dafydd said. "Certainly, we couldn't have defeated Arawn without King Cadwaladr. He is *sidhe* and carries a magic sword."

"There you go." Angharad allowed the cloak to settle onto her lap in folds. "Magic has its uses."

"I never said it didn't," Dafydd said. "But just think what could happen if this cloak fell into the wrong hands."

"Mabon's hands."

"Those hands wouldn't have to be Mabon's to do great damage."

"It would be of benefit to a thief at the very least," Angharad said.

"To anyone who planned mischief," Dafydd said.

Angharad carefully encased it in its pillow once again. When she finished, she clutched it to her chest and just stared at Dafydd. He didn't know her well enough to read her eyes as yet, but surely there was uncertainty there, as well as calculation.

"You were right," Dafydd said. "This is a more dangerous and precious thing than I could have imagined. More so even than a sword. No wonder your father refused to give it to Mabon."

"But he wants to leave it in King Cadwaladr's keeping." Angharad looked down at the pillow. "Why?"

"Because even if your father didn't use it himself, he doesn't want Mabon to have it."

"And why didn't my father use it for himself?" Angharad grabbed Dafydd's pack without asking his permission and stuffed the pillow into it. Before he could protest, she answered her own question. "Maybe it was too tempting. Like misers who count their gold but never spend it. Their possessions haunt them, even as they can't enjoy them."

"I suspect your father didn't feel he *could* use it," Dafydd said, "or else he wouldn't have given it to you to keep."

"Perhaps," Angharad said.

Dafydd settled himself back onto the log, the strap to his pack in his hand. He didn't know what to do with it. He daren't let it out of his sight and would probably have to actually *use* it as a pillow from now on, just to keep it safe. "I'm wondering why Mabon wanted it. He disappeared during the fight in the hall all on his own. He doesn't need a magic cloak to become invisible."

"And although he had a magic sword, it didn't do him any good either," Angharad said.

"What do you mean?"

Angharad gestured to Dafydd. "You defeated him."

"That's because his sword wasn't magic—or at least not the way Dyrnwyn should be or King Cadwaladr's Caledfwlch is." Dafydd went to his horse and pulled out the sword. He looked down at it, tracing the writing etched into the blade with his eyes. The swirls were impossible for him to decipher and he'd dismissed them as meaningless, just like the sword. He held it out to Angharad but she put up her hands and backed away.

"No, not for me."

"It's all right," he said, still urging it on her. "It won't hurt you. It feels lifeless when I hold it."

"Then you hold it," Angharad said. "Besides, why would it respond to you? You're not a god like Mabon."

Dafydd swallowed hard, finding that her criticism hurt. He'd hoped they were beyond that. Then he met her eyes and realized that she wasn't disparaging him. She honestly didn't know the mythology of the sword. "Only a noble man can wield Dyrnwyn," he said. "Those who fall short will find that the hilt burns their hand and they can't hold it."

"And because it doesn't burn yours, you think it isn't the true sword? Maybe you are worthy of it."

Dafydd was suddenly feeling much better. He decided telling her the truth about his experience with Dyrnwyn wasn't boasting, but instead was necessary so she could understand what they faced. "I held Dyrnwyn in Arawn's cavern. I pulled it from King Cadwaladr's belly after Arawn thrust it through him. At the time, it allowed me to hold it, that's true, but it certainly didn't feel this comfortable in my hand. This can't be the same sword. This one is a fake."

"Why would Mabon bring a false Dyrnwyn to Castell Clydog?" Angharad said.

"I don't know," Dafydd said. "To frighten us? Mabon sent two demons to Deganwy Castle to get Dyrnwyn, since he believed King Cadwaladr had it. When this sword lit in your father's hall, it didn't make me happy, but I merely assumed that he'd found it after all."

"Yet he didn't."

"So has he given up the search? He came to Castell Clydog seeking this cloak," Dafydd said.

"And almost found it," Angharad said.

"But again, didn't," Dafydd said.

"He seems to be looking for magic items, my lord; ones that might be useful to us if we found them first or kept them from him."

"What else might he be seeking—and why?"

15

Goronwy

Caerleon in Gwent, a fort the Romans called Isca, was as far away from the Isle of Man where Goronwy had grown up as he'd ever been. At thirty, with over ten years of fighting on the mainland under his belt, it had been a long time since he'd thought of Man as home. Leaving the island had been the right decision, for him and for Dafydd. The island was too small for so many brothers to share, and it was their eldest brother, Merfyn, who would succeed to the throne upon the death of their father, Cynin.

It was fortunate that Merfyn, Goronwy, and Dafydd, each born to a different mother and many years apart, felt no animosity towards one another. Goronwy had understood since he was a small child that the kingdom would never be his and he would have to make his way in the world on his own merits, with no land to claim and no inheritance, other than the sword he carried and the training to use it.

Still, memories of his childhood came increasingly back to him the older he grew and the longer he stayed away. If he survived the coming confrontation with the Saxons, he'd make a trip home to see his family one more time before his father died.

Goronwy passed a marking stone and traced the writing on it with his eyes. Few knights knew how to read these days. It seemed that knowledge had left Britain with the Romans, except for a few bastions of learning. Like all royal sons on the Isle of Man, however, Goronwy had learned Latin, for no other reason than because his father believed that a man wasn't educated unless he knew Latin *and by God his sons were going to be educated!*

Goronwy was Christian enough to find the language—and the religion that came with it—useful, whatever Taliesin thought. He appreciated the way the language gave shape to his thoughts that his Welsh couldn't properly express. But the Romans were gone now and all that remained of them were their roads and ruined forts. The Welsh still used the roads, though only a few lords and kings were brave enough to rehabilitate their forts. Clydog, the man to whom Dafydd had been sent was one. King Arthur of Gwent, a man Cade called his uncle, but who was actually a slightly more complicated older relation, was another.

The fort of Caerleon was a huge and sprawling complex of buildings. Goronwy couldn't see how Arthur could possibly defend it. It lay in a bend of the River Usk, less than five miles as the crow flies from the sea, though longer by boat along the winding river. Goronwy passed through the open gate into a bustling courtyard that was more small city than fort.

"Welcome, my friend!" King Arthur's great voice boomed from the entrance to one of the main buildings. "Pardon the crush, but it's market day."

"I'm glad to see things are going well for you." Goronwy dismounted and allowed Arthur to hammer him on the back. The man was fifty if he was a day, but was still as broad and strong as the bear for whom he was named.

"To what do I owe this pleasure?" Arthur clasped Goronwy's forearm while one of the stable boys led his grey stallion away.

"I'm here on behalf of King Cadwaladr of Gwynedd," Goronwy said.

Arthur's eyes lit. "Ho! King Cadwaladr of Gwynedd, is it? Doesn't that sound fine?"

Goronwy laughed. "That's the way the dice have fallen."

"That boy has rolled a deuce more times than I can count," Arthur said. "Come inside and tell me more."

Goronwy followed King Arthur into the great hall. On every side, tapestries adorned the walls and fresh rush mats covered the floor. They sat at a small table to the rear of the hall, lit by a bank of windows, the shutters open to let in the spring air. And then Arthur confessed the truth.

"The market is doing well, but it's like spitting into the wind to hold it. I hope it will last but I fear we are nearing the end. We soon will be dust like those who left those Roman marker stones you passed on your way in."

"I assume you are referring to the threat of the encroaching Saxons?" Goronwy said.

"I've lost nearly all of my eastern lands," Arthur said. "And it isn't just me. The Saxons cross the Wye River as if it were a creek. Every lord between here and Brecon is at risk."

"That's why I've come," Goronwy said. "The Saxons under Cerdic of Wessex and Penda of Mercia mass troops at Shrewsbury. I know that's far to the north of here, but if we lose in the north, all of Wales could fall to them."

"And Cadwaladr wants the High Kingship," Arthur said.

Goronwy shrugged noncommittally. "He wants Wales united. He doesn't much care under whom."

"He's not his father's son, then," Arthur said. "No man lusted after power more than Cadwallon."

Goronwy pursed his lips and didn't answer immediately. This wasn't the version of events he'd heard, but he'd been only a young boy when Cadwallon had died. Cadfael had wanted the High Kingship, thinking it his right as King of Gwynedd, and all talk had been of him more than of the man he usurped. "I wouldn't know."

"I would," Arthur said. "Cadwallon was an arrogant bastard with a pole stuck so far up his arse it kept his chin raised and his nose pointed at the sky. His transparent allusions to his Saxon allies and what they would do to us if we didn't declare him High King were all that kept him on the throne. No one should have been surprised—least of all Cadwallon—when he died so far away from home, leading good Welshmen against Saxons in Saxon lands. About which we cared nothing."

"He felt that they were our birthright. The Saxons took those eastern lands from Vortigern—"

Arthur guffawed his disagreement. "Vortigern let them in and when they turned on him, paid for his stupidity with his life. Don't talk to me about what the Welsh used to have. That was two hundred years ago. The world is a different place now. I just want to keep what I have. Cadwallon was a fool."

Goronwy studied Arthur. "Don't tell Cade that. He worships him—or at least the memory of him."

"How could he not?" Arthur said. "The man is dead. Besides, I'll grant that he knew how to fight. But he was a fool to trail all over Britain fighting Saxons for Penda who was a Saxon himself. Cadwallon gained nothing for Wales but his own glory. The man was a prick, as I said. He and I would be the same age, if he'd lived."

"You could have been High King," Goronwy said.

"Ach," Arthur said. "I would have had to talk to all those other idiots. Better to hold my own lands and let my nephew worry about unity."

"But now..." Goronwy said.

"Yes, you have the right of it." Arthur grunted, scoffing at his predicament. "Now I can't even do that because we don't have a High King and none of those other pretenders to the throne care about anyone but themselves. You're telling me this Cadwaladr is different?"

"Yes," Goronwy said.

Arthur gazed at Goronwy, rubbing his chin with one hand. "Just like that? No equivocation? Just 'yes'?"

Goronwy nodded.

"Things have been quiet for the last month," Arthur said. "It might be worth coming with you to see what a real High King looks like."

"We need your men too," Goronwy said.

"Ah. Now we come to the reason for your visit," Arthur said. "My *teulu* will put their swords where I tell them. I can leave these lands in the hands of my son until we return."

"I can't promise that you will return," Goronwy said.

Arthur's eyes brightened at that. "One can always hope."

* * * * *

In Arthur, these words weren't mere bravado. That evening, he stood in front of his men and passed his crown to his son, Caradoc. "To you, I entrust the well-being of my people and these lands."

"Thank you, Father," Caradoc said.

Goronwy detected a hint of relief *and* ambition in Caradoc's eyes—and Goronwy couldn't blame Caradoc for feeling either. What son didn't want to test himself in his father's shoes before he was too old to wear them? Caradoc was a few years older than Goronwy himself. It was hard when fathers lived too long, and perhaps that was what was giving Arthur the impetus to come with Goronwy now.

They left the next morning, a host of men jostling along the road. Arthur's men had fought more battles than they liked of late, and some of them hadn't been happy to ride north with Arthur. Arthur, however, was in high spirits.

"We'll have to take the western roads to Caersws, rather than those to the east. They'd be faster, seeing how the lands are flat."

"But full of Saxons," Goronwy said.

Though Goronwy had been deadly serious, Arthur laughed. "You've the right of it." His good mood was contagious and some of his men laughed with him. Goronwy had ridden in a company such as this more times than he could count, and still he was glad to feel the camaraderie and participate in their jests.

Boom!

A concussion split the air and Goronwy's horse reared. Men shouted and spun their horses, looking for the threat. Goronwy's horse danced full circle. When he got him under control and came back around, the real danger became clear.

"Well, well, isn't this pleasant."

"Mabon!" Goronwy reined in, a black pit forming in his center. This was the last thing he wanted or needed. But in truth, hadn't he expected it? Mabon's men had gone away from Deganwy unsatisfied. His companions were fools if any one of them—Cade included—had thought they could evade him forever.

"This is the famous Mabon?" King Arthur said. "He doesn't look like much."

Which was patently untrue but Goronwy admired Arthur's brave stance. "What do you want?" Goronwy said.

"Such disrespect." Mabon's tone was casual and amused, but his eyes glinted and narrowed. "I just want to speak with King Arthur."

"So speak," Goronwy said.

"Look what surrounds you." Mabon gestured to the dozens of men who hemmed Arthur's company in. Somehow—out of nowhere—Mabon had conjured a company of men, dressed in black as he was. "I would rethink your tone if I were you."

Goronwy glanced right and left, calculating what it would take to free himself and Arthur. Arthur put a hand on Goronwy's arm to stay him. "What can we do for you, my lord?" he said.

Mabon puffed out his chest. "Give *it* to me."

"Daughter of Christ," Goronwy said, though this time under his breath so Mabon couldn't hear. "Not *it* again." And then out loud: "We don't have Dyrnwyn, Mabon."

Mabon sniffed. "That's not at issue." He pointed his chin at Arthur. "*He* knows what I want."

Arthur's jaw clenched. "No."

Mabon laughed. "I will take it over the dead bodies of your men."

Arthur pulled his sword from his sheath and held it above his head. "I dare you to try!"

Both sides took that as the signal Arthur intended: to fight. The men behind Goronwy roared and he barely had time to register that they'd gone from peace to war in half a heartbeat. He cleared his sword from his sheath in time to meet an oncoming warrior in black. The man wasn't demon, however, and died just as all men did when a sword sliced through him. Spurring his horse forward, Goronwy launched himself towards Mabon, who hadn't moved, perhaps not expecting one of Arthur's men to challenge him directly. Mabon flailed at Goronwy with his sword, but held his ground.

They hacked at each other a few more strokes before three men charged through the ranks, heading for Arthur, who already was fighting two men at once. Goronwy disengaged and spun, urging his horse after them. He managed to unseat one, and then threw himself from the saddle into the torso of a second who had an open path towards Arthur's exposed neck. They went down together. The man landed with a terrific crunch, and although Goronwy was on top of him and wore his helmet, his head connected with a rock on the edge of the road and everything went black.

16

Goronwy

Goronwy didn't know how long he'd been out—whether moments only or hours—but the silence around him when he awoke didn't bode well for Arthur and his men. Groaning at the effort, Goronwy pushed onto his knees, his head hanging. Everything ached—muscle, bone and sinew—but his head hurt the worst. He pulled off his helmet and dropped it. It landed with a clunk and rolled away, into the ditch that lined the road.

"Goronwy—"

Goronwy peered in the direction from which Arthur's voice had come. It wasn't evening yet, but a fog had rolled in. At least it wasn't raining. A figure crouched over another in the center of the road. At first Goronwy was afraid it was Mabon, sending Arthur to his death, but then his vision cleared and he realized it was a young woman of perhaps five and twenty in hood and cloak.

"Hurry," she said. "He wants you. He hasn't much time."

Goronwy crawled the fifteen feet that separated them. When he reached Arthur, Goronwy grasped his hand. The woman had opened Arthur's coat, revealing a gaping wound in his right abdomen. Goronwy glanced at her and she shook her head. He nodded back, understanding that Arthur had gotten his wish and would not return to Caerleon.

Arthur had his own concerns and didn't notice their muted looks. "Take it," he said.

"What—what do you want me to take?" Goronwy said.

"The stone," Arthur said.

Goronwy didn't mean to be dim, but he didn't understand. He would have asked again, but Arthur moaned and turned his head. His sword and shield lay on the ground beside him, the shield split just under the leather-wrapped haft. Arthur flopped out an arm towards them. Goronwy thought he wanted him to bring his sword to him, but when he reached for it, Arthur shook his head.

"Not the sword, the shield."

Goronwy picked it up and brought it to Arthur. "It should go to your son."

"No," Arthur said. "Take it to Cadwaladr."

"To Cadwal—"

Again the moan and the shake of the head.

Goronwy tried again. "I'm not deliberately trying to misunderstand, Arthur. You're telling me to take this to Cadwaladr? Is it this shield that Mabon wanted?"

"Not the shield, the handle."

Goronwy turned the ruined shield in his hands. He couldn't see what Arthur meant, but the woman reached for it.

"Here. Let me." She picked at the end of the leather wrap that bound the handle and unwound it, revealing a black, rectangular stone that couldn't have been comfortable to hold, even within its leather casing.

"It's a whetstone." Goronwy glanced from the stone to Arthur. "Why do you have it as the handle to your shield?"

"To keep it safe." Arthur closed his eyes. "I've used it twice, both in times of great need."

The woman gazed at Arthur, awe in her face. "It's the Stone of Tewdrig. I can't believ—"

"It has been my family's honor to keep it for many years. But that time is over." Arthur turned his head to the side.

"Arthur!" Goronwy slipped his arm under Arthur's shoulders and lifted him, but the great king had passed away. Goronwy closed Arthur's eyes and then turned to the woman. "What is the Stone of Tewdrig?"

"The most treasured artifact in Gwent," she said. "Our mothers tell stories to us of it from the cradle, but I thought it was legend only. Everyone did."

"Many legends have arisen to walk the earth of late," Goronwy said. "What's special about this one?"

"The story goes that if a worthy man sharpens his blade on this stone, it will kill his opponents with one slice, but if he is an unworthy man—"

"—it fails utterly. Goronwy finished the sentence for her. "Typical."

"Obviously King Arthur believes it to be true," the woman said.

Which made Goronwy finally focus on her instead of the circumstances in which he found himself. "Who are you?"

"I was out gathering herbs when I came upon the wreckage." She gestured around at the dead men and horses. "I am Catrin. My hut is a few yards distant. The magic drew me." She said this matter-of-factly.

Goronwy narrowed his eyes at her. "Are you telling me you're a witch?" He touched her sleeve. "Is this a *glamour* you project?" She wasn't beautiful necessarily, but rather striking with her soot-black hair, lithe body, and gray eyes that seemed to penetrate his thoughts with a single glance. She made him more than a little uncomfortable.

Catrin canted her head. "I don't do magic, only feel it. That was enough to make men wary of me. Although people come to me for healing, they don't want me in their village." She paused and studied Goronwy. "But I see you're not afraid of me. Why?"

"My lord is *sidhe*. I have seen things in the time I've served him that are too strange to speak of, even to a witch," Goronwy said. "I have few fears left, at least not for myself."

"Who did this, then?" the woman said. "Surely he is one to fear. The aura of magic remains, though it was stronger when I first arrived, and was more than that which comes from the Stone."

"Mabon, son of Arawn and Arianrhod, was here. He wanted Arthur to give him the Stone."

Catrin took in a sharp breath. "It is a wonder you survived!"

"Mabon is a coward and a bully," Goronwy said. "Unfortunately, he is also a god with a long reach. I wonder where he found his men and where he's got to now?"

"That I don't know, but you need food and rest if we are to travel north to find King Cadwaladr."

Goronwy blinked at her as he processed all that she'd said. "Did you really say 'if *we* are to travel north'?"

"Of course," Catrin said.

Goronwy laughed. "There's no 'of course' about it. You don't know me; I don't know you and I'm not sure I want to. Why would I let you accompany me?"

"Even I, in my isolation, have heard of the great Goronwy ap Cynin, and besides, you need my help."

"I don't—"

"If Mabon searched Arthur and his men—including you—for this stone, he didn't find it. He might accost you again if he realizes you have it," Catrin said. "It wouldn't be safe for you alone. At the very least, how would you sleep with nobody to keep watch?" Her gaze was steady as she looked into Goronwy's eyes.

"It occurs to me that you could be working for Mabon." Goronwy kept his eyes on her face. She didn't drop his gaze. "It seems that other men and even gods do his bidding now."

"That's Mabon's style, is it?" she said. "To ask a woman for help?"

"Not in the least," Goronwy said. "But nobody said he couldn't learn."

"He hasn't once in all the years of his existence," Catrin said.

Goronwy's skin turned cold. Catrin seemed so sure. The more he looked at her, the less likely he thought she was evil, but at the same time, the less sure he became of what or who she really was.

Then a new thought struck him. *Could this be Arianrhod?* He'd touched her and she'd felt real to him, not the ethereal goddess that Rhun had described. But she could have become the creature who came to Cade in that cave in the guise of a beautiful woman. Catrin wasn't beautiful like that, but still ... could he refuse a goddess? Cade didn't think it wise.

Goronwy bowed his head. "I must give way." His head ached. The task Cade had set him had suddenly grown far more difficult and serious. He was going to have to trust Catrin. For now.

* * * * *

"If you really intend to come all the way to Caer Fawr with me, I have a friend you should meet when we get there," Goronwy said.

He lay reclined on a pallet near the fire, sipping a cup of soup Catrin had made. He'd watched her carefully from the first, trying to discern any waver in the humanness she projected. If she really was Arianrhod, she was doing a good job at pretending not to be. She even spilled some soup on her hand and sucked at the burn. He couldn't imagine a goddess being clumsy.

"Really?" Catrin said. "And who might that be?"

"Taliesin," Goronwy said.

Catrin looked up. "The bard? He's still alive?"

Goronwy laughed. "Last time I looked. You'll like him. He talks only in riddles and obscure references to past events you've never heard of, or future ones you probably don't want to know about."

"Are you mocking me?"

"Is that what you think?"

Catrin sat back on her heels. "You don't like me, do you?"

"As I said before, I don't know you," Gorowny said. "In this world, I trust few people and none on first acquaintance."

"Except for your lord," she said. "Except for King Cadwaladr."

Goronwy thought about that. "I trusted him to do what he thought was right from the first. His good intentions were transparent. Whether or not he was a good leader, however—whether or not he could lead men in battle—that I didn't trust until later."

"And you tell me he is a *sidhe*. And that we have demons as well as Mabon to worry about as we travel."

"And maybe other gods too," Goronwy said. "I haven't yet told you about our encounter with the boar at Caer Dathyl, who Taliesin thought was Camulos in animal form."

"Camulos is never far from his cousin Barinthus."

"And both are associated with Mabon." Goronwy caught Catrin's eyes. "Do you know how to fight?"

"I have a knife." She studied Goronwy in return and he let her. "Perhaps we ought to use the whetstone."

Which told Goronwy all he needed to know about her own opinion of herself. *Maybe she really is Arianrhod.*

17

Hywel

"Are you sure you're ready for this?" Bedwyr said.

"No," Hywel said, finally giving him honesty instead of the false face he'd been employing since they left Deganwy.

"So what exactly did your father say when you last saw him?" Bedwyr said.

"Not to come back until I'd learned better manners," Hywel said.

"When was this?"

Hywel couldn't help smiling. He'd been such a child when he'd stormed out of his father's house. "Two days before we fought the demons at Llanllugan."

Bedwyr stared at him and Hywel shrugged. "Didn't you notice that I was a bit green?"

"You're telling me that you fell in with King Cadwaladr by chance? That—what?—you were riding north through the countryside and happened upon Geraint and his men an hour before Cade showed up to fight the demons?"

"It was more like a quarter of an hour, actually," Hywel said.

Bedwyr barked a laugh. "That was a trial by fire, wasn't it?"

Hywel couldn't help but laugh with him. "It was. When I found myself beside King Cadwaladr, it was the culmination of an impossible dream. I thought I knew what battle was. I thought I knew who I was. But then, fighting back to back with him, my entire life came down to my sword and his—it was all or nothing."

"*All*, I'd say," Bedwyr said. "Will your father be pleased that King Cadwaladr has taken you into his *teulu*? Surely he will see the honor in that?"

Hywel shot him a sour look. "He has never approved of anything I've done. As I told King Cadwaladr before he sent us on this journey, it may be that my father doesn't support him out of sheer perversity, in that it would imply approval of my ventures."

"Families are complicated," Bedwyr said.

"You have the right of it," Hywel said.

Bedwyr had kept him entertained all the way from Deganwy with stories of his home on Anglesey. He had fourteen brothers and sisters and from the sounds of it, Bedwyr had been lucky to have them. Hywel wished he'd had siblings to take some of the pressure off of him. As it was, he'd grown up in a far quieter household, with only him and his older sister. His father's hopes and demands had fallen entirely on Hywel.

Hywel's home lay in a bend of the Wye River, not far from the Roman road. He and Bedwyr followed a track wide enough for two carts to pass. Trees overhung the road and Hywel felt his breath easing out and his shoulders relaxing for the first time in four days. He was coming home and his heart knew it, even if his stomach roiled at the thought of confronting his father again. Maybe it would go well. Hywel squashed the thought the moment it entered his mind. Better to have no expectations at all.

"Legend has it that Vortigern himself retreated to my family's castle after failing to contain the Saxons and ultimately died here," Hywel said.

"Is that good or bad?" Bedwyr said. "I mean—is it something of which your father is proud or something I should refrain from mentioning?"

"Vortigern didn't do the Welsh any favors by inviting the Saxons in," Hywel said, "but he was a great ruler and my mother is numbered one of his descendents."

"Ah," Bedwyr said. "Then perhaps your father thinks himself in line for the throne of the High King? He might not be well disposed to seeing Cade in his place."

Hywel should have known better than to think he could hide something like that from Bedwyr. "Not him, but for all his despair of me, my father thinks the High Kingship should come to me, through my mother."

Bedwyr shot Hywel an amused look. "I suppose you told this to Cade before we left."

"Of course," Hywel said.

"And what did the King say?" Bedwyr said. "My guess, it pleased him in a perverse way."

Hywel couldn't deny it. "He laughed and clapped me on the back. He said that of the two of us, he'd be just as happy for me to become High King as him, as long as someone he trusted held the post. He doesn't want the headache inherent in the job."

"Much easier to be a knight in the High King's guard," Bedwyr said.

"That is no jest," Hywel said. "Despite my father's aspirations, he has no idea what he's asking of me. He sees only the power, and not the price to attain it or keep it."

A mile later, the two companions approached the fort. It exploited a strong natural crag overlooking the Wye to the west and south, and was defended on the north and east by rock-cut ditches with a causeway on the north-east leading to the main gate. A strong wall followed the edge of the bluff on the river side, making it impossible for an army to ascend from the river, not to mention a straight drop down for anyone choosing to depart the castle that way.

Bedwyr pulled up twenty yards from the causeway. "Impressive. Your father is rebuilding in stone."

"The exterior walls, anyway." Hywel raised a hand to a soldier on the battlements whom he didn't know and wondered how much had changed in the weeks since he'd left. The man returned the greeting with a measured stiffness that didn't bode well for the rest of the visit. Then the double gate opened. Hywel glanced at Bedwyr. "No time like the present."

By the time Hywel and Bedwyr reached the great hall, Hywel was so stiff and uncomfortable—with his back teeth clenched so hard—he had to force himself to relax lest he pass out. That wouldn't do at all at his first entry into his father's presence as a knight. His father, Deiniol, sat in his carved wooden chair at the head of the hall by the fire. A dozen tables were scattered around the room. The servants would put them together for formal dinners, but more often than not, meals were served more haphazardly than that, according to need.

As it was, they were alone except for Deiniol and Hywel's mother, Nest, who sat beside her husband, worrying at her skirt with two fingers. It made Hywel think his father had sent all his men away so there'd be no witnesses to Hywel's dressing down. It was kind of him, if that was indeed the case. Then again, perhaps he was afraid Hywel had something to show for his absence, and didn't want anyone to witness his own capitulation.

Deiniol sat unmoving, one hand to his chin while his eyes followed their progress towards him. He didn't rise—and didn't greet his son.

"It seems I'm not yet forgiven," Hywel said under his breath, as he and Bedwyr came to a halt ten paces from Deiniol's chair.

"My lord." Hywel sketched a bow. Bedwyr followed suit.

Deiniol gestured towards the tunics they wore, both showing Cade's red dragon crest. "You've come from Gwynedd, have you? Lord Morgan has informed me of recent events, including the death of King Cadfael."

"Then he would have also told you how King Cadwaladr and his men, your son included, saved this region of Powys from Saxon and demon marauders," Bedwyr said.

Deiniol's face was a frozen mask. Beside him, Nest looked close to tears. She hadn't looked at Hywel either, which was even more disconcerting. His father had always been a hard man—and even harder on Hywel than on his own men on whom he was hard enough—but if Hywel had an ally in his own house, it had always been his mother. Occasionally—very occasionally—she'd been able to temper his father's harsh decrees. It wasn't any wonder that Hywel's sister had left home with the first man who offered for her, thinking anything was better than another day under Deiniol's thumb.

It wasn't any wonder that Hywel had left when he did.

"Are you well, Mother?" Hywel took a step towards her but as his movement, she jerked her hand, pushing him away. Hywel stepped back.

Deiniol cleared his throat. "You are not welcome here. Neither you nor an entreaty from your king."

"You support the Saxons, then." Bedwyr's jaw bulged, his anger barely contained. "I'll be sure to let them know that they have your permission to pillage your lands at any time."

While Hywel appreciated Bedwyr's support, he regretted that his friend had spoken. Deiniol gritted his teeth, but otherwise didn't respond to the taunt, other than to meet Hywel's eyes for the first time. Deiniol withdrew his attention so quickly, however, that Hywel wasn't sure he'd even seen it.

Hywel was about to turn away, so disheartened that he felt his insides had melted, when he realized what he'd missed: One of his father's arms hung loose beside his chair, his fingers almost to the floor. All the while they'd been talking—or not talking—he'd been speaking to Hywel in their family's coded battle language.

Enemy near, his father's hand said. *Danger.*

"Forgive me, my lord." Hywel put his feet together and bowed stiffly. "I hadn't realized I wasn't welcome in my own home. Now that I understand we are not wanted, we will not impose on you any longer." He turned away.

"Hywel—" Bedwyr said.

"I'd hoped you would have matured in the time you've been gone," Deiniol said to Hywel's back. "Your mother had prepared your old room for you, but it seems no one will sleep there tonight after all. Your sister will be sorry she missed you."

Hywel froze in mid-stride, his hand on Bedwyr's coat pulling him with him. He processed his father's words, and then continued down the gap between the tables towards the doors to the hall. Thankfully, Bedwyr didn't ask questions, having caught the strange undercurrent between Hywel and his father. Then Hywel and Bedwyr mounted their horses and passed under the gatehouse. They took the eastern road from the castle.

"What was that about?" Bedwyr pulled up once they were half a mile from the fort."

"Keep going a little longer," Hywel said. "We need to circle back among the trees."

"Your father's fingers moved in code," Bedwyr said. "I didn't notice until the very end. He was trying to cover his signals with his cloak, and was so successful I almost missed it."

Hywel nodded. "Did you also note that my father wasn't wearing his sword?"

"I didn't," Bedwyr said, "or if I did, I didn't think anything of it at the time. What did he say to you?"

"That we were in danger and an enemy is near," Hywel said.

"An enemy?" Bedwyr said. "What kind of enemy? No Saxons were in the castle or we would have seen signs."

"The threat comes from within the fort. Only my parents sat in the hall. Where are our men? What has happened to the garrison? To the servants? At first I thought he'd sent them away so he could meet with me in private."

"But he hadn't."

"No," Hywel said. "Whoever has cowed my father wanted him to get rid of us quickly. My father took advantage of our estrangement to make it look more real than it really is."

"It looked real to me," Bedwyr said. "Fathers and sons ..."

Hywel shot him a dry look. "I'm sure after you and I deal with whomever has frightened him so badly that he no longer controls his own house, we'll be back to our old ways. But for now—"

"—for now he needs you and trusts you enough to believe that you *will* do what needs doing," Bedwyr said. "So what's the rest of the code? The bit about your room and your sister?"

SARAH WOODBURY

"The only way into the fort other than through the front door is from the river. Once, on a dare, I scaled the rocks and then the wall around the fort to my sister's room, which is built directly into the curtain wall."

"And where is she?"

"She married Rhys ap Morgan, whom you've met, although she's well into her second pregnancy and could not come to the wedding at Deganwy."

Bedwyr wrinkled his nose in distaste.

"I know," Hywel said. "Rhys wasn't my first choice either. I said as much to my father at the time."

Bedwyr barked a laugh. "I'm sure he appreciated the advice."

Hywel laughed too, genuinely, and then sobered. "If someone is watching, from either inside or outside the castle, they'll think us no threat. Meanwhile, we need some equipment and I know where to get it."

A few yards further east, Hywel led Bedwyr off the main road to a track heading north, that looped back towards the Wye River. It came out on a stretch of water above the castle and some three hundred yards to the north.

"I'm not going to like this, am I?" Bedwyr said as they came to a halt on the bank.

"Not if you're opposed to getting wet," Hywel said. "The fort is built on a particularly difficult stretch of the river, and as it's almost April, the water is running high." Hywel checked the sky, eyeing the clouds above their heads. It rained almost every day here in the spring. Those clouds would release their rain just as soon as the sun set.

"That's exactly what I didn't want to hear." Bedwyr dismounted on the bank. "What are you looking for?"

"A friend of mine," Hywel said. "He's fished in this river every day of his life, regardless of whether or not he catches anything."

"Or if his lord might object?" Bedwyr said.

"That too," Hywel said.

Then he saw him. Goch stood in the river above a short waterfall, barefoot, shirtless, his breaches above his knees. He held his hands below the level of the water and Hywel waited for him to move before he disturbed the silence. In a moment he'd know whether or not his old friend had caught or lost the fish.

"Damn," Goch said.

Hywel smiled and moved towards him.

Goch glanced up. "Oh aye. You've come home."

"Not for long," Hywel said. "Just to sort out some trouble."

"Oh, aye," Goch said again. "You'll be wanting to get inside the back way."

"How'd you know?" Bedwyr's tone was full of suspicion.

Goch nodded at Hywel. "Goch knows his boy. Men in black have been in and out o' the fort the last few days. I didn't like the look of them so I stayed away."

"Men in black?" Bedwyr said. "Hooded and cloaked?"

"No. Regular soldiers from the look, with helmets and swords. Not your father's men, my lord," Goch said.

"Have they hurt anyone in the village?" Hywel said.

"Not so much hurt, my lord, but they ransacked every home," Goch said.

Hywel frowned. Whenever Goch began 'my lording' him, that meant he was upset. Often it was the only way to tell. The old man waded out of the water, still fishless, and Hywel handed him his shirt.

Goch brushed a hand through his nearly white hair, with only a few strands that had once been red remaining. "Looking for something, they were."

"Something they obviously haven't found, or they wouldn't still be here," Bedwyr said.

Hywel squared his shoulders. "Right. Goch—we need rope and a hook to help us up the wall, if you have them, and then I need you to let my parents know we're coming."

"You two against a dozen?" Goch said.

"We don't have time to find more help, even if any help were available," Hywel said.

"Besides he's a knight now." Bedwyr grinned. "No telling how many men that's worth."

Goch barked a laugh. "This way, my lords. We've much to do before it starts to rain."

18

Hywel

"It may be," Hywel said, "that King Cadwaladr didn't send me alone like he did Goronwy and Dafydd because he didn't know if I was up to the task, but I thank you for sticking by me anyway."

"Ah, boy," Bedwyr said. "I don't think that's it at all."

"Then what?" Hywel said.

"The others weren't straying so near Saxon lands is all," Bedwyr said. "Less need to set a watch. Cade said as much to me when he sent us out."

Hywel studied his friend. Bedwyr seemed sincere, but he'd had long practice in telling untruths to any number of lords before he'd fallen in with Cade. "All right. Either way, I'm glad you're here now because it evens the odds a bit."

"Two against a dozen sounds even to you, does it?" Bedwyr said.

"Better than one against a dozen," Hywel said. "With my father, we'll have three, and more if we free my father's men from wherever these men in black have hidden them."

"We've got some killing to do," Bedwyr said. "These aren't demons, you know. You might have been in battle, but not against humans, not recently anyway. Are you sure you're up for it?"

Hywel took a deep breath and let it out, not taking offense at Bedwyr's question or begrudging his right to ask it. "I am. We'll do what needs doing." He glanced at Bedwyr. "But no more or less, if you understand my meaning."

"Same as King Cadwaladr, I kill only when I have to," Bedwyr said.

Hywel looked up at the darkened fort, a black bulk above them against the deep gray of the sky. They'd come down the river, in the river, which meant treading through two small waterfalls on the way. Even that hadn't been easy and Hywel was reminded that when he'd done this as a youth, it had been summer, daylight, and not raining. It had been a lark that time, not in deadly earnest.

Good as his word, Goch had driven a wagon into the fort and made contact with Hywel's parents. Soldiers had stabbed their swords into the hay piled into the back of the cart before admitting him to the castle, which made Hywel glad he'd not chosen that route as means to get back inside. What the soldiers had missed was the coiled length of rope and hook that now hung from the upper window in the fort. Hywel tugged on it and then glanced at Bedwyr.

Both of them were soaked through, having left their cloaks with the horses in Goch's hut. They'd dressed in black, which was Bedwyr's normal gear but Hywel had to borrow from him and his shirt was larger than he liked, though as the rain had plastered it to his body, the size was no longer so noticeable. Hywel hoped that their black clothing would give them a moment of grace before the enemy guards recognized them. In that space of time, as short as it might be, he and Bedwyr would disarm, disable, or kill them if they could. In preparation for the task of climbing, which they had to manage first, Hywel wore gloves, had slung his sword over his back by the leather belt, and left off his armor.

"Time to go," Bedwyr said.

Hywel grasped the rope and began to climb up the sheer cliff face, hand over hand, his feet searching for purchase in the crevices in the rock. He reached the point where the curtain wall joined the bedrock and rested on the six inch wide landing afforded by the top of the cliff face. In Vortigern's time it might have been wider, but whatever grass and dirt might once have embedded itself there had eroded away.

Hywel tugged again on the hook.

"Steady," Bedwyr said, the sound coming out a harsh whisper.

"I'm good." Hywel back tipped his head to see up the wall. His sister's window showed twenty feet above him. Rain blew in his face, forcing him to close his eyes against it. The weather *had* turned out to be a blessing: its patter on the stones was so loud, coupled with the rushing river, that it disguised the sound of their movements. It also discouraged the enemy from putting much effort into scouting the exterior of the castle.

Goch had knotted the rope every foot to help with the climb and now Hywel abandoned the quest for crevices and merely climbed straight up the rope with the strength of his arms. Shortly thereafter, he flung one arm over the window sill, rested a moment just hanging on, and pulled himself inside the room. As Hywel's father had promised, no one slept in the bed. A single candle stood on a table by the door, flickering in the breeze that came through the open window.

The instant Hywel's weight left from the rope, Bedwyr began climbing. Hywel leaned out the window, watching for his dark head to reach the level of the sill. It felt like a longer time than it had taken Hywel, but Bedwyr was a much larger man and hadn't ever climbed this way before. And it was probably just Hywel's imagination anyway.

At last, Bedwyr flung a boot over the window frame, swung the rest of his body up and into the room, and collapsed on the floor with a muffled *thud*. Hywel was already at the door, but Bedwyr held out a hand to stay him.

"Give me a moment." His breath came hard and he bent over, gripping his knees. "I don't know that I could hold a sword just now."

Hywel channeled his impatience by closing his eyes and breathing deeply and evenly, talking himself through what they might face on the other side of the door. Bedwyr straightened and Hywel opened his eyes.

"Once I open this door, there's no going back," Hywel said.

"I know," Bedwyr said.

"Are we searching the fort separately or together?" Hywel said.

"Separately," Bedwyr said. "Point me in the proper direction and I'll do what needs doing—just as I know you will."

"I find it likely that whoever has taken the fort will have placed men along the wall walk," Hywel said. "To reach it, once you're through this door, turn to the left. The corridor leads to a door at the end of the hall which opens onto the battlements. I will go to the right—to my father's room."

Bedwyr held his knife, rather than his sword which he'd buckled again at his waist in preparation for a fight. Hywel did the same, tightening the leather and loosening the sword in its sheath. They shared a glance, Bedwyr nodded, and Hywel carefully opened the bedroom door. He muffled the sound of the latch with one hand as he'd learned to do as a boy when he wanted to leave his room without waking his nanny or his father.

The door opened inward. Hywel eased past it and poked his head into the hallway. Quickly he pulled back. A man stood guard outside his parents' room. The man had his shoulder braced against the wall but was looking towards the stairs, not down the hall in Hywel's direction. The guard had the expectant set to his shoulders of a man waiting for his relief.

Hywel held up one finger to Bedwyr before stepping around the doorframe on tiptoe. The guard in front of him still hadn't moved—perhaps too focused on the stairs—which was his bad luck. In two strides, Hywel reached him. Before the guard had a chance to turn or shout the alarm, Hywel wrapped his arm around his head, stuffed the curve of his bracer between the man's teeth, and twisted. The man's neck cracked.

Hywel grasped the body under the shoulders and Bedwyr came around to lift the feet. Rather than drag him, which would have made noise, they carried him into the bedroom they'd just vacated. They laid him on the floor, mindful of Nest's unstated preference for not spoiling the bed.

"Quickly now," Bedwyr said.

Through the doorway again, they moved in opposite directions. Hywel glanced back once to see Bedwyr open the door to the battlements and disappear through it. Hywel pulled the latch to his parents' bedchamber, praying that his father expected him, and nudged the door open. His father stood in the center of the room, fully clothed, watching for him. He grimaced as Hywel entered. But for once, not in disappointment at Hywel.

"We're dealing with madmen. I've never felt so helpless in my life." It was the most honest statement Hywel had ever heard from him.

"Whose men are they?" Hywel said.

"I don't know. All they do is keep asking *where is it?* and nothing else. As if I would ever tell them."

In friendlier times and because Hywel was his father's only son, Deiniol had confided in him, so now Hywel nodded his understanding. "They want the knife."

"It appears so," Deiniol said. "But I still don't know *who* wants it."

"Perhaps I do." Hywel glanced around the room. "Where's mother?"

"Seeing to a woman in the village," Deiniol said. "Births continue, whether the men in black want them to or not."

"And you made sure they asked for her," Hywel said. "Even if the woman only *thought* the baby might come tonight."

His father tipped his head in acknowledgement of this deception.

"We've three of us now." Hywel pulled his sword from its sheath and handed it, hilt out, to his father. "Use this."

Deiniol gazed at the sword, at his son, and then reached for the weapon. "I knew you'd come."

Hywel gaze held a wary cast. "I would hope so."

"We've exchanged harsh words in the past, and will again," Deiniol said. "Nothing's changed."

"I've changed." Hywel turned from his father and strode to the door, looked out, and waved a hand for his father to come beside him. "I killed one. Bedwyr is attending to the guards on the battlements. Goch said a dozen men had overtaken the castle. Is that accurate?"

"There are ten of them," Deiniol said. "I may never allow a stranger in the door again."

"How did they overpower the garrison?"

"They didn't," Deiniol said. "They asked for hospitality and I admitted them, not knowing why I shouldn't. It wasn't that we weren't prepared, but ..." He paused and pursed his lips.

Hywel studied his father's downturned head, waiting.

Deiniol nodded. "No, you are right, though I thank you for not saying it. We *were* unprepared. They were Welsh and no Welsh lord has challenged me in many years. They murdered half the garrison in their sleep and poisoned the rest."

"I don't judge you, Father," Hywel said. "Anyone could have made the same mistake."

"Including King Cadwaladr?"

Hywel gave him a grudging laugh. "Perhaps not him. But betrayal is a recent memory for him. His father was murdered by one of his own lords who then usurped the throne and married his mother. It isn't easy for him to trust."

"And yet he allowed Cadfael to ambush him and kill all of his men, including his foster-father, Cynyr of Bryn y Castell."

"As I said," Hywel said, "yours was a mistake anyone could have made." He led the way out of the bedroom and down the stairs, keeping to the wall, his knife extended. Below him in the hall, men snored in a cacophony of sound.

"Five watch, five sleep," Deiniol said. "It's been this way for three days."

"All ten die," Hywel said.

He and his father stepped into the hall. Hywel pointed to two men opposite each other, asleep with their heads on the table, their glasses of mead empty.

Those are yours, Hywel's hand said. He took the three at a near table. Two slept as the others, while the last sprawled on his back on a bench.

His father nodded and moved toward the sleeping men. When they'd reached the tables, father and son gazed at each other for half a heartbeat. Then, Hywel put the knife between his teeth and held up his hand to count with his fingers: *one, two three*. He killed the first sleeping man as he had the guard in the hall: with a hard twist that snapped his neck.

Then, recapturing the knife, Hywel leapt on the table and kicked at the head of the second sleeping man with such force that it threw him backwards of his bench. The third man died with his throat slit. It wasn't a clean death, however. When blood spattered all over Hywel's clothing, he had to swallow the bile that threatened to unman him and finished the job with an awkward slash that nearly severed the man's neck.

His father, meanwhile, had dispatched his first opponent, but was having trouble with the second, who'd woken in time to pull his belt knife from its sheath and fend off Deiniol's attack with it. He grabbed a spindle chair that had been set against the wall behind him to keep Deiniol at bay.

Hywel strode towards the soldier. "Surrender and you'll live."

Deiniol glanced at him, a flash of skepticism in his eyes, but Hywel ignored it. He believed King Cadwaladr would have given the man a chance.

The man didn't take it. "Never!"

Before the soldier could do something they all might regret, the front door burst open and Bedwyr strode in. Blood, distinguishable from the black of his water-logged shirt only in that it glistened in the torchlight, covered his front.

"Are you all right?" Hywel said.

"A minor head wound." Bedwyr brandished his sword, also coated in blood. He took in the scene with a glance, then walked toward this last enemy soldier. "You have a death wish, eh?"

The man refused to cower, but he was trying to look out of the corners of both eyes at the same time, to keep Deiniol, Bedwyr, and Hywel in view. He was outnumbered, however, and his three opponents were in accord. Deiniol grabbed the leg of the chair the man held while Bedwyr prodded him in the back with the tip of his sword. "Put up the knife."

The man raised his hands in surrender and Hywel stepped forward to grasp his arm at the wrist. The knife clattered to the floor. "Who is your master?" Hywel said. "You should at least be able to tell us that."

"I serve Barinthus, the mighty."

"Who?" Hywel said. The word came out instinctively and Hywel cursed himself for showing ignorance. It was a mistake to appear weak and he'd been holding himself together hard for the last hour, even if throughout the entire adventure he'd worried that a puff of wind would pull him apart at the seams.

Deiniol leaned in, his voice low. "He is a charioteer to the Underworld."

That explained a lot.

"And whom does *he* serve?" Hywel said.

"Mabon, lord of the worlds." The man was a font of information.

Bedwyr smirked. "That's what he's calling himself these days?" He shook his head. "Such cheek."

"And what is Mabon up to now?" Hywel said.

"I don't know," the man said. "He told us to ask for *it* and when Lord Deiniol gave it to us, to bring it to him."

"Where?" Hywel said.

"A Saxon place. Near Shrewsbury."

Hywel and Bedwyr exchanged a look and Hywel said, for his father's benefit, "It is near Shrewsbury that the Saxons gather, and at Caer Fawr where we are to meet King Cadwaladr."

"I wonder what Taliesin would have to say about this?" Bedwyr said.

"I don't like this meddling from the world of the *sidhe*," Deiniol said. "I have heard many rumors these last weeks, with King Cadwaladr at the center of them."

"Some might even be true," Bedwyr said.

Deiniol flushed red and he put his face right into the captive's. "You're telling me that this Mabon is responsible for the death of my men and the terrorizing of my people?"

The man swallowed and then gave Deiniol a slight nod. Deiniol glared at him for another count of ten and then stepped back, his color subsiding. He glanced at Hywel. "If even a fraction of what I've heard is true, King Cadwaladr might be one of the few men who can stop Mabon."

"I believe he can," Hywel said. "I ask your leave to go to him."

Deiniol had been studying the captive again and now faced his son fully. "You do not need my leave."

"But I would like it."

"Then you have it," Deiniol said.

Just like that. As if the two of them hadn't spent the last fifteen years fighting about what Hywel could and could not do.

Deiniol gestured to Barinthus' man. "What do I do with him?"

Hywel shrugged. "Let him go. He has failed in his mission. Either Barinthus or Mabon will find him. We all might prefer it if he wasn't here when that happens."

"No! No!" The man fell to his knees at Hywel's feet. "You can't send me out there alone!"

"What you planned for my family was far worse," Hywel said.

The man's face took on an even more desperate look. And then before Hywel realized what he was doing, he grasped Hywel's hand with both of his and thrust himself upon the knife that Hywel still held. Hywel staggered to one knee under the man's weight while blood from the wound poured over their hands. Deiniol grasped the man's shoulders to try to pull him away, but by the time he managed it and laid him on the floor, death had taken him.

"I don't understand what this gains the poor bastard," Bedwyr said. "He's dead. Now he goes to Arawn, Mabon's father, in the Underworld."

Hywel chewed on his lip as he looked down at the body. "I think he has unknowingly given us a gift."

Bedwyr glanced at his friend. "What do you mean?"

"Mabon has been with Arianrhod since she took him out of Arawn's cavern at Caer Dathyl. Thus, we can't assume that Arawn knows what Mabon has been doing since then."

"But now he does," Deiniol said, understanding in his face. "This man will tell him."

"You do realize that Arawn could approve of his son's activities," Bedwyr said.

"I wouldn't be so sure that he will," Hywel said. "Arawn has spoiled Mabon, but meddling in the human world as Mabon has—in pursuit of his own power, possibly at their expense—is not something any of the *sidhe* take lightly. Taliesin told me that the truce between the children of *Don* and the children of *Llyr* is predicated upon none of them using the human world as a tool or a shield."

Bedwyr toed the body. "Would someone mind telling me why Barinthus sent men here? What is *it*, this time?"

19

Dafydd

They'd traveled through two nights and days, hardly stopping for rest, but now they had to. Dafydd's wound ached more with every hour that passed. He was trying to keep his pain a secret from Angharad, but wasn't sure he was succeeding, and even more, wasn't sure how much longer he could go on pretending he was fine.

Fear. He'd known it before, of course. The bitterness of it caught in the back of his throat. He'd been afraid for himself and Rhiann at the battle by Llanllugan. Only peripherally had he the consciousness at the time to be afraid for all the people behind him, though those thoughts had preoccupied Rhiann's mind. Fear had nearly overwhelmed him again in Arawn's cavern and that time it had been for his friends, more than himself, and specifically for Cade. Blood had pooled in Cade's mouth, but Dafydd had tasted it in his.

Now, it was not for himself that he was afraid, but for Angharad, who was nearly as innocent has he'd been when he left

Orkney over a year ago. There had been times, as they passed through the mountains that formed a barrier across Wales, when he'd thought about using the cloak—for protection, for relief from the fear of prying eyes—but something had always stayed his hand. He was afraid that its use wouldn't be without consequences. At the back of his mind, he even wondered if wearing the cloak wouldn't make him more visible to Mabon, that in joining the unseen world of the *sidhe*, the *sidhe* could see him more clearly.

He wished the cloak was at least warm. He could have risked swinging it over both of them if it could have provided them with something to keep the cold at bay. He'd slept outside plenty in his life. Why he was so cold tonight he didn't know, even with the blankets they shared. But now his arm ached so much that it threatened to drive everything else from his mind. Angharad had checked his wound again and there was no pus within it, but his arm felt *wrong*. Over the last two days, he'd been able to use it less, not more, as it supposedly healed.

They lay side by side. Dafydd hadn't offered to bring her into the circle of his good arm, though he'd thought about it. So they lay back to back instead, each gazing into the darkness beyond their immediate circle of trees.

"I'm glad I came with you, my lord," Angharad said.

Dafydd had hoped she was asleep. He scootched a little and rolled onto his back. "I can't imagine why. This has to be the worst two days of your life."

"I've never done anything important before." And then she paused. "No one has ever needed me to."

Dafydd thought about that for a moment. "That was true for me as well, before I left the Isle of Man. I think feeling that way is part of growing up."

Another pause and Angharad felt for Dafydd's hand and squeezed it. "I'm glad it's you I'm with."

A stick snapped in the forest, which saved Dafydd from having to answer.

"What was that?" Angharad said, her voice a whisper.

Could some of Mabon's men have tracked them all this way? "Stay down." Dafydd put his hand to Angharad's shoulder, listening hard, and then got to his feet.

Angharad didn't obey. Instead, she rose with him and slipped her hand into his useless one. "I don't want to get separated."

He didn't want that either. It would be easy enough for an enemy to draw him away from her into the woods and then attack the camp. They'd left their supplies on the horses for just that eventuality. Dafydd's fingers lay lifeless in Angharad's and he wished he could tighten his grip.

Dafydd scanned the trees, grateful he hadn't dared to light a fire. He swung his pack over his shoulder and then unsheathed his sword.

"Are we in danger?" Angharad said.

"I don't know yet." He glanced down at her, although all of her he could really make out was a darker shape among the trees. "Take out your knife."

She obeyed and, leaving the horses, they crept from tree to tree, circling in ever deeper spirals away from the campsite.

A whisper came to him. It was more sense than sound and he froze. Angharad instantly stilled with him. After listening for a dozen heartbeats, Dafydd risked taking a step. Unfortunately, it was directly into the tip of a sword. It poked him in the breastbone and it was like his heart fell through his chest into his boots. That, and he felt like puking, but then, he'd felt like that ever since Mabon had sliced his arm.

"Do not move."

"Jesus, Goronwy!" The exclamation burst from Dafydd the instant he recognized the voice.

Goronwy stepped back and both men sheathed their swords.

"I had no idea that you might have followed the same path we did," Dafydd said.

"I might say the same for you. Not that I'm not pleased to see you, of course," Gorowny said. He squinted into the murk in Angharad's direction. "And your friend."

Dafydd pulled Angharad forward. Without thinking about it, his arm slipped around her waist. "Goronwy, this is Angharad ferch Clydog of Ceredigion. Angharad, this is Goronwy."

"What of the men you were supposed to find for King Cadwaladr?" Goronwy said.

Dafydd shook his head, reluctant to put into words his failure in that regard.

Angharad stepped in front of Dafydd. "Circumstances have changed, Lord Goronwy. Sir Dafydd is bringing King Cadwaladr something far more valuable."

Dafydd almost laughed, her tone was so fierce. "It's all right, Angharad. Goronwy is my elder brother, and also serves King Cadwaladr." He grinned. "And I see that he doesn't have any men with him either, despite a similar mission to mine. What of the armies of King Arthur?" Dafydd lifted his chin and looked past Goronwy. A woman stood in a small clearing thirty paces behind him. A ray of moonlight pierced the cloud cover overhead and shone directly down on her. She had a knife in her hand.

"King Arthur is dead," Goronwy said. "Along with the men he hoped to bring north to fight with us."

Dafydd stared at Goronwy. "What? All of them? What happened?"

"Mabon paid us a visit on the road," Goronwy said.

Angharad spun around to gaze up Dafydd, one hand on his chest and pressing hard. He looked into her eyes, which glinted up at him, and then back at his brother over her head. "Mabon came to Ceredigion. When you saw him, did he ask you for something— *it* again like at Deganwy? Something that King Arthur possessed?"

"How did you know?"

"Because he asked the same of Angharad's father," Dafydd said.

Goronwy gazed off into the distance for a long moment. "This just gets worse and worse. Bring your things to our fire. We need to talk."

Angharad strode back through the woods to their campsite and Dafydd followed. Her shoulders were back and her chin up. He read anger and determination in her. When they reached the place they'd been sleeping—or not sleeping—she picked up her pack, swung it over her shoulder, and then snapped. "What does Mabon think he's doing? He's mucking about with everybody's lives as if he has a right to them."

Dafydd found himself relaxing in the face of her anger, partly because it wasn't directed at him, and partly because he liked her so much more this way: defending him and talking to him as if he were a friend, rather than a potential suitor she treated badly at Lilwen's urging. "Mabon is a god, the son of Arawn and Arianrhod. He does what he likes."

"And destroys everything in his path in the process?" Angharad said. "It was one thing to come into my father's house. My father had men prepared to withstand him. But King Arthur was an old man."

"It is as you said. Mabon does what he likes. Two months ago, he had King Cadfael, Queen Rhiannon's father, killed," Dafydd said. "He sees nothing in taking a human life."

"Well, I for one hope that King Cadwaladr can do something about it." Angharad grabbed her horse's reins and began leading him towards Goronwy's campsite. Still bemused, Dafydd followed. They'd just reached Goronwy's camp when Angharad stopped and looked back at him. "Wait a moment, my lord. You've held Dyrnwyn. You fought with King Cadwaladr.

What happened the first time he faced Mabon? Why didn't the king deal with him then?"

Dafydd snorted a laugh. "One *sidhe* at a time, Angharad. The King banished Arawn to the Underworld. Cade's foster brother, Rhun, skewered Mabon with a knife through his throat, but—"

"But it didn't kill him," Goronwy said, from his seat on a log near the small fire, smokeless as Dafydd's had been when he'd dared light one. Dafydd was glad to see that Goronwy's skills hadn't deserted him, even if he rarely had to use them anymore. Goronwy had taken Dafydd on his first adventure into the wild, the week before Goronwy had left the Isle of Man for Gwynedd. Dafydd had been six, Goronwy eighteen, both of them trying so hard to be older than they were.

Goronwy gestured to the woman. "This is Catrin, a healer, who saved my life in the south."

Dafydd stepped forward, his right hand out. "Thank you for that."

She took his hand and canted her head. "My pleasure, for all that your brother resented needing it."

Dafydd laughed. Goronwy and Catrin were getting along about as well as he and Angharad had at first. Probably something to do with traveling with a woman with ideas of her own she didn't mind sharing. But Goronwy surprised him.

"I did thank you," he said, looking at Catrin.

Catrin canted her head, giving nothing away, though she answered politely enough. "You did. And agreed to allow me to accompany you to Caer Fawr. King Cadwaladr might have need of both of us."

Goronwy turned to Dafydd. "Catrin is more than just a healer. She can sense the use of magic. If Mabon is near, we'll know it."

"That's a relief," Angharad said, obviously still feeling a bit tart since the comment came out sarcastic rather than genuine.

Catrin shot Angharad a look of amusement and patted the space on the log next to her. Dafydd took the reins Angharad held and led both horses to where Goronwy had picketed his and Catrin's. He didn't recognize either beast.

"I lost Cadfarch in the battle against Mabon's men," Goronwy said, coming to stand with him. He stroked the nose of the new addition. "We found these two in the woods. I think this one is King Arthur's own."

Dafydd rubbed his horse's nose with his knuckle, then glanced at his brother. "Did Mabon himself fight?"

"He left it mostly to his men," Goronwy said.

"Ah, yes, how noble of him," Dafydd said.

Goronwy spoke in an undertone. "Did you fight him?"

"Yes," Dafydd said.

"And won?"

Dafydd shrugged. "Yes." Dafydd fell silent. He rested his head against the horse's and closed his eyes.

Goronwy placed a hand on Dafydd's shoulder. "This wasn't the walk in the woods we'd hoped it might be, was it?"

Dafydd turned to his brother. "When Rhiann and I shot the demons at Llanllugan, lives other than our own hung in the balance. I knew it, of course. But this was different."

"Because you, alone, had to make the decisions," Goronwy said. "Angharad's life depended on your choices, not another's."

Dafydd nodded. "What is most strange to me is why Mabon insists on interfering in our world. As Taliesin once said, he is like a child, clumsily knocking over blocks to get to what he wants."

"He lacks understanding of his own actions," Goronwy said. "And that makes him dangerous."

"Can't we—" Dafydd paused. "No, that's stupid."

"What?"

"Can't we talk to someone? One of the *sidhe*, I mean. What about Arianrhod?"

"She can't control Mabon," Goronwy said. "At least that's how it appears to Cade. Besides, how would that work? I've never encountered one of the *sidhe* in my life before Caer Dathyl and now they're everywhere."

"Something must have happened," Dafydd said. "In the Otherworld I mean. Something has changed that has pushed Mabon upon us. Or made him think that he wants to live among us."

"I couldn't say." Goronwy was looking at him curiously and Dafydd ran a hand across his brow, not sure what his brother was seeing. "Come. I have an *it* to show you."

Dafydd managed to nod, though as they'd been speaking, Goronwy's shape had wavered in front of his eyes. He blinked his weakness back. "And I you, if Angharad will let me."

Goronwy looked closer. "What's wrong?"

Dafydd drew his right hand down his left arm. "I don't feel well. Mabon's sword cut me—"

Goronwy grasped Dafydd around the torso as he staggered. "Catrin!"

An instant later, Catrin was on Dafydd's other side. "I thought something was wrong the moment I laid eyes on him. His aura wasn't right."

Between the two of them, they managed to get Dafydd to the fire and lay him down on a blanket near it. Dafydd wanted to tell them that the wound was healing, but they talked over the top of him.

"You mean you sensed magic?" Goronwy said.

Catrin shook her head. "It wasn't that clear. I thought it was coming from the stone, since I've felt it nudging at the back of my mind all day." She turned to Angharad. "Where is he hurt?"

"His upper arm," Angharad said. "I've checked it every day. It doesn't fester."

"How did he get it?" Goronwy said.

"From Mabon's sword." Angharad had fallen to her knees, a step beyond Catrin and Goronwy. She waved a hand in the direction of Dafydd's horse. "Mabon dropped it when Dafydd defeated him and we brought it with us."

Catrin unwound the bandage and gazed at the wound. Dafydd watched her through half-closed lids and a haze of fever. She met his eyes and then looked up into Goronwy's. "I—I've never seen anything like this before. There are some things I can try..."

"There's only one thing I can think of that can counter a magic sword," Goronwy said, "and that is another one. We must get him to King Cadwaladr."

20

Rhiann

Rhiann had tried to convince Cade that he couldn't possibly travel to Caer Fawr without her. It was, in effect, their first fight and Rhiann had lost it.

"I can't tell you that this is the right course, Rhiann," he'd said. "But it *feels* right."

"You sound like Taliesin!" Rhiann had said.

Taliesin himself stepped forward at that, putting in his nose where Rhiann didn't want it. "But this time, Taliesin agrees."

Rhiann had stared at him, aghast. "Why?"

Irritatingly, Taliesin had refused to answer.

But his words had clinched it for Cade. "Right. You're staying where it's safe." What had started out as a hopeful proposal on his part had turned into an opportunity to exert his husbandly authority over her.

"It isn't safe anywhere, Cade," Rhiann said. "And if I'm not safe with you, how can I ever be with you?"

"The Saxons are gathering at Shrewsbury *today*," Cade said. "We have a week at most, Taliesin thinks, before they drive west across the Severn River."

Rhiann had glanced at the bard to see how he was taking this. He'd given her a mild look that told her nothing. She'd liked him better when he couldn't *see*.

They'd left her. Even Geraint had gone, riding north and west to gather more support for Cade. Out of desperation, she'd turned her attention to making Dinas Bran habitable, even if she ground her teeth all the while. On her own, she'd hired a few local women from the village of Llangollen as servants, along with an army of workmen who swarmed all over the fort. In the three days since Cade and Taliesin had departed with the bulk of their men, they'd made substantial progress. Enough so, that Rhiann was beginning to think it could be a kind of home again.

"I see things are going well here." Madog, a villager in his middle forties, pushed open the door to the hall.

The hall was the only part of the complex that had sustained minimal damage from lack of attention in the years since Cade's father had fallen. Rhiann was using it as a work space, until a more private office could be refurbished for her.

"They are," Rhiann said from a table near the fireplace. At Madog's approach, she stood. She didn't like this self-appointed 'counselor to kings' as he called himself, for all that he was the leader of the village elders. He claimed to have been away when they'd first arrived, but had appeared almost immediately after

Cade had left. Rhiann suspected that Madog had correctly perceived that Cade wouldn't have tolerated him.

She, however, didn't feel that she had the authority to go against the wishes of the villagers, if indeed they'd appointed him their leader as he'd said. Certainly, none of the women questioned his assertion, even if they did scurry out of his way. *She* would have scurried too, if it wasn't her duty to speak to him.

His first smarmy visit had set Rhiann's teeth on edge, and she'd had the same reaction each day thereafter. He claimed to be checking on the progress of the work. The garrison captain, a man named Alun who was one of the five soldiers Cade had left to mind the fort, leaned in to speak into Rhiann's ear. "Shall I get rid of him for you, madam?"

"Yes." The word hissed through Rhiann's teeth.

While Alun strode to intercept Madog and usher him back out the door, Rhiann turned away. "I hate that man! I hate being here alone! I can't believe Taliesin backed Cade up..." Rhiann gathered the leftover cups from an earlier meal onto a tray so she could return them to the kitchen. It wasn't necessary. They had servants for that but she'd been a servant once and still remembered how it was done.

Then she heard a step behind her. She stopped, the tray in both hands, and turned. Madog, apparently having evaded Alun's arresting arm, halted five paces from her. She couldn't ignore him.

He bowed. "My lady."

"What is it?" Rhiann peered around him looking for someone—anyone—to aid her, but Alun had disappeared. She was on her own.

"I informed your captain of a small matter with one of the workmen. He is seeing to it," Madog said.

Rhiann narrowed her eyes at the man. That didn't sound right. "What do you want?" She was done with being polite, even if it got her off on the wrong foot with the villagers. "It's time you went back to wherever you came from."

Madog blinked, and then his face contorted. "How is it that you see through me when your husband isn't even here?" And then between one heartbeat and the next, Madog transformed into the more familiar form of Mabon.

Rhiann took a step back, trying not to let Mabon see the panic rising to her throat. He had confused her bravado for certainty. She swallowed hard and then threw off her fear. Dafydd had shared with her his theory that for all his pride and grandeur, Mabon didn't have any power in the human world but what humans—or his father—gave him. If there was any time to put that to the test, it was now.

"I ask again, what do you want?" she said. "Why are you here?"

Mabon sniffed. "I admit I was disappointed to find your husband already gone when I arrived. I'd hoped we'd have a chance for another chat. Where is he, by the way?"

Mabon's question appeared casual, but it raised Rhiann's hackles even more. *Why wouldn't he know and how should she answer?* "South. Fighting the Saxons as you should well know."

"Ah, the Saxons. They are always so malleable," Mabon said.

This time, instead of stepping back, Rhiann took a step forward, her blood running cold. "Are you working with the Saxons? What have you done?"

Mabon's face took on a look that Rhiann could only describe as gleeful. "I guess your husband will find out, won't he?" Mabon turned on his heel and headed for the kitchen, leaving Rhiann aghast and speechless. Before he left the room for the stairs, however, he reached out a hand and set a carved image of a king, one finger in length, on the edge of a table the servants used as a sideboard during meals. "Give your husband this, if you will—with my regards." Mabon shot Rhiann one more grin and disappeared down the stairs.

Rhiann ran after him, afraid of what havoc he might wreak in her kitchen. She rushed through the doorway, but skidded to a halt at the three pairs of eyes that looked up at her from the chopping board and cooking pots. "Did a man in black come through here just now? Madog was his name, from the village."

"No, my lady," Gwen, the head cook, said. "Not that I've seen."

Rhiann looked back up the stairs to the hall. Mabon, as usual, had disappeared at his whim.

"I grew up in Llangollen and I don't know of any man named Madog," Gwen said.

"I thought as much." Rhiann gave her a tight smile and nodded her head. "Thank you."

Back in the hall, Rhiann crouched so she was eye level with the little king, which appeared to be nothing more than an ordinary carving. Hesitantly, she touched it with one finger. Nothing happened. She straightened and picked it up. The carving lay quiet in her hand, so finely crafted she could make out each spire in its crown. She stared down at it, wishing that Cade had left her even one of her friends to talk to. *Why hadn't he?*

The answer came to her instantly. *Because he trusted her.* And now she was going to betray that trust and ride to Caer Fawr. Hopefully, her husband would understand.

Part Three

21

Cade

"You're telling me there are thirteen of these things to worry about?" Cade sat on the edge of a work table, with Dafydd beside him. Every now and then, Dafydd reached out a hand to touch the hilt of Caledfwlch. Cade had made it clear that he was to stay close and use it if he needed it. Goronwy had brought Dafydd in time, and Cade had healed his wound, but Dafydd still didn't feel quite right. None of them—not Cade, Dafydd, or Taliesin—could explain it.

Just as with the black shadow in the cavern beneath Dinas Bran.

Cade glanced at Taliesin, whose expression was unreadable. Now that he could *see* again, Cade had been able to get even less out of him than before, about the shadow or anything else.

"That is my belief," Taliesin said, answering the one question Cade had asked out loud. "You won't like the rest of the story any better."

"Better tell us quick, then." Goronwy peered through the slit between the door and the frame. They had gathered in a storage shed off the courtyard. "Rhys will be noticing you're gone and start to wonder."

Cade had included the two women, Angharad and Catrin, in the consultation: Angharad because for generations her family had owned the cloak she'd brought and she deserved to have a say in its future, and Catrin because ... well ... because Taliesin thought he should.

Cade too eyed the door. He'd arrived with Taliesin and his *teulu* the previous evening. The other lords of Wales had trickled in over the course of the day, but by the time the sun had set, the trickle had become a flood. Rhys and his men, Geraint and the lords of southern Gwynedd, with their knights and archers, and then a hundred others had arrived to fill the fort and its surrounding plateau with men. Only Rhun and Tudur were still missing. Cade was hugely relieved to know that he would have men to counter the Saxons. He'd called a Council session for within the hour.

Cade had chosen Caer Fawr as the place to meet because of its extensive defenses, its access to water close to the fort, and its proximity to Shrewsbury. He hoped the Saxons had never read Tacitus, for it was this spot that Caratacus had chosen for his last stand against the Romans. The fort was naturally defended such that they could cover every entrance and exit, with steep slopes on all sides and rings of an ancient rampart and ditch system of which Cade intended to take full advantage.

Caer Fawr had once been a great fortress, but now like Dinas Bran, lay half in ruins. The curtain wall, which followed the natural shape of the mountain, was one of the few works of stone that remained and enclosed a space of nearly three acres. In addition, a fifty foot wide extension at the southern end of the complex took up the base of the hill. Cade had posted watchers there and had ordered others to continually circle the mountain. If the Saxons came, Cade would know.

"The tale begins and ends with Arianrhod." Taliesin leaned on his staff, both hands clasped at the top and his chin resting on his fists.

Cade crossed his arms across his chest, prepared to be annoyed. "As it always seems to these days."

"As you say." Taliesin gestured to the items on the table. "These are some of the Thirteen Treasures of Britain which she kept, at one time or another, in her home on the Isle of Glass. Some of them she commissioned, some she merely acquired or inherited."

"I know this story," said Dafydd. "It includes a prophecy about one who will gather the Treasures and in so doing, restore the Welsh to their former glory. To a time before the Romans came."

"Is that why Mabon wants them?" Angharad said. "Because he sees himself as a savior of the Welsh?"

Taliesin moved his head noncommittally. "His desire would be the power the Treasures would bring him."

"Of course it would," said Goronwy. "How could it not?"

"With every Treasure he collects, his power grows. He wouldn't even need to gather them all to find himself ruling not only the human world, but the world of the *sidhe*."

"Ah," Cade said. "Understanding dawns at last. Mabon is in the human world because the Treasures are here. But it's power among his own kind that he wants."

Dafydd shifted beside Cade. His hand went to Caledfwlch's hilt and he held it as he spoke. "No wonder the gods are taking sides. Do they know what Mabon has in mind? How many of the *sidhe* are with him and want him to overthrow Beli, who rules the *sidhe* council?"

Almost imperceptibly, Taliesin lifted one shoulder. "I'm not privy to those answers."

"So what are they, these Treasures?" Cade said. "Do you have a list?"

Taliesin licked his lips, glanced once at Cade, and recited just loud enough so that everyone in the hut could hear:

"Dyrnwyn, the flaming sword,
lost for centuries beneath the earth.
A hamper that feeds a hundred, a knife to serve twenty-four,
A chariot to carry a man on the wind,
A halter to tame any horse he might wish.
The cauldron of the Giant to test the brave,
A whetstone for deadly sharpened swords,
An entertaining chess set,
A crock and a dish, each to fill one's every wish,

A drinking horn that bestows immortality on those worthy of it,
And the mantle of Arthur.
His healing sword descends;
Our enemies flee our unseen and mighty champion."

Silence descended upon the companions. Cade's hand clenched around a husk of bread, which he'd brought with him from the meal he'd interrupted to confer with his friends. As had become common of late, he was more hungry than he felt comfortable admitting, though that was far better than gaining energy by killing.

Goronwy broke the silence. "Why all the secrecy on Mabon's part? This foolishness with *it*. Why not name them?"

"Because naming has power?" Taliesin said. "Because he knows to whom the items were given, but not which Treasure each man possessed? His motivations remain a mystery to me, beyond that he seeks these items for his own power."

"Well, if they're a mystery to you, I don't see how we can hope to understand him," Cade said.

"Maybe we shouldn't try," Dafydd said.

Goronwy cleared his throat. "So, at this juncture, King Cadwaladr has collected Caledfwlch, the mantle, the knife, and the whetstone. Four of thirteen, since the fake Dyrnwyn doesn't count."

"So it seems," Taliesin said.

"All of which Mabon is seeking and because of Mabon, we now possess these in one place," Dafydd said.

"Again, yes," Taliesin said.

"None of this helps us in the slightest against the Saxons," Bedwyr said.

"No," Cade said. "The treasures comprise a separate issue, unless we have to fight Mabon for them at the same time as we fight the Saxons for our freedom."

"I hope that is not the case," Taliesin said. "Time is not the same to Mabon as to us. He's just as likely to disappear for a week as to know where we are and *when* it is to us."

"And Mabon isn't as powerful as he thinks he is," Dafydd said. "He's not a good swordsman. For all that he injured me, it was his sword that did the damage, not some invincibility or strange power of his own. He can't hurt you unless you let him and give him power over you. I don't understand him at all. I don't understand the world of the *sidhe* at all."

"Probably better that you don't," said Geraint.

"Perhaps his only real power stems from his association with his mother or father, and since neither are aware of his activities, he has only his *glamour* to fall back on," Dafydd said.

"He can do a lot with *glamour*," Goronwy said.

Geraint jerked his chin towards the door. "It's time to go."

"Just a moment." Cade gazed at the Treasures on the table and then swept up the cloak. He met Taliesin's eyes for a heartbeat and then swung the cloak over his shoulders.

Catrin gasped.

"Can any of you see me? Taliesin?"

"No," Taliesin said.

Cade pulled Caledfwlch from its sheath. "And now?"

"No again," Taliesin said.

"What are you thinking?" Dafydd said.

Cade almost laughed to see him looking at a spot a hand's span from Cade's eyes and a foot higher. Cade walked to the door, opened it wider, and peered out.

That got more of a response from the others. Bedwyr said, "You don't really think ..."

Cade shot Bedwyr a grin he couldn't have seen. "No time like the present!" Cade slipped out the door and into the daylight. He left the door wide so they all could see him, were he to start burning up, or be struck by lightening, or experience any of a number of events Cade deemed unlikely.

Instead, what Cade thought might be true, was. He stood still for a long moment, his neck bent forward, staring at the ground, and then spread his arms and tipped his head back to look up into the sky. A ray of sunshine pooled against the curtain wall and Cade deliberately stepped into it.

Nothing.

Restraining an urge to whistle, Cade strolled back to the hut. He slipped off the cloak and dropped it onto the table. "The mantle of Arthur will protect the King of Gwynedd, once again."

"Do you see any harm in me wearing it, Taliesin, if the need arises?" Cade said.

Taliesin gazed at the swath of fine wool. "All magic comes at a cost, but I think the price for this one has already been paid."

"As with Caledfwlch," Cade said.

Taliesin bowed his head. "As you say."

Now it really was time to go. "Taliesin, a moment," Cade said. "The rest of you—I need you to keep your eyes and ears open. I don't trust Rhys, for all that he appears to side with us now."

"Yes, sir." Dafydd had his hand at Angharad's waist in what Cade saw as a proprietary fashion, and steered her out the door towards the hall. Bedwyr saluted him as he left.

"And Goronwy," Cade said before he departed with the others, "I'll see you in the hall for the Council Meeting."

Goronwy halted in the doorway. "Why me?"

"You are the eldest of Cade's knights, the son of the King of the Isle of Man, and a leader of men in your own right," Taliesin said. "Your own father could claim the High Kingship if he chose."

Goronwy muttered under his breath and then raised his voice so they could hear him. "The question was rhetorical."

Cade smiled and shot him an amused glance. "If I have to suffer through another one of these meetings, so do you."

Goronwy grimaced and left.

Cade turned to Taliesin. "What am I to do with these?" He fingered each item in turn—the cloak, the knife, the whetstone, and the false Dyrnwyn—that remained on the table. "They can't stay here; I'm not going to stay here and who shall guard them when I'm gone? Will I have to bring them with me everywhere I go?"

"That is going to be a problem, but it is for another day," Taliesin said. "If you like, I could take one, or all, or none, as you see fit."

Cade studied his friend. "To what end? Are you leaving me again?"

"Mabon is seeking the remaining Treasures," Taliesin said. "Someone has to counter him. Your tasks are many, with what you have before you today, this week, and this year, without concerning yourself with this task too."

"Do you suggest we scatter them again to keep them from him?"

"That might be wise," Taliesin said. "But we have to think about the manner in which we do it. Whoever scattered them the first time thought they'd be safe with the families with whom he entrusted them."

"And they were," Cade said. "For a time."

"It might have even been the great King Arthur who did this, before his death," Taliesin said.

"Before we follow in his footsteps," Cade said, "we must understand how Mabon found the location of each of the Treasures in the first place." Cade picked up the knife and dropped it, frustrated as always by his lack of knowledge. He might be a *sidhe*—some of the time—but he was not on a par with the gods, no matter how powerful he might appear to his fellow men. He scoffed at his pretentions under his breath, but then a slight sound from Taliesin had him looking up.

Taliesin was gazing at him with an unreadable expression.

Cade gazed back, uncertain as to what his friend was seeing. "What's wrong?"

"You haven't mentioned gathering the Treasures for yourself," he said. "Not even once."

"Why would I want them?" Cade said. "It's Mabon who seeks that kind of power, not me. Never me."

"It would greatly enhance your ability to influence the High Council, not to mention enable you to control Mabon and whoever else opposes you in the world of the *sidhe*."

At that Cade laughed. "If that is true, I may reconsider! I would give much for that kind of power."

"And," Taliesin said, "they would help you fend off the Saxons. There is every reason to want to gather them to yourself."

"You're not seriously suggesting this? You of all people?"

Taliesin shook his head. "I'm not suggesting it as much as putting the choice out in the open. If you reject the opportunity—if you choose to gather the Treasures but not use them—you need to know what you're giving up."

"When have I ever had that kind of ambition?" Cade said. "It's a fool's quest. A man could go mad pursuing them. Perhaps Mabon already has."

"Be that as it may, are there others besides Caledfwlch you would keep, at least for now?" Taliesin said. "The items were created because they were useful, after all."

Cade spoke without hesitation. "The cloak. It uniquely serves my peculiar needs. The whetstone may help us defeat the Saxons this one time, but too many men aren't worthy of it and the men who are worthy of it are precisely the ones who don't need it. The knife is useless in battle. While I appreciate the fact that with it, I have the ability to feed my men, whole villages would benefit from it in times of famine. It would be wrong to keep it to myself." Cade glanced at his friend. "You should take that one with you on your travels."

"You know me well." Taliesin gestured to the fake Dyrnwyn. "And this sword?"

"Even if it were real, I have a sword that suits me." Cade patted his hip.

Taliesin traced the ornate designs on the sword's hilt with one finger. "I believe Dafydd is mistaken. This is the real Dyrnwyn, my lord."

Cade glanced at him, surprised both at his words and at his uncharacteristic use of Cade's title. "Really?"

"The magic of Dyrnwyn is not easily discerned," Taliesin said. "Arawn bore it and bent it to his will, but did not master it. Gofannon, the divine smith, forged it, along with the horn of immortality. The latter he gave to his sister, Arianrhod, while he gave the sword to his brother, Gwydion, the great warrior."

"Your patron," Cade said.

"Indeed."

"And why do you say this is that same sword?" Cade said. "I saw it in Arawn's possession; I held it afterwards and it flamed for me. Even Dafydd was worthy to draw it. We've both held *this* sword and it lies in our hands, limp."

"Did Dafydd hold it with the intent to use it?" Taliesin said. "Have you?"

Cade went still. "No. Neither of us." Cade gazed down at the sword and like Taliesin had done, traced the writing on the hilt and then along the blade. "Why do you say it's the real one?"

"I read the inscription: *only thou who art noble in heart may wield me.*"

"Remarkably self-explanatory, if anyone could actually read the words," Cade said.

"There are few of us left," Taliesin said.

"There's one left, you mean," Cade said, gently.

"Perhaps."

"Having found it, through considerable effort, why would Mabon leave it behind?"

"Didn't Dafydd say that Mabon appeared not to know how to wield a sword? That he sweated as he held it? Dyrnwyn does not bestow allegiance lightly. Mabon might have realized that claiming this particular Treasure, at least, was a mistake."

Cade nodded, still fingering Dyrnwyn's hilt.

"Try it," Taliesin said.

Cade had told Taliesin that he wasn't tempted to keep the Treasures and that was the truth. Power as Mabon understood it was overrated, in Cade's opinion. Love was much harder to come by. But still ... Cade straightened his shoulders and picked up Dyrnwyn. He respected Taliesin's foresight, so braced himself for the possibility that he was right. He spun on one heel, slashing the blade through the air as if decapitating an unseen opponent.

The hilt warmed, and then in a flash of fire and light, blazed from hilt to tip. A storm of power filled the room and words echoed in the small chamber: *Hail Cadwaladr ap Cadwallon, King of the Britons!*

Cade dropped the sword on the table so fast he feared in retrospect that it would burn the wood. It didn't. Nor had it burned him. Still, his hands trembled. "Did you hear that?"

"I heard it," Taliesin said, "although no one else could have. The voice came from the world of the *sidhe*. What do you think Mabon might have heard when he drew it? Something, perhaps, that frightened him into abandoning it? Some say these Treasures have minds of their own."

Cade stared at Taliesin, his eyes wide. "This changes everything."

"Everything, and nothing," Taliesin said.

Without looking at his friend, because he couldn't quite bear to see the wisdom in his eyes, Cade wrapped the priceless artifacts in the cloak and tucked them under his arm.

"The Saxons will be here in two days," Cade said.

"Yes," Taliesin said.

If only Cade could have been as certain of victory.

22

Goronwy

Goronwy had taken all of a dozen breaths in the hall—or what passed for a hall since half of it was open to the air—before he found himself grinding his teeth and regretting every moment that he spent among these supposed allies.

"How do we know that you are not in league with the *sidhe* more than us?"

That was Rhys again, who seemed to feel that he had become the spokesman for all of the lords of Powys. Goronwy wished Arthur could have come, or Hywel's father, or even Angharad's. Any one of them would have been preferable to having to listen to Rhys and his father, Morgan.

But Arthur was dead and the others had felt it impossible to leave their people while Mabon—or the Saxons—were so dangerous. Hywel had led the contingent of his father's men and been proud do it. But in the eyes of the lords here, he was a boy. Goronwy glanced at Cade—who himself was only twenty-two.

Cade didn't meet his eyes. Goronwy's stomach sank into his boots: Cade needed Goronwy himself to speak.

Goronwy rose slowly to his feet. "I have something to say."

He was pleased that a palpable sense of relief wafted throughout the room. He wasn't the only one who was sick of Rhys' pronouncements and answers masquerading as questions.

"By all means." Morgan made a welcoming gesture. "The son of the King of Man has every right to speak in this company."

"I confess to being confused by this meeting," Goronwy said. "Are we here to fight the Saxons, or to fight among ourselves?"

Rhys snorted. "The Saxons, of course."

"Then what is the question at issue?" Goronwy said. "Who shall lead us? Surely that is a simple matter." He turned to Cade. "Only one man has defeated an army of Saxons in recent memory, and that is the King of Gwynedd."

Cade's teeth were clenched, but he did the right thing, which was lift his hand in acknowledgment of his achievement.

Goronwy turned back to the company. Nobody else had said anything. "If the issue at hand is the High Kingship, which so far nobody has openly spoken of, then surely that is an issue to be decided another day. If we do not defeat the Saxons here, whomever we've chosen as High King will rule over a country that doesn't exist."

"Well said." Morgan stood. "But I differ with you as to who should lead." He nodded his head at Cade. "While I admit to King Cadwaladr's recent triumphs, where are his men? I have brought far more than he and I believe that my son, Rhys, should unite our forces here."

"The men of Gwynedd are here!"

Beside Goronwy, Cade sighed as Tudur and his brother-in-law, Pod, marched into the room.

"We follow King Cadwaladr," Tudur said. "There is none whom we trust more to lead us."

"Such is the sentiment of every man here, regarding his overlord." Morgan's voice was smooth though Goronwy was sure he saw unhappiness in Morgan's face at Tudur's arrival. Wouldn't he rather have more men to fight the Saxons, even if it meant his son didn't lead the Welsh forces?

"But we must counter the Saxons," Morgan continued. "I propose a compromise. King Cadwaladr shall lead his men in battle." Morgan bowed his head towards Cade. "Rhys shall lead the men of Powys. No one shall be forced to follow someone he does not trust."

Goronwy stared at Morgan, appalled. It was like having two cooks in the kitchen. It never worked and everyone suffered from burned food.

"I do not object to such a decision," Cade said.

Goronwy glared at him, wanting to throttle his king. They both knew who was the better leader. Every man in the room knew who was the better leader. But Cade wasn't willing to create disunity at the cost of his own ascendancy and the other men didn't want to go against Morgan. Goronwy looked back at

Morgan, who had a smile of satisfaction on his face. There was something wrong here, currents that Goronwy couldn't follow.

Morgan smiled. "Is that settled, then?"

* * * * *

"Christ on the cross! Why didn't you say anything?"

Goronwy and Cade stood alone on a lower rampart. Dawn was coming, and they watched the eastern plains for a sign of the Saxons. Goronwy had slept fitfully, cursing himself for how the meeting had turned out, but not knowing what he could have done to change it. In the darkness, he'd gone looking for Cade, who hadn't slept at all. That was normal for him, of course, but Goronwy thought he saw a haggard look in Cade's eyes. Sleep might have refreshed him.

Cade lowered his hands. He'd been cupping them around his eyes so he could see further. Goronwy had found that this helped him less lately than it used to.

"What would you have had me do?" Cade said. "Lose all of the men of Powys in a fit of pique? We can work with Rhys. Morgan is leaving Caer Fawr at first light, along with most of the older men on the Council. Without his father to bolster his opinion of himself, Rhys is malleable."

"You think so?" Goronwy said. "More likely, he decides he's infallible and kills us all in some stupid gambit he thinks will defeat the Saxons."

Cade turned fully to Goronwy who clenched his fists to keep his hands from shaking. So rarely did he find himself this angry, he didn't quite know what to do.

"You really think I was wrong, don't you?" Cade said. "That I should have asserted whatever authority I had to push the council towards appointing me?"

Goronwy took in a deep breath and eased it out. "I respect your judgment, my lord, more than any man's, but your greatest fault is that you don't recognize your own strengths as fully as you should."

"I would not rule men against their will." Cade pointed east, to the Saxon forces they couldn't yet see. "Not when death sits on the horizon and I'm a *sidhe*."

"I understand that this power you have is not something you've chosen," Goronwy said. "But Arianrhod gave it to you anyway. She chose you. To deny that of which you are capable is to lie to yourself. I'm not saying that your humility is false, but that it is misplaced."

Goronwy didn't like the discomfited look he saw in Cade's eyes, but he didn't look away. Someone had to tell him the truth. Even Taliesin hadn't in this instance.

"Those are strong words, Goronwy," Cade said.

"But truthful ones as I see it."

Cade rested his elbows on the turf wall of the rampart, his chin in his hands. "Yesterday, Taliesin offered me the Thirteen Treasures as a means to gather power to myself. To rule all Britain as no man as done since the days of Arthur."

"And you refused him," Goronwy said.

"Of course," Cade said.

"I don't necessarily disagree with that decision," Goronwy said. "Meddling in the affairs of the *sidhe* never results in a predictable outcome. That's not to say, however, that is the same thing as using the gifts that God has given you."

Cade scrubbed at his hair with both hands, leaving it standing on end, and then dropped them to his sides. "You are right. Of course you are right."

"I don't want to be right," Goronwy said.

"Worse, because I failed to take up the mantle of leadership here, it will be my fault if we lose men over Rhys' poor decision-making."

Goronwy swallowed hard. "I wouldn't have put it that starkly..."

"But that is what you're saying, isn't it?"

"Rhys' decisions are his own," Goronwy said. "Each man makes his own choices and his are not your fault, my lord."

"Even if I could have averted them?" Cade said. "What use is honor and nobility if somebody dies because I failed to put Rhys and Morgan in their place."

"Then again, even had the Council named you general in this battle, that's not to say Rhys or his men would have followed you. Perhaps they would have left us, as you feared," Goronwy said. And then swallowed hard, for he realized he was arguing for a position he hadn't before considered.

Cade eyed him and now it was Goronwy's turn to feel discomfited. Goronwy sighed. "Which is why you didn't force their hand. I am chastised. Forgive me, my lord."

"My lords."

Goronwy and Cade turned to see Catrin standing ten feet away with downturned lashes, having kept her distance from their conversation. It had been heated, however, and if she'd stood there any length of time, she couldn't have failed to hear what they'd said. She held a tray with food and drink for them. Despite the lingering unease at the exchange he'd just had with Cade, Goronwy was pleased that there was enough food for ten men. That meant there'd be enough for him, even if Cade ate his fill.

"Thank you, Catrin," Goronwy said.

Catrin approached and set the tray on the wall beside Goronwy. She kept her eyes towards the ground but she didn't fool Goronwy with her show of temerity.

"You heard us," he said, not as a question.

"I apologize, my lords, but I couldn't help it."

Cade glanced upwards to the rampart above them that protected the fort proper. "Did others?"

"I don't believe so, my lord," Catrin said. "It wasn't loud as all that. Besides, the men in the fort are preoccupied with the coming battle."

"And what do you think about what Goronwy had to say to me?" Cade said.

Catrin looked at Cade for the first time. "You're asking me?"

"Why not?" Cade said. "Rhiann isn't here to give me her opinion. Yours will have to suffice."

Catrin shot Goronwy a piercing look he couldn't quite interpret. "I agree with Lord Goronwy that we would be better off with you as our commander, but that does not excuse Rhys his mistakes, when he makes them. It was his choice to press so hard for the role. It is his choice to take advantage of your lack of ambition."

Goronwy studied Catrin. She'd raised her head as she'd continued speaking, no longer feigning a retiring nature—any more than that was Cade's true personality. Lord and witch exchanged long looks, before Cade nodded. "I give way," he said, "though it is too late to change the Council's decision. However, I will not allow Rhys to ruin our chances of victory out of ignorance."

"How are you going to stop him?" Goronwy said.

"I'll think of something."

"I think you have to be prepared to overrule Rhys if need be," Catrin said, looking at Cade with a steady gaze. "It might be possible to persuade him of the proper course of action, but the time might come when he refuses to listen."

"Understood," Cade said.

Catrin's shoulders relaxed. Goronwy managed to catch her eye and nodded encouragingly.

"What is the mood of the men?" Cade said. "Perhaps you have a thought on that too."

"They are ready to fight," she said. "They haven't seen the Saxon force yet, of course, so that could change."

"And that means I must speak to Taliesin." With a nod at them both, Cade strode away, back up to the fort.

Cade hadn't touched the food Catrin had brought and now there was too much. "Stay and eat with me," Goronwy said.

"I would like that." Catrin hitched herself onto the rampart beside her tray. "Angharad and I have been run off our feet in the kitchen."

Goronwy leaned against the wall. "It will get even busier up there once the fighting starts. We will need your healing skills then."

Catrin bowed her head in acceptance. "It would be an honor to assist in any way I can." She turned her head to look where Cade had gone. "He is a ruler whom a man could follow to the ends of the earth. As I understand you have."

"He's married," Goronwy said.

Catrin choked on a swallow of mead. She spit and coughed until Goronwy had to clap her on the back to loosen her throat. "I'm fine," she said—finally—laughing through her tears. "You mistake me. I have no designs on your lord."

Goronwy's eyes narrowed. "Then what?"

"You can learn much of what you need to know about a man by the lord he chooses to follow." Catrin spoke with that disconcerting frankness that had marked her from the first moment they'd met. "You, Dafydd, Taliesin ..."

As she said Taliesin's name, Catrin jumped lightly down. Then, she spun on her heel to march away, back towards the fort.

Goronwy had to smile. *Taliesin.* While Goronwy was pleased he was such a good judge of his fellow man—or woman, rather—he almost felt sorry for Taliesin. He had no idea what he was in for.

23

Rhiann

Rhiann had ridden the whole way from Dinas Bran with fear at her heels, terrified that she wouldn't reach Caer Fawr before the Saxons did. The worst thing in the world would be to watch from a distant hill as enemies slaughtered her people. Not that she could be the one to save them, but if they were going to die, perversely, she wanted to be with them. Besides, she didn't believe it was going to happen. Cade was too good a commander and his men had promised to come.

She and the three men she'd brought with her, including the garrison captain, Alun, crested the last rise before Caer Fawr and pulled up. The moon lit the sky from horizon to horizon. The mountains of Wales lay to the west but more were below, for Caer Fawr sat on a lonely hilltop, with the Severn Plain and the Breidden hills in the distance to the southeast.

Cade had told her that a spring precipitated from the peak and flowed down the hill near the west entrance to the fort. That was the one for which she and her companions would aim.

"They come." Alun pointed with one finger. Torches massed in the distance to the east. It could only be the Saxon army. She wasn't quite too late.

"But why?" Rhiann said. "Caer Fawr is impregnable. Even they should know that."

"They don't know mountains, do they?" Alun said. "Maybe they hope to starve us out."

"That doesn't sound like Penda, though, does it?" Rhiann said. "Cade has studied Penda's victories. Aggression is his trademark, although he's not been above treachery and assassination too."

Alun had fought with her father and his Saxon allies before Cadfael's death and knew what she was talking about. He barked a laugh. "Penda *is* more likely to favor a frontal assault."

It was nice to laugh, even in the face of the Saxon army. Rhiann didn't know how many men Penda had, couldn't begin to count them, but it was surely thousands. She hadn't understood the scale of what the Welsh were facing. Cade had known, if only because his own father had fought among the Saxons for so many years.

Then again, so had hers.

Rhiann and Alun gazed east, gauging the distance between Caer Fawr and the Saxon force. "They seem to be resting where they are, but I predict they'll move at first light," Alun said. "The Saxons will reach us by noon."

"We'll be ready."

Then, as they'd descended from the hills, the hundreds of men who filled the valley Caer Fawr guarded came into view. Cade might not have the thousands upon whom the Saxons could draw—but maybe he had enough. Rhiann's heart lifted.

The sun was just peaking over the eastern horizon when Rhiann and her companions made their way through the men camped to the west and behind the fort and up the hill to the hall. Most of the flags sported the crest of Madog of Powys and his son Rhys. But Tudur's flag was there, and Hywel's. Men ran back and forth from the fort to the encampment, shouting at each other.

"The Saxons! The Saxons!"

"I thought we had until noon?" Rhiann said.

Alun pursed his lips as he gazed down at the encampment. "We have some time, yet. That's just fear you're hearing."

Rhiann hoped he was right, but didn't like the idea that men were already desperate, inside the fort or out of it. Rhiann had never known Cade's men to panic.

Another shout came from the ramparts above them and Rhiann looked up to see who called to her. Bedwyr waved a hand. She returned the greeting and hurried through the gate. More men ran from hall to barracks to stables and back again.

"This way." Bedwyr helped Rhiann from her horse and took her elbow. "The sun has forced Cade to retreat inside."

Rhiann could read the tension in the set of Bedwyr's shoulders so she didn't question him as she went with him up the steps to the door, which swung open before she reached it.

Goronwy waved her inside. "He's not going to like it that you're here."

"I know," Rhiann said. "But I have news that couldn't wait."

"And you couldn't send another to deliver it?"

"I'll take chastisement from my husband, Lord Goronwy. Don't you start too!"

Goronwy surprised her with a laugh. "He's missed you. Perhaps you can put him in a better temper."

"I hope so too, but I wouldn't count on it." Rhiann passed among the dozens of men who milled about the hall until she reached a table near a caved-in dais. Cade leaned heavily on his hands, a plan of Caer Fawr and the lands around it spread before him. She hesitated, still some yards away, drinking him in. He'd pulled his nearly black hair into a leather thong at the base of his neck and wore a rich blue shirt that exactly matched his eyes.

"I'm sorry, Cade—"

Cade bent his head over the table, gripping the edges with both hands. "I heard what you said to Goronwy." Then he growled and straightened. "Come here, girl."

Rhiann went to him. Her heart had lightened at the mere thought of him. The reality was so much better. She wrapped her arms around his waist and put her face into his chest. "I missed you so much."

He lifted her arms to place them around his neck and bowed his head to touch hers. "When the lookout said you were coming, I was so angry... I didn't want you here. But now ..." He kissed her and she hung onto him for dear life.

When they drew apart, just a fraction, she said, "Mabon visited me. I didn't feel like I had any choice but to come."

"I don't want to hear this." Cade gripped her arms tightly, his tension returned, though thankfully no longer directed at her. She'd rehearsed what she was going to say to him the whole way down from Dinas Bran and she eased out a breath, glad she'd read him right. Then, he lifted his head and waved to Goronwy and Bedwyr that they should approach. "Get the others. Rhiann has brought us more bad news."

* * * * *

"So what can I do?" Rhiann said.

Angharad and Catrin looked up from their work. They were sorting through dozens of scraps of linen. It was always the one aspect of warfare that men forgot—or perhaps they didn't want to remember. Men would die in this battle but some would be wounded, and someone needed to attend them.

"I'm sure you don't need to help us, my lady," Angharad said. "The Queen of Gwynedd—"

"Hush," Rhiann said. "Don't be ridiculous. You need every hand that can be spared."

Angharad subsided and now Catrin smiled at Rhiann. "We have more than enough work to keep you occupied, my lady, if you're looking to hide from the King."

"Call me, Rhiann." Catrin's casual acceptance of her presence lifted some of Rhiann's worry. "My husband wasn't so mean as that. But I am on a short leash." Rhiann moved towards the pile of linen. Sorting it wasn't a difficult job, just necessary.

Angharad still hesitated to begin working again. "But surely, as the Queen of Gwynedd ..."

"As I reminded myself the other day before Mabon visited me, I was a serving wench long before I turned queen." Rhiann gestured to the bandages. "Many of these are dirty. We'll have to clean these before we can use them on the men."

"I asked King Cadwaladr's permission to leave the fort, to wash them in the river," Catrin said. "He was reluctant to give us leave with all these men about whom he doesn't know."

"But surely—" Rhiann thought for a moment. "The spring begins its flow just outside the western gate. There must be a spot not far from the walls where we would be safe." She held up a cloth, revealing the scrape of dirt across the middle of it.

"These aren't much use as they are," Catrin said. "But your lord won't be happy if you leave the fort."

"I'll speak to him," Rhiann said.

"He's in council with Rhys," Catrin said. "Taliesin is with him."

Rhiann thought she heard a hitch in Catrin's voice when she said Taliesin's name and made a mental note to get to know Catrin better if she could. If they had the time.

"Lord Hywel went to inventory our stock of arrows," Angharad said. "But Dafydd might be free help us."

Rhiann smiled to herself at Angharad's obvious regard for Dafydd. She was more transparent than Catrin. Still, Rhiann had only been at Caer Fawr a few hours. She didn't know if either man was aware of the interest they'd engendered. And maybe they'd never know, if the coming fight didn't go well for them.

"We'll find him," Rhiann said.

Dafydd proved amenable, so it was he and the three women who left the fort by the western gate and wended their way among the ramparts, heading steadily away from the fort. Soon they came to a rocky outcrop, from which the spring precipitated. They followed a narrow path beside it that cut through the remaining ramparts until it neared the bottom of the hill. There, a few stubby trees still grew that Cade hadn't ordered taken down. Further on, perhaps two hundred yards, Rhys' men camped.

A hillock hid the companions from the river. Before they came around it on the path, however, Rhiann pulled up short. "I hear a woman singing." She turned to the Dafydd. "We'll need to bring the camp followers inside the fort before the battle begins."

"I'll see that the word goes out," Dafydd said.

The lilting tones carried through the mid-morning air, but in words that Rhiann couldn't make out. Rhiann picked up the pace, anxious to see who it was that sang so beautifully, but Catrin grabbed her arm. "No. Don't."

"Why not?" Rhiann said.

Catrin's face had drained of all color and her eyes had gone a silver grey. Then she blinked and the impression was gone but still, Catrin held Rhiann's arm. "I can feel magic and the world of the *sidhe*," Catrin said. "It's all around us in the fort, of course, because of King Cadwaladr and the Treasures, but my sense of it had faded as we'd traversed the path, but now…"

"Now you feel it again?" Rhiann looked ahead. The singing continued. "We must go on, if only to find out who it is."

Dafydd unsheathed his sword and stepped in front of Rhiann. "Come on."

Ten paces later, they came around the outcrop. An old woman laundered clothes on a spit of gravel in the middle of the river. She wore a gray dress and cloak and her beautiful voice was a sharp contrast to her beaked nose and scraggily hair.

Dafydd pulled up short. "It's just an old wom—"

"No it isn't!" Rhiann threw herself past him and into the channel that separated them from the old woman. She went under the surface and came up sputtering. Seeing Rhiann's mistake, Catrin raced along the grassy bank, coiled herself in preparation, and leapt across the channel. She landed on the gravel bar in the middle of the stream a dozen yards from where the woman washed.

Rhiann hauled herself out of the water, scrabbling at the rocks. She planted herself in front of the woman. "How dare you!" She snatched a shirt from the woman's grasp before turning to Dafydd and Angharad. "Help Catrin get the ones she's already washed!"

Catrin had spared herself the initial dunking, but now flung herself into the water to grasp one tunic after another before they floated downstream. Angharad and Dafydd gaped at both of them, not understanding.

"It's Arianrhod!" Rhiann said. "She's washing the tunics of the men who will die in battle this day."

That spurred them into action. Meanwhile, the crone pointed her finger at Rhiann. "You, of all people, should know better. You cannot avert your fate."

"It isn't fate!" Rhiann said. "This is your choice. Why are you doing this?" Unwanted tears leaked from her eyes and she brushed them away.

Arianrhod only cackled. "You can't save them all." She'd been watching the actions of Rhiann's friends but now turned back to Rhiann. "Would death be easier to accept if I looked like this?"

Rhiann didn't have time to take in one breath before the woman had transformed herself into the form she'd always shown to Cade, that of a beautiful woman. Then in another flash, she crouched again over the washing, a crone in tattered grey.

Not looking at her, not caring that she was openly defying the goddess, Rhiann gathered the tunics from the basket that the Arianrhod still had left to wash. "You would have every one of these men dead? Why? They are your people! Why not hamper the Saxons instead of us?"

Arianrhod laughed. The tinkle of it was in sharp contrast to her earlier cackle. "I would not deprive your husband of his fight, my dear." She had returned to the shape of a beautiful woman.

Rhiann shivered. She couldn't bear to look at Arianrhod and clutched the twenty tunics she'd gathered. She was just reaching for the last item in Arianrhod's basket, when the goddess laughed again. Against her will, Rhiann's chin came up so she had to look at her. "I am the goddess of the cauldron, of war and battle, of the silver wheel of life and death." Arianrhod gazed at Rhiann and it was as if Rhiann's breath froze in her chest. "And life is what you care about, isn't it?"

The chatter of Catrin, Angharad, and Dafydd, gathering the tunics that Arianrhod had already committed to the depths, came muffled to her ears, as if she and Arianrhod stood in a crypt by themselves. Outside sounds echoed without penetrating the rock.

"Wha-what are you saying?"

Arianrhod's face was wreathed in light. She pointed to the tunics Rhiann held. "Would you trade just one of those, not your husband's of course, but Dafydd's perhaps, or Bedwyr's? Just one, for the chance to bear a son for Cade?"

Rhiann tried to swallow, but her tongue stuck to the roof of her mouth. "You ask me to exchange a friend's life for ... a baby?"

"For Cadwaladr's child." Arianrhod spoke the words as if they were nothing, as if she was asking Rhiann to pass the butter.

"No." Rhiann found her head shaking back and forth, back and forth. "You can't ask that, you can't offer me that."

"But I just have." Arianrhod took a step towards Rhiann. "No one would know. We would keep it between us." She leaned closer and lowered her voice. "Just close your eyes and choose."

"No!" Rhiann threw out her arm in a gesture of denial and backed away, but the stones behind her tripped her up and she fell among them, half in and half out of the water.

Arianrhod stood over her, smiling though the smile didn't reach her eyes, even in the *glamour* she had donned.

"So be it," Arianrhod said. "Perhaps you are worthy of *him* after all."

Rhiann gaped at the goddess, who smiled serenely back.

"Rhiann!" Dafydd raced towards them.

Arianrhod shimmered, glanced back once at Dafydd, and then seemed to melt into nothingness. As Dafydd reached her, Rhiann looked around, feeling like she'd just woken up from a dream. Her hands were empty, too. Everything Arianrhod had brought to the river—the tunics, the basket, the scrubbing brush—were gone. Instead, an arrow lay among the rocks where Arianrhod had been standing. At least a yard in length, the wood was silver-grey, like the crone's dress, but with black feathers and tipped in silver.

Rhiann crawled towards it but didn't pick it up. Catrin crouched beside her and they studied the arrow together.

"Is it safe?" Rhiann said.

"A gift from the goddess is never safe," Catrin said.

Rhiann reached out a finger to touch it. As with the chess piece, when no lightning struck her, she picked it up.

"Where did Arianrhod go?" Dafydd said.

"There." Catrin pointed to the channel on the far side of the gravel bar. The goddess had assumed the shape of the crone again, solid and ugly as she trudged through the river. Her dress was soaked to her waist, but her hands were empty. She disappeared into the woods on the other side.

24

Dafydd

Rhiann was shaking so hard Dafydd was afraid she would fall out of his arms. He clutched her more tightly. Catrin and he had supported her through the water and up the bank, but she was trembling so hard she couldn't walk. Not long ago, he would have been thrilled at the thought of holding Rhiann so close, even if she was in peril, but now, all he wanted was to find Cade and pass her off. But Cade couldn't walk in the sun. Dafydd checked the sky. It would have to be someone else and he hoped he would come soon.

"Angharad—do you have the arrow?" he said, over his shoulder.

"Yes, my lord," she said.

He tsked through his teeth. She'd taken to calling him 'my lord' in the last few days and he couldn't seem to get her to stop. "Give it to Catrin and run ahead. The path is too steep and too far. I won't make it."

And that was another thing he would have been loathe to admit two months ago. But a man was not measured by whether or not he could carry his queen a hundred yards straight up a mountain. Another few feet and a watcher finally spotted them. Dafydd's legs had started to tremble with the effort, and then Bedwyr arrived to rescue him.

His jaw set and grim, Bedwyr took Rhiann from Dafydd and strode away. Goronwy had come too. He took the arrow from Angharad and then escorted Catrin, still carrying their dirty cloths, the rest of the way to the fort. They'd never gotten the linen washed, but Dafydd didn't think they wanted to go back to the river to finish the job. They did have Caledfwlch after all. The sword would heal anyone who would accept Cade's help. It was just that there would be men who needed to be kept alive until Cade could help them.

Dafydd bent forward, his hands on his knees. All he could see of Angharad was her boots and the hem of her skirt. Like him, she was soaked to the waist.

"I don't understand any of what just happened," Angharad said. "Who was that woman? And what kind of hold did she have on Queen Rhiannon?"

Dafydd straightened and took in a deep breath. "You know that King Cadwaladr is a *sidhe*?"

"Yes, of course."

"Arianrhod—the goddess of time and fate, and of war—made him what he is. She has been known to visit, especially recently."

"And that's who the crone was at the river?" Angharad said. "I thought Arianrhod was a beautiful woman."

Dafydd shrugged. "She takes many forms. Legend says that before a battle, Arianrhod washes the tunics of men doomed to die in that battle." Dafydd looked at his hands, empty now of any proof of what they'd seen and done.

"I couldn't get them all," Angharad said. "Some floated away in the faster currents."

"I know," Dafydd said. "I didn't want to look but I couldn't help it. Many of them bore the crest of the boar."

"Rhys' men?"

Dafydd bit his lip. "Goronwy and I wear the eagle badge, when we don't wear Cade's red dragon. Did you see—" He broke off, realizing that he didn't want to know the answer, but Angharad was looking at him steadily.

"The crone had one such tunic with her and Rhiann tore it from her hands."

Dafydd swallowed again. This magic, this world of the *sidhe*, was not a world that he wanted anything to do with. The moment of a man's death should be a mystery, or at the very least, not determined by the opaque reasoning or whims of a feckless goddess. The moment the thought formed in his head, he struggled to suppress it. Who knew if the goddess could read his thoughts? Dafydd hoped not.

Angharad looked over the ramparts towards the stream. "Arianrhod didn't have to wash the tunics here."

"What do you mean?" Dafydd said.

"Of all the rivers in Powys to wash them in, she chose this one? Perhaps she wanted Rhiann to find her."

"I'd like you to be right," he said. "I'd like to think the goddess is on our side, at least a little bit."

Angharad turned back to him. "The news is worse than this, though."

Dafydd snorted a laugh. "How could it be worse?" And then he sobered because he realized she was serious.

"When we were coming up from the river, I overheard some of the men who passed us going the other way. Rhys has ordered his men to move out within the hour. They will meet the Saxons in the fields below Caer Fawr."

Dafydd stared at her. "He can't be serious." Dafydd looked east. "They outnumber us. To meet them in open battle loses all advantage of the high ground. That's why King Cadwaladr chose to gather his troops at Caer Fawr in the first place!"

"Rhys is preparing to march. With all of his men and ours."

Dafydd caught Angharad's arm. "You must leave. Now. Go with Catrin and Rhiann and head directly west. You have enough of a head start that they won't catch you."

Angharad tried to wrench her arm away. "I will not! You need us. I won't leave you."

Something shifted in Dafydd just then. Maybe it was her adamancy. Maybe it was her upturned nose and the freckles scattered across it that Lilwen had tried so desperately to hide. She wasn't Rhiann, but maybe she didn't have to be. He wasn't Cade either. Without thinking about it, before the impulse deserted him,

Dafydd caught Angharad's hand. She looked down at their interlocked fingers and then back up at him.

"I don't want anything to happen to you," he said.

"I don't either," she said. "But how would leaving here help? The entire world is dangerous. Besides, Mabon knows that I last had the cloak. I'd be more vulnerable out there than in here."

The sound of drums and marching feet were evident as the men in the camp below them fell into lines on Rhys' orders.

"I hate to admit it," Dafydd said, "but you may be right."

25

Cade

"And your honor says that you must fight alongside Rhys?"

Rhiann asked the question from a curled position on the pallet that was all that adorned their chamber. King and Queen of Gwynedd they might be, but they had no more in the way of luxuries than anyone else, barring the privacy of a room.

"He is determined to face the Saxons on what he calls *his own terms*," Cade said. "I think he's trying to prove to his father that he can lead."

"He seeks to upstage you."

"When all it does is show him a fool and endanger all of us." Cade scrubbed at his hair with both hands and turned to look at his wife. That Arianrhod had appeared to her was terrifying. He'd found himself more angry—at the goddess, and the fates— than he'd ever been in his life. And he'd taken out some of that anger on Rhiann, to his regret. "I am bound—"

"You are not." Rhiann's words came out sharp and taut. "You swore no allegiance to Rhys or Morgan. You agreed to share command at Caer Fawr. That is all."

"A fine point—"

"Don't make me hurt you, Cadwaladr ap Cadwallon!" Rhiann picked up the pillow on which her head had been lying and threw it at him.

Cade caught it and then moved to her side. He knelt to wrap his arms around her. "You could never do that."

"I could," Rhiann said.

Cade looked into her eyes and his heart twisted to see tears starting in them again.

"Arianrhod wanted me to hurt you," she said.

"Something about the tunics?" he said. "I still don't understand what happened down at the river. It doesn't make sense."

"She spoke to me, Cade," Rhiann said. "I didn't want to tell you in front of all the others, but Arianrhod spoke directly to me."

His eyes narrowed. "And what did she say?"

"She offered me a bargain." Rhiann had her face pressed into his arm, refusing to look at him. Cade had never seen her like this before.

"What kind of bargain?" Cade felt his temper rising again at the idea. It was one thing for Arianrhod to speak to him, to demand his services. It was quite another for her to upset his wife.

"She offered to trade the life of one of your men, one of our friends, for a child. Our child."

Cade took in a deep breath and then swallowed down the first three things that came to his mind. He studied his wife's downturned head and then stroked back a lock of her hair that had come loose and tucked it behind her ear. Only after he'd gained some measure of control, did he speak. "And she actually thought you'd make such a bargain with her?"

Rhiann clutched his hand. "She pressed on me. Her eyes bored into me. I wanted to accept so badly, but ..."

Cade tugged on Rhiann's braid. He heard and accepted the pain in her voice. But that Rhiann would choose such a thing wasn't possible. Arianrhod should have known that. "Is a child so important, Rhiann? We've been married only a few weeks. We've not even discussed it other than in passing."

"It doesn't matter how long we're married, Cade." Rhiann finally looked into his face. "We will never have a child. You know that."

"I know it," Cade said. "But I didn't realize how much you were thinking of it already."

"Soon, everyone will begin to look askance at me," Rhiann said. "They will wonder when I will give you a son, and when I prove incapable of it, they will say that it's my fault. They'll question your decision to marry me. They'll wonder what it will take to convince you to put me aside. For the sake of Wales."

"They would be fools to think or say it," Cade said, "but I grant that biddies in the solar are often fools." He rubbed the back of her hand with his thumb. "This war has left many children fatherless. Motherless too. And there will be more after today. We could bring such a child into our house, if you like?"

Rhiann lifted her head. "Do you mean it?"

"Of course," he said. "Wasn't I mothered and fathered well by people who weren't my birth parents? Wasn't I loved as much as Rhun?"

Rhiann sat up and threw her arms around Cade's neck. She hung on, holding him tightly. "Yes. You were. And we could do the same."

* * * * *

Which was all very well and good, and Cade was delighted that Rhiann was happy, but meanwhile, they had Saxons to fight. Disaster loomed on the horizon. He left Rhiann asleep and entered the great hall. And stopped short. Hywel—alone among all his men—had chosen to confront Rhys. Cade hesitated on the threshold, wondering if he should interfere, but then thought better of it. Hywel was Rhys' brother-in-law. He had a right to speak his mind.

Hywel held Rhys' arm in a tight grip, even as Rhys tried to twist away. "You can't order your men into the field. It is suicide."

"It is the only way to show them that we are not afraid." Rhys' face showed defiance. He was either sure of himself, or wanted to be sure and was using bravado to appear so. Cade moved silently along one wall until he came abreast of the pair.

"You fought for the right to command the forces here," Hywel said, "and your first move is one that everyone counsels against? Where's the sense in that?"

"I do what I think is right," Rhys said. "As does your lord, does he not?"

Cade had come to rest just within Rhys' line of sight and Rhys' eyes flicked to him and then away. Cade, for his part, kept his face impassive. He'd already had this conversation with Rhys. Cade's choice, now, was to allow Rhys and his men to die unsupported, or to die alongside them.

"This is how you treat a member of your family?" Rhys said, deflecting the issue. "No wonder your father hasn't spoken a civil word to you in two years."

"We've spoken," Hywel said. "How did you think I arrived with a hundred of my father's men?"

"I would hope you'd be thinking of your sister," Rhys said. "Of what you owe her—and by extension, me, as your brother-in-law."

"I *am* thinking of my sister when I stand on the battlements of this keep and see five thousand Saxon soldiers within two hours' walk of this fortress!" Hywel said. "I am thinking of her when I tell you that she will be ashamed to discover that her husband allowed so many men to die for no reason! We can devise a plan to defeat them, but it won't be with on a field in front of Caer Fawr, out of arrow range of the fortress and with too few cavalry to make a difference."

"You are wrong," Rhys said. "We march now." He wrenched his arm away from Hywel's grip. Hywel's fists clenched at his sides and Cade thought he would strike Rhys, but Taliesin moved in and caught Hywel's arm, stepping between the two men and blocking Rhys' view of Hywel with his body.

"Let him go," Taliesin said. Although he lowered his voice for the next words, Cade read his lips. "Death is not the only possible future for us. We can win despite Rhys' idiocy."

Hywel stepped back. "You mean this, truly?"

Taliesin nodded. Meanwhile, Rhys glared at Taliesin's back, spun on his heel, and marched down the hall to the double doors at the far end. He waved a hand at the half dozen retainers who'd watched the scene with considerable interest. "We go! Who rides with me?"

Before Rhys' men pulled open the doors, Cade was there. Rhys hadn't seen Cade coming, but then, Cade could move quickly when he wanted to. "And what is the role you have for me?" Cade said. "I cannot ride with you. I cannot fight while the sun shines."

Rhys sneered at Cade and it was so reminiscent of the look that Mabon's face usually held that Cade faltered. Was there more to this show of force than bravado, or a son's desire to prove himself worthy of his father?

"Then you can watch our victory from the safety of the guardhouse," Rhys said.

"And if you are wrong, what then?" Cade said. "You leave us to defend Caer Fawr against a great Saxon force that will surround us. At our defeat, they will run free through Wales, picking off our castles and our lands one by one. Including your father's." Cade jerked his chin at Hywel. "Sir Hywel is right. As I predicted, Penda won't be able to resist a frontal assault. If we stay inside Caer Fawr, the Saxons will come to us. We will have the high ground, and the archers to counter any who come against us."

Rhys's teeth clenched. He gripped Cade's shoulder and for the first time, met his eyes. "We can't win from inside Caer Fawr, no matter how many men we have."

Cade's eyes narrowed at him. "Why do you say that?"

"You are not the only one whom the gods have favored with a visit," Rhys said.

"What are you saying? Who of the gods came to see you?"

"I have found favor where you have not. I am assured a victory."

Cade's mouth tasted of acid. "I'm very glad to hear it. Tell me who it was. Surely not … Mabon?"

The smirk was back and Cade considered wiping it off Rhys' face with his fist.

"The gods ally with these Saxons, but against *you*, not me, and not my men." Rhys pushed past him and into the sunlight of high noon. Cade stayed where he was. Safe but impotent.

Hywel came to stand beside him. "As I see it, we have three choices: you could kill him now, though his men might riot and we'd be no closer to victory than before, we could stay safe inside the fort and let him and his men die, or we could fight alongside them and pray for a miracle."

Cade turned his head to meet Hywel's eyes.

Hywel nodded. "You'll need the cloak."

Cade tensed his shoulders and then released it. "For all I am *sidhe*, I am only one man. This is going to be a slaughter."

26

Goronwy

"**H**elp me!"

"God damn it!"

"That's my leg, you piece of dung!"

The words of the men around him clung to Goronwy's ear as he hacked away at the Saxon force. It was no good, of course, had been no good almost from the start, and he was hoping to God that soon Rhys would see it. If he still lived, that is.

Cade was somewhere off to his right, Bedwyr to his left. Thankfully, Cade had insisted that Hwyel, Rhiann, and Dafydd stay on the rampart with their bows. When it came to the retreat, they could defend it with their arrows.

"Fall back!"

Goronwy didn't have to be told twice. He swung his horse around and made for the gate that cut through the northern rampart. Just ahead, a foot soldier was struggling to help a friend who'd lost the use of one of his legs. Goronwy leaned down to collar the foot soldier, while Bedwyr grabbed the wounded friend by the arm and hauled him up behind him.

"Praise God! I thought we were goners." Goronwy's rescued pikeman clutched him around the waist.

Goronwy grunted at that, for he'd thought so too—about a dozen times in the last hour. He leaned over his horse's neck, averting his eyes from the setting sun. Darkness couldn't come too soon for Goronwy.

"Rhys is dead," the man said. "I saw him fall."

And for that, Goronwy had no answer. He risked a look back. Behind him, the bulk of their men had taken to their heels and were running full out for Caer Fawr.

"Why don't the Saxons follow?" Bedwyr said, also looking over his shoulder.

And then Goronwy saw why. The Saxons hadn't brought cavalry to the fight—Penda's men never fought on horseback—and that gave the single horseman who raced his horse between the Welsh retreat and the Saxons advance a tremendous advantage. Especially because that horseman was the King of Gwynedd. Although Goronwy couldn't see Cade due to the cloak, he knew he was there by the glow the cloak couldn't suppress, even in the brightness of the late afternoon sun. Cade blazed between their fleeing men and the bulk of the Saxon lines and his invisible sword cut down every Saxon who attempted to follow them.

Goronwy reached the stream that ran between the rampart and the battlefield and pulled up short. Taliesin shouted at Bedwyr while stabbing a finger in Cade's direction. "Get that fool back here right now! We need him!"

Bedwyr shoved the soldier he'd rescued off his horse and was away again, back the way they'd come. He cut through the lines of retreating men, who opened a path for him through their ranks. Fewer than half of those who'd gone out were returning.

Meanwhile, Taliesin, Dafydd, and Hywel were working furiously with sticks and rope among the trees on the near side of the stream.

Goronwy allowed the pikeman to drop to the ground and dismounted himself. He handed the reins to the young man. "Care for him with your life. This was King Arthur's horse."

The man sketched a bow. "My life belongs to you as it is." And with an insouciant grin, which told Goronwy how pleased he was to be alive, he was off.

"What are you doing?" Goronwy said to Taliesin.

"Creating a surprise for the Saxons, should they decide to continue the assault." Taliesin threw a glance at Goronwy over his shoulder. "We could use the help."

Which is how Goronwy found himself suddenly changed from knight to serf as Taliesin ordered them all about during the time it took for the last of the able-bodied men to reach the gatehouse.

"You've never shown us this type of magic before," Goronwy said.

Taliesin glanced up from his work and then back to the series of complicated knots he was tying. "We've never needed it quite this much before." Goronwy didn't know about that, and was about to say so, when Taliesin added, "Anyone who uses magic pays a price. It wouldn't do for me to use it unless in absolute need, nor for any of you to come to rely on it." One more glance. "And I'm stronger now than I was."

Last of all, Cade and Bedwyr came flying across the field towards them.

Cade reined in under the darkness of the trees and removed his cloak so they could see him. He stood in the stirrups to look east. "The Saxons will come. I'm sure of it. But we have a little time." He lifted his chin to indicate the complex weaves of ropes that Taliesin had painstakingly crafted and his friends had interspersed among the trees. "What's this?"

"When the Saxons come, you will see." Taliesin looked up at Cade. "You fought well. You saved many men."

"It helped that the Saxons have no demons among them this time," Cade said. "It leaves me with a prickling at the back of my neck. Perhaps Mabon is waiting for his chance to hound me the moment I put my guard down."

"We'll just have to do our best until then." Taliesin said this absently, his tongue peeking between his teeth as he concentrated on the task he'd set himself.

"How can you—" Cade bit off the words and looked away, back across the fields littered with Welsh fallen. Crows and birds of prey gathered above them, spiraling down in ever smaller circles to come to land. "We can't even bury our dead."

"We have a war to fight," Taliesin said. "It's time to get on with it."

Dafydd moved closer. "The men who can count have done so and come up with long odds."

"I know," Cade said. "We've had long odds before."

"But not under these circumstances," Goronwy said.

"We have enough food to last us, what with the knife," Cade said. "We can survive on half-rations for a long time."

"To what end?" Dafydd said. "We hold out until the Saxons give up or falter from illness? How long will that take? And how long, then, are we penned in here like sheep in a stockade while other armies lay waste to our lands?"

"We still haven't heard from Rhun and Siawn," Goronwy said. "They will come."

"If they can," Cade said. "Another army just like this one could be marching out of Chester as we speak. The northern barons have had their hands full too, in recent months."

Taliesin shook his head. "This is useless wondering and unlike you—all of you." The bard checked the sky. "They'll come as the sun sets. We have an hour, maybe two. Let's use it. We all have work to do."

And that was that.

"I'll save any wounded man I can." Cade turned his horse's head and trotted back towards the field, draping the cloak around himself and disappearing just before he hit the sunlight beyond the trees.

"Why are you so calm?" Goronwy said to Taliesin. None of them had mentioned the despair and rage that Goronwy had been feeling ever since he learned the size of the Saxon force and that Rhys intended to march against them.

"And what would I gain by despair?" Taliesin said.

"Did you know this would happen?" Goronwy said.

The bard stopped working. "My gift is neither clear nor certain," Taliesin said. "I see a host of possible futures. Sometimes that is almost worse than seeing none at all." He shrugged. "Almost. Every choice made both reduces and expands the possible futures. It's when they narrow to only one that I begin to worry."

"And have they? The paths you see?" Goronwy said.

Taliesin studied him. "Not yet."

"So you don't know what will happen?" Gorowny said.

With a slight shake of his head, Taliesin went back to his weaving of rope. "Only what could."

27

Hywel

Hywel glared over the ramparts at the oncoming force and barked a laugh. It was too late for second guessing. "A few hundred men from Gwynedd against a host of Saxons we've barely stung."

"But it's the same men we had when we fought the demons outside Caer Dathyl," Dafydd said.

Hywel fingered the arrows in his quiver. "Yet this time, we fight against a far greater, and less stupid, opposition." And with too few arrows. They always had too few.

"What's the accounting?" Bedwyr stepped up to the rampart to look with them. The sun would set behind the hills in a moment, falling into the sea they couldn't see from where they stood. The last rays shone in the Saxons' eyes. Cade would give the order to fire the moment the Saxons came within arrow range.

Hywel gestured to one of the baskets of arrows under the rampart. "Some two thousand of them. It will still be hand to hand, far sooner than I'd like."

"At least the Saxons don't have archers," Bedwyr said.

"Or not many," Hywel said. "They hunt with bows; they just don't fight with them."

"Nor horses," Bedwyr said.

"Our advantage," Hywel said.

"Not our only one," Bedwyr said. "We have the high ground."

Hywel turned to Bedwyr, trusting him more than he had ever trusted any man, barring his father and King Cadwaladr at times. "Were we fools to follow the king? We could have left. Lived to fight another day."

"And what of Rhys and his men?" Bedwyr said. "Should we have left them to fight unsupported?"

"Either way, the Saxons will be free to pillage our lands, kill our people, without any check," Hywel said. "Penda will now happily pick the other kings off one by one."

"You assume we are going to lose," Dafydd said. "King Cadwaladr doesn't think so."

"Doesn't he?" Bedwyr said. "Or is he putting on a brave face?"

Hywel stared again at the Saxon force. Caer Fawr was protected by a system of ramparts. Two ran on each side of the fort (eastern and western) and as many as six on the southern and northern sides where the gates lay. Hywel and his friends stood on the rampart that formed the defenses for the lowest level, but was still a twenty foot high wall of mounded earth, with a ditch on the other side that meant the Saxons would have trouble no matter how they tried to go over it. This was where the first attack would come. Here and at the north-eastern gate.

Below him further, Cade was marshalling an initial force of archers and swordsmen at the extension to the fort that looked southeast. The Saxons had to know that the Welsh numbers were reduced. Hywel hoped that they didn't know how far.

Hywel turned around to find that Bedwyr was gone, replaced by Taliesin who was looking at him gravely. "What, no bit of poetry to mark the occasion?" Hywel said.

"Is it necessary? Because I could find an appropriate word if you needed it."

Hywel coughed on a laugh. "No."

"I meant what I said in there," Taliesin said.

Hywel sobered. "Am I going to die? Is that why you're here?"

"We are going to live, whether in fact or memory," Taliesin said. "I don't look ahead that way with my gift. But I do have a task for you, one that is dangerous, but one I feel you are uniquely suited to."

"What is it?" Hywel said. "And does it mean I'll miss your fireworks?"

Taliesin gave him a small smile. "King Cadwaladr asks that you enter the Saxon camp to speak to Penda."

Hywel stared at him. "What? Why? To what end? Penda smells blood. He won't back off."

"He might reconsider, if he knew what I know."

"And King Cadwaladr wants me to deliver this message—one that Penda is sure not to like?" Hywel said.

"He needs someone who speaks Saxon, as you do, and is smart enough to get in without being seen and out without dying," Taliesin said.

Hywel licked his lips. "King Cadwaladr knows I speak Saxon? Does he also know—" Hywel broke off, reluctant to finish the sentence.

"That your father is also Saxon? That he was one of Penda's staunch allies until the killing sickened him to the point that he fled for Wales? You forget that Cadwaladr's own mother is Penda's sister. There is little he doesn't know."

"If Penda discovers who I really am ..."

"He might kill you," Taliesin said.

"You've seen it?"

"It is one possible future, but I don't think it likely."

Hywel bit off a comment about how that was all well and good for Taliesin, but it was *his*—Hywel's—life they were talking about. "That's a relief."

"I suggest you don't tell him,"

"What *am* I to tell him?"

"What I have *seen*."

"And that is?" Hywel said. It was like pulling teeth to get Taliesin to give him any solid piece of information. He could be so infuriating at times, as if everyone else could *see* too and he only had to allude to some future event and everyone would understand. Either that or he enjoyed the suspense. Hywel suspected that was just as likely.

"That Oswin of Northumbria has gathered an army on the northern border of Mercia. If Penda takes the time to fight here and loses many men, he won't have a country left to defend or enough men to defend it, even if he defeats us."

"King Cadwaladr thinks he might withdraw?" Hope sparked in Hywel's chest, which he instantly suppressed. Penda would never withdraw. He would look a coward.

"No," Taliesin said. "But he might think better of a fight to the death. He might see a thousand men fall to our arrows and believe that what I saw was true."

"And is it true, in fact?"

"True enough," Taliesin said.

Whatever that meant.

28

Dafydd

"You're letting her fight?" Dafydd forced himself to back away rather than get right in Cade's face as he wanted. Cade's office was so small, there wasn't much room as it was. Dafydd clenched his fists. "Are you out of your mind?"

"She is not your wife, Dafydd," Cade said. "This is not your decision."

"I fought with her in Llangollen and at Caer Dathyl," Dafydd said. "I know better than you of what she is capable and I don't want her put at risk again. She shouldn't even be here!"

"I couldn't agree more," Cade said. "But she is here. Are you telling me you don't need another bow?"

"Of course we do—but not hers! She should stay with Angharad and Catrin among the wounded."

"What's gotten into you, Dafydd? You've never objected to her fighting before." Cade folded his arms across his chest. Dafydd had been in love with Rhiann, he knew, but his behavior towards Angharad had seemed proprietary. *What am I missing?*

"What's gotten into me?" Dafydd paced around the small room. "Why are women here at all? They've no business on the battlefield, even if we have twenty-foot walls surrounding us. We should have sent them away while we had the chance. *You* should have sent them away."

"And where would they go? Rhiann is the wife of the King of Gwynedd. Penda has already tried to corral her once and marry her to Peada. Do you think any place in Wales will be safe for her if I fall?"

"What if the Saxons break through? How safe will our hall be then?"

"They won't—"

"Damn right, they won't!" Dafydd said.

"Ah," Cade said.

Dafydd glared at him, not liking the sudden knowing tone. "What?"

"You think this is your fault, don't you?" Cade said. "It was you who brought Angharad here, and now you are afraid for a woman like you've never been afraid before."

Dafydd stopped his pacing, glared at Cade, and strode from the room, slamming the door behind him. Cade barked a laugh through the door but Dafydd kept going. He crossed the great hall at a trot, determined to get outside as quickly as possible. He didn't want to talk about his disagreement with his king, and particularly not the role Angharad had played in it. As far as

Dafydd was concerned, King Cadwaladr saw far too much. If Dafydd had thought Rhiann was willful, she had nothing on Angharad. *I sure can pick them...*

Leave it to Angharad, however, to notice his flushed face and move to intercept him. He slowed and forced a calmer expression. But when she came abreast, she had something else on her mind. "Taliesin wants you on the ramparts."

He glanced at her. "Why?"

"They're coming. Now."

Dafydd picked up the pace. "I just left the King. Does he know?"

"Rhiann went to tell him."

"So why does Taliesin want me?" Dafydd said.

"Something about you needing to shoot an arrow to start it off," Angharad said.

Dafydd didn't know what that meant, but he didn't argue, just hurried across the courtyard and through the gate to the spot on the rampart where Taliesin waited, looking east at the oncoming Saxons. As it turned out, it wasn't the main force after all, but a party on horseback, perhaps looking to probe the Welsh defenses.

"What do they think they're doing?" Dafydd said. "They'll be within arrow range shortly."

"I've asked Cadwaladr to let them come," Taliesin said.

"How close?" Dafydd said.

"You know exactly how close. You helped me set the traps." Taliesin eyebrows practically met in a look that told Dafydd he thought Dafydd was an idiot but was too polite to say so.

"Rope and sticks were all I saw," Dafydd said.

"Well, you'll see more shortly," Taliesin said. "I'll need you to shoot an arrow, one of my own design, exactly where I tell you to. We don't have much time before it's full dark."

Dafydd gripped his bow, hoping Taliesin's trust wasn't misplaced. Angharad and Catrin hovered on the margins of their conversation. Taliesin looked over and waved them nearer. "There's nothing to fear. At least, not for you up here."

"I can feel your magic," Catrin said. "It's rising."

For the first time ever, Taliesin actually looked discomfited and then his expression smoothed. "As it should be. You might be a better judge even than I am of when I should release it."

Catrin surprised Dafydd by nodding her agreement. He wasn't sure how he felt about having both Catrin and Taliesin next to him. There were undercurrents here he'd last felt only in Arawn's cavern.

The Saxon cavalry neared the line of bushes that followed the little river. Dafydd split his attention between them and Taliesin who brought out a three foot long, slender stick and held it out across his palm. He muttered words Dafydd didn't catch in a language he didn't understand. Dafydd found himself growing dizzy watching him, as if the stick were wavering between the world of magic and his own.

"Dafydd!" Catrin caught his bow arm and he jerked back to himself to find Taliesin gazing at him, a smile twitching at his lips. The stick had become an arrow with a golden point, which he handed to Dafydd.

"Press it into the bow," Taliesin said.

Dafydd didn't ask him to say *please*. He fitted the arrow to his bow and pressed into it. Then Taliesin, his staff in his left hand and his right hand outstretched, pointed his index finger at the tip of the arrow and uttered a soundless incantation. It lit with a purple fire.

The ropes they'd positioned at Taliesin's direction also glowed purple and Taliesin pointed at a spot on the ground on the far side of the creek. "There!"

Dafydd loosed the arrow. It flew through the air and hit—

Whuf!

The bushes exploded and the concussion that followed had Dafydd on his knees with his hands over his ears. Angharad fell into him as the wave of power passed over them. With his arm around her, Dafydd staggered to his feet.

The magic had torn the earth on the far side of the creek asunder, the trees and scrub that had lined it were in flames, and all but three of the two dozen Saxon cavalry were down. The remainder raced towards the Saxon lines.

Cade ran down the path between the ramparts, his eyes wide. "What was that, Taliesin? You said you had a surprise for them but ..."

Taliesin's eyes were bright. "That went better than I expected. I'd only done a small trial earlier to see if it worked. If I'd known it would go so well, I would have saved it for when the bulk of the army marched on us."

"You could do it agai—" But Dafydd cut off his words at the sudden whiteness in Taliesin's face. The bard staggered and would have gone down if Cade hadn't caught him.

"Power has a price," Catrin said.

Cade bent and threw Taliesin over his shoulder. "Warn me next time, will you, Taliesin? You're the king of understatement." Cade strode back to the keep with Taliesin on his shoulder.

Dafydd would have laughed if Taliesin didn't look so ill.

Angharad slipped her hand into his and they turned back to the devastation below them. "Here's hoping the price he pays is worth it," she said.

29

Hywel

Hywel crouched in the trees. Darkness had fallen, made even thicker by the heavy cloud cover that had blown in with it. The first raindrops fell. Above him on the hill, his own men shouted to each other about Taliesin's handiwork, while the Saxons gathered two hundred yards away. That they were Saxon and not demon, he had no doubt. He didn't know where Mabon was in all this, and by now he didn't much care. He had a job to do.

"Thought you'd try this without me, did you?" Bedwyr's gruff voice sounded in Hywel's ear. He didn't bother turning to look at his friend, since he couldn't see anything anyway.

"King Cadwaladr sent only me," Hywel said. "This isn't your task."

"Ach," Bedwyr said and Hywel felt the accompanying shrug. "I told him he was an idiot for letting you go alone."

Now Hywel did turn, searching for Bedwyr's face in the murk. "And what did the King say?"

Bedwyr guffawed—quietly. "He laughed. He knew I was right. I told him that I couldn't let you die before you'd found a girl to come home to."

Hywel scoffed. "Like Dafydd? He's taken to Angharad pretty quick."

"They rode north together for two days. It doesn't take long. Besides ..." Bedwyr peered over Hywel's shoulder. "This is what I do best."

And that, Hywel decided, was probably true. Bedwyr hadn't been raised in a castle, nor to the sword, though he fought as well as any of the other knights. He'd fallen in with Goronwy not long after Goronwy's arrival in Gwynedd. They'd fought together ever since and when Goronwy had learned of Cade's existence, Bedwyr hadn't considered letting him join Cade's *teulu* without him.

"Then let's do it," Hywel said.

At a crouch, the two men raced forward, skirting the Saxon lines to the west and staying within the trees that lined the little river that separated Caer Fawr from the rest of the valley it overlooked—and that Taliesin had so effectively destroyed.

They peered at the camp from underneath a bush. A steady drip of water fell on both of them and Hywel's front was already muddy to his chin. In the time it had taken to reach this point, the Saxons seemed to have gotten themselves together again. The explosion had been a shock, but they'd lost fewer than two dozen men. They'd be more cautious from now on than they would have been, but it looked like they hadn't changed their minds about their attack.

Maybe Hywel could help Penda with that.

"We've barely dented their numbers, Bedwyr said.

"Rhys was a fool," Hywel said.

"He's in the Otherworld now," Bedwyr said. "He can tell Arawn all about his defeat and how he ignored Cade's best judgment. And got so many good men killed."

Hywel suddenly had a cold feeling in his belly. "Arawn isn't powerless, you know, for all that Gwyn guards the cauldron and will not let him out. He roams freely in the world of the *sidhe*."

"So?"

"What if Rhys speaks to him of our efforts here? What if he tells Mabon where we are?"

"Didn't you hear what Rhys told Cade?" Bedwyr said. "Mabon came to Rhys already and assured him of victory."

"Lied to him, you mean." Hywel shook his head—and then shook off his worries, glad his tasks were more grounded than Cade's. Hywel agreed with Dafydd: he'd had enough of the world of the *sidhe* and everyone in it. It was time to get on with what he could do and could control.

Bedwyr pointed to less well-lit spot, equidistant from the firelight at the center of the camp and the torches on the perimeter. "Your best bet is to run across the field at a crouch and fetch up between those two tents there. I'll be here when you're done, and if you don't return, I'll see to Penda's death myself."

"Good to know I'll be avenged when I'm on Arawn's rack." Hywel shot Bedwyr a grin he probably couldn't see and was off, crouching low as Bedwyr had said, scuttling across the field more like a thief than a knight. The Saxons had packed down the grass so it provided little cover. Hywel had to hope that the Saxons' night vision would be hampered by their own lights and the rain.

Ages later, but only a dozen heartbeats really, Hywel crouched behind the closest tent and then peered around it, still keeping low to the ground. Men bustled near a large tent twenty yards away.

Hywel straightened and adjusted his helm so it hid most of his face. He and Bedwyr had scavenged Hywel's entire outfit off a dead Saxon on the far side of the field. They hadn't had as many men to choose among as Hywel would have liked (far too many fallen Welshmen surrounded them) but the armor and helmet fit well enough. After this was over, he thought he'd hang onto his new axe, which had felt comfortable in his hand before he'd slotted it into his belt. He'd left his sword with Bedwyr, along with his surcoat sporting Cadwaladr's red dragon crest.

Hywel waited until the flow of men in and out of the tent subsided and then strode forward, Taliesin's parting words echoing in his ears, words that for once were clearly stated so that Hywel couldn't misunderstand: *Act like you belong there and know what you're doing. Nobody will question you. The men around you will see what they want to see: a fellow Saxon soldier.*

Loud shouts in Saxon carried on the breeze from the western end of the camp where Penda's captains gathered their men. Ignoring them, Hywel threw back the door flap and stepped into Penda's tent. The only light came from a lantern on a stubby table. Penda was alone, leaning over a map spread out in front of him, but looked up at Hywel's entrance. He looked back to the map, instantly dismissing Hywel, before bringing up his head again. "I don't know you."

"No, my lord," Hywel said in Saxon. "I have a message for you."

Penda looked past Hywel to the door of the tent, but none of his servants came through it. Hywel kept his hands loose at his sides, hoping that Penda wouldn't decide to run him through. He had a sword and Hywel wasn't accomplished yet in the use of his new axe.

"What is it?" Penda said.

Hywel bowed. "My name is Hywel. I bring you news from the King of Gwynedd."

"So Cadfael seeks peace, does he?" Penda said. "He snubbed my son, refusing him his wayward daughter. He has not responded to any of my messages and rebuffed my councils. It is too late for peace."

Hywel almost choked on his tongue. Could Penda not know that Cadfael was dead? That Cadwaladr was king? And yet, it appeared so. Hywel swallowed hard. This was not the news he'd thought he was bringing Penda. "My lord, I-I-I—" Hywel found himself stuttering.

"Why does Cadfael even bother with this charade? He must fear defeat. He must think he can turn his magician in my direction and I'll turn tail and run away. No." Penda shook his head. "I will crush Cadfael beneath my boot and all Wales will fall to me before the year is out."

Hywel finally marshaled his thoughts. "It is not Cadfael who sends you word. Cadfael is dead."

That seemed to shake Penda out of his complacency. He tsked through his teeth. "Not Cadfael? Then who? My sister never gave Cadfael a son. Who has taken the throne?"

"Your sister didn't need to," Hywel said. "She'd already given one to Cadwallon."

Penda's mouth opened in surprise. "The boy lived? I would have thought Cadfael was smarter than that. If I had been he, I would have scoured Gwynedd for every year-old son, just as Herod did in the Christian Bible." Penda laughed openly. "If all the rulers in that religion had his spine, I might join that faith myself."

Penda was definitely not the type to turn the other cheek.

"His name is Cadwaladr ap Cadwallon, soon to be High King of the Britons." Hywel's chest swelled at the thought. Here was a name—and a king—that could shake even this great lord of Mercia.

Penda's eyebrows furrowed. "You imply that because another man leads the Welsh, the game has changed? Why would I treat with him if I wouldn't have spoken to Cadfael?"

"Cadwaladr is your nephew."

"He thinks to bind me with blood?" Penda said. "I haven't spoken to my sister in fifteen years. Is that all you have for me?"

"King Cadwaladr sent me to warn you."

"Warn me? Enough of your riddles." Penda scoffed under his breath. "Give me your message and I might allow you to live."

"Oswin of Northumbria gathers a force on your northern border. If you do not withdraw from this fight, you may not have a country left to defend."

Penda crossed his arms across his chest and tapped a finger to his lip. "How does your king know this? Perhaps this is a trick."

"It's no trick," Hywel said.

"Withdraw, eh? He must be more afraid of me than I hoped, to think that such a ruse could possibly work. We outnumber you. You are locked in your little fort and cannot get out, with too few men to win the day. Or night."

Hywel kept his face impassive but Penda laughed again.

"I see I am right."

"You are wrong. King Cadwaladr sends me to you because he would prefer an enemy he knows on his border than one he does not. You might not die yourself today, but if you do not withdraw and turn your attention to Oswin, your army will never recover. You will not have the men to defeat him. And you yourself will not live out the year."

Penda stared at him and Hywel realized that his voice had changed as he'd spoken those last words, deepened into a rhythmic chant reminiscent of Taliesin. What had come over him? For Penda's part, he gazed at Hywel for several heartbeats.

"You resemble your father more than a little. Is he well?"

Another swallow. "He is," Hywel said.

"But the rest of your message is not that he comes to join me? To beg forgiveness for deserting me when I needed him most?"

"No," Hywel said. The word came out short. He forced himself not to glance towards the door, knowing that it would indicate weakness to Penda. Hywel had very little time. Bedwyr was waiting. From the looks of it, they still had a war to fight.

But Penda was done too. "Go. If I see you again, it will be your death."

Hywel didn't need to be told twice.

30

Rhiann

The Saxon torches sputtered and spit in the pouring rain, barely penetrating the cloak of darkness that had descended on Caer Fawr. Rhiann gazed over the rampart. Dafydd stood beside her, extreme tension in his shoulders. For Rhiann's part, she felt a strange sense of dislocation—as if what she was seeing wasn't real—and if it was, she was watching the scene from the point of view of someone else. The Saxons outnumbered them at least four to one. Maybe more. The defenders didn't have enough arrows. It was as simple as that.

Cade had told Rhiann about his argument with Dafydd. What Cade hadn't told Dafydd was that he'd listened, and had insisted to Rhiann herself that she keep as safe as possible. Whether or not Dafydd knew it, Cade was punishing him just a little by making him stay with her. They stood on a raised platform behind a palisade, overlooking the southwestern gate. By splitting their force to directly assault both gates at the same time, the Saxons had forced Cade to split his as well.

Rhiann was torn between horror at what was coming at them and an absolute refusal to believe that they were all going to die. If they couldn't hold the Saxons off long enough to prompt Penda to rethink this action, it would be hand-to-hand along the ramparts soon enough and there was no way the Welsh would win that battle.

"Aim for the neck or heart," Dafydd said.

Rhiann glanced at him. "I'm glad you've found Angharad."

"Can we not talk about it?" Dafydd said—and then proceeded to talk about it. "She's smart, and she doesn't talk too much, and she says she loves me. I have no idea why."

"Don't be foolish, Dafydd," Rhiann said. "I loved Cade before I met you. It doesn't mean you weren't worthy of love. Such modesty doesn't become you." She elbowed him in the ribs to take the sting out of her words.

"Remember Caersws?" Dafydd said.

"How could I forget?" Rhiann said. "I'm staring down at an overwhelming force where the odds don't favor us."

"And yet we won the day," Dafydd said. "Just the two of us."

"We did, didn't we?" Rhiann found courage at the memory, though that had been a different situation. These weren't mindless demons, chasing confused villagers across Powys. These men followed a commander who knew what he was doing and had won more battles in the last thirty years than any Mercian king before him.

"We have King Cadwaladr," Dafydd said. "Maybe they don't understand what that means."

"According to Hywel, they hadn't realized my father was dead," Rhiann said. "They are truly behind the times."

"Here they come." Dafydd raised his bow.

Because of the rain, they'd waited to tie their bowstrings until the last instant. As it was, the strings would soon be soaked and unusable. Rhiann had two spares. Like the arrows, she could only pray that they would be enough.

"They're coming!"

"Why didn't Taliesin save his explosion for now?" Dafydd said. "He could have killed two hundred of them instead of twenty."

"He bought us time." Cade said, coming to stand beside them, his own bow in his hand. Then, Cade lifted his voice above the grunting and marching of men. "Fire at will!"

Rhiann obeyed. At first, she focused entirely on the feel of the bow in her hand, the physical act of pressing and loosing arrow after arrow, and the concentration needed to aim it. She didn't even bother to see if her arrows hit anyone, so quickly did she reel them off. As it was, the Saxons were pressed so close together, accuracy was immaterial, and the first waves of arrows devastated the initial ranks of marching Saxons.

"Watch out!"

Cade launched himself at Rhiann and pulled her to the ground, cushioning her fall with his own body.

"What—what happened?"

"They have their own bowmen," Cade said. "I didn't expect it."

"They have one fewer now," Dafydd said.

Cade pushed to his feet but kept a hand on Rhiann's shoulder to keep her below the level of the rampart. "Stay there!"

He released six arrows in the time she could have gotten off one.

"Cade, this is ridiculous—"

"Not to me," Cade said. "And anyway, you can get up now. They're all down." He pulled her to her feet and into a quick hug, squeezed once, and set off at a run toward the rampart above them.

Rhiann went back to work.

It was a brutal business. Rhiann shot, and shot, and shot again, feeling that same welling up of fear—and the draining out of everything she cared about. As at Caersws, she became one with the bow, the string, and the arrow that she shot from it. She lost track of the number of arrows she loosed or the Saxons she hit.

Rhiann continued to shoot, mindful of her emptying quiver. Each archer had brought at least two dozen of his own arrows with him, but if Rhiann's were nearly gone so were everybody else's.

A call went up from the archers who held a more easterly position. "More arrows! We need more arrows!"

A moment later, Angharad appeared behind Rhiann and stuffed a handful of arrows into her quiver, and then more into Dafydd's.

- 310 -

"Taliesin is keeping count." Angharad's breath came in short gasps. "Take care of these. We don't have many left."

Angharad ran back to the stockpile.

"We've made headway against the Saxons, but how long can we hold out?" Dafydd said. He muttered under his breath, calculating the number of arrows, by the number of archers, by the Saxons they needed to kill.

His bow loose in his hand and unstrung, having run all the way from the northern gate, Hywel skidded to a halt behind Rhiann. "We've turned them back!"

"Are you sure?" Rhiann aimed carefully at a Saxon who had the temerity to creep into the ditch at the base of the wall below her. From what she could see, they'd only killed the first ranks of Saxons—not even a thousand men. And even that thought sickened her, knowing that she'd been responsible for many dozen all by herself.

"Hold!" Cade's call came from above them. "We can't afford to waste even one arrow." He landed beside Dafydd and Rhiann with a thud, having jumped the distance from the upper rampart. "Hywel's right. They've retreated from the northern gate. I don't know yet whether or not they intend to renew the assault there, or if they're going to concentrate only on this gate."

Rhiann lowered her bow. She didn't believe it. For every Saxon they'd killed, another had come to take his place. And yet, in the few moments she'd spent talking to Cade and Hywel, the Saxons below her had also backed off from the lowest rampart, to a point just out of arrow range, having faced just enough opposition to prevent them from laying their siege ladders against it.

"Maybe Penda is rethinking his decision to attack," she said.

"I don't think so." Dafydd pointed a finger which didn't actually tremble, even though a slight waver appeared in his voice. "The Saxons are bringing their wagons forward."

They peered together into the murk. "What's in them?" Rhiann said.

"Soil and ladders," Hywel said. "I saw them when I was in the Saxon camp. Penda must have been working his men like dogs to have managed this so quickly. He knows what he's about."

Cade waved to Goronwy who commanded the men in the portion of their defenses Cade had taken to calling 'the annex'. It was the bit of rampart that protected the entry gate on the southwest side of the fort, just below where Dafydd and Rhiann stood. "Cease firing! I need more bowmen on the first rampart. We must make each shot count!"

Rhiann pushed the sopping wet tendrils of hair that had come out of her braid out her eyes and gazed down at the oncoming Saxons with something that felt worse than horror. It filled her mouth with bitterness. The carts rolled right over the bodies of the Saxon dead.

"Is Penda mad?" she said. "Doesn't he see the carnage right in front of him?"

Cade wrapped an arm around her and pulled her to him. "He thinks to defeat us now, and that is worth any number of dead to him, if he can accomplish it before dawn."

"Surely doubt has seeped in by now," Dafydd said.

"If he finishes us off, he has no western flank to defend," Cade said. "He thinks he can handle Oswin as he has in the past."

"That we are defeated won't help him if he doesn't have an army left," Rhiann said.

"That's what I told him," Hywel said.

"Penda is an experienced commander. He will have realized that the pace of our arrows slowed, just before he withdrew his troops." Cade said. "In fact, that's probably why he withdrew. He knows that we are running out. He wants to give us time to contemplate our mortality."

"Would he honor a flag of truce?" Rhiann said.

"No." The three men spoke in unison, with no hesitation.

"And I wouldn't show one," Cade said.

Rhiann looked from one to the other. Each man had the exact same expression of grim determination on his face.

Catrin raced up to Cade, breathing hard. "Goronwy says one-third of his force protects the inner wall. If the Saxons crest the lower rampart, he'll be able to shoot them as they come up the pathway. But we need to take them down before they reach that point."

"Agreed." Cade lifted his own bow.

Side by side with Cade and Dafydd, Rhiann shot, and shot, and shot again. *Press. Loose. Press. Loose.*

But too many Saxons came at them. Now, for every Saxon casualty, two more came to take his place. The Saxons gradually filled the moat, even if the dirt they'd piled high in the carts was interspersed with the bodies of the dead. Another half an hour and the stockpile of arrows was gone. Each archer had a half full quiver, and was staring into a full frontal assault by the Saxons.

"Ladders!"

Two men holding the base of the first scaling ladder slammed it into the ground, while others swung it up against the rampart.

"Shoot them before they reach the top!"

But it wasn't really possible. The initial Saxon climbers fell but others took their places, swarming up the ladders like a waterfall in reverse.

"How many are there?" Rhiann said, her voice going high. She gazed across the wall at the oncoming Saxons.

No one answered her.

Dafydd tossed his bow to the ground and pulled out his sword. The Saxons had placed their ladders a few feet apart such that in total it seemed there were a hundred of them side by side.

Cade handed his bow to Rhiann. "Be safe, *cariad*. Get yourself to the hall. There's nothing more you can do here."

Rhiann stared at the bow. She clenched her jaw, wanting to deny him, but she felt Dafydd's eyes on her and knew it would be foolish to do so. "Yes, my lord."

Rhiann ran away. With every step she cursed and wept at the same time, tears streaming down her cheeks, hating to leave her husband and her friends but knowing that her skill with a blade would be inadequate to the task. She would only get herself killed along with them.

31

Goronwy

The first Saxon had just pulled himself to the top of the wall when an arrow pierced his neck. He screamed and tumbled forward off the ladder. Goronwy had a moment of relief, but shook it off the next moment. There was no hope here.

Another Saxon replaced the first, and then another, and surely there were hundreds more waiting at the foot of the ladder to take the place of those who fell. When the next Saxon appeared, Goronwy hacked him with a down sweep of his sword. He too fell back. And then so many faced him in succession Goronwy stopped counting.

Geraint moved up beside him and they fought back to back, in concert with the dozen other men who'd staked out this portion of the rampart. Goronwy knew many of them. He'd taught some of them sword play, but now, when it was no longer play, it was he they looked to for courage. As had been the case in the council hall, his lord was counting on him. Goronwy smiled grimly as he hacked away at another Saxon neck. He was better at fighting than talking.

On the other side of him, Bedwyr slashed at a Saxon who came up the ladder one over from the one Goronwy was protecting.

"To the wall!" Goronwy hoped they'd prove a bold sight to the other Welsh fighters, encouraging them to think they had a chance, even if Goronwy himself knew better.

He, Geraint, and Bedwyr leapt onto the rampart itself and swung their swords at the necks of first men who poked their heads over the top of the rampart. If Goronwy could maintain his position, he could stop every Saxon who reached the top of the ladder. The rain hindered both defender and attacker, making the sod wall of the rampart soft and mucky and the ladder slippery. More than one man's foot slipped off a rung and plunged him down onto the soldiers below him. It seemed every man tried a different technique for reaching the top, whether climbing one-handed with an axe in one hand, putting a blade between his teeth, or with a weapon slung along his back.

But none could reach the top of the wall more quickly than Goronwy could chop them off it. At the same time, not every defender was as skilled or as quick as these three and they didn't have enough men to replace those that fell. Bedwyr cursed steadily beside him. At one point, Goronwy turned just as a Saxon came up behind Geraint and slashed at his head. Goronwy shoved at his friend and met the Saxon's blade with his own. But the few heartbeats he'd taken to protect Geraint had allowed a Saxon to reach the top of the ladder and leap down to the path behind it.

Goronwy swung around, panicked that he'd lost the rhythm of the fight. If he got behind the pace, the Saxons would overwhelm them. But in this instance, Bedwyr was there. Then once again, the friends fought together. As time passed, Goronwy lost track of all sense of himself, fiercely holding on with two hands to the hilt of his sword. He was aware only of the succession of blood-shot eyes of the Saxons in front of him.

"Retreat! Pull back!" The call came from the rampart above and behind them. The Annex had been a bold, initial line of defense, but they couldn't hold it.

Geraint obeyed instantly. Gorowny shoved his sword through a last Saxon, but then had to drag Bedwyr along the pathway towards the main gateway to Caer Fawr.

"Come on! Run!" Dafydd had posted himself at the top of the rampart above the gate and he screamed the words over and over as they ran.

"Loose!"

That was Cade from the level above, ordering the remaining archers on the inner rampart finally to release the arrows they'd saved. The barrage of metal held the Saxons back long enough to allow the exhausted Welsh to secure themselves inside the lower walls. The gate slammed closed behind them.

"Christ on the cross!" Bedwyr ripped at a strip of cloth from the hem of his tunic and wound it one-handed around a slit in his upper arm.

"Damn it! I thought we had them there for a while!" Goronwy said.

Goronwy sputtered and spit his anger, but after a skeptical look from Bedwyr, had to acknowledge that Cade was right to sound the retreat, and if he'd waited any longer, it might have been too late. None of them would have made it back.

Goronwy leaned against the inner wall and rested his head against the sod. Cade remained on the wall above him, shouting and pointing at men, one after another, each running off to do his bidding. From up there, he would have seen the heavy toll the Saxons took on the defenders.

Cade glanced down at Goronwy, who didn't even have the energy to lift a hand in acknowledgement of his king. Cade jumped the distance instead. "You were the last to leave the balustrade, I see."

"We had to leave the dead and a few of the gravely wounded to the Saxons," Goronwy said.

Cade put a hand on his shoulder. "I know. Several of the men wanted to retrieve them, but I refused."

"The Saxons will slaughter the wounded," Geraint said.

Cade's face was drawn and as grim as Goronwy had ever seen it. "I know that too." He tipped his head to indicate the pathway that led to the gate in the second rampart. "Come. We have another wall to defend."

* * * * *

Goronwy and Cade ran up the pathway to the final gatehouse that protected Caer Fawr proper, this wall was ten feet higher than the lower one they'd been defending. The Saxon ladders wouldn't reach the top of that wall, no matter how many they crammed into the space. Possibly lashing two ladders together would do it, but whatever the Saxons decided it would take time—and give the Welsh time—to breathe until the Saxons regrouped.

"How many men have they lost?" Goronwy's breath was just beginning to ease. He glanced back towards the gate behind them. It held firm. For now.

"Many, but a lower percentage than we have," Cade said. "I had hoped that Penda would have reconsidered by now."

"He wants you dead, my lord," Goronwy said. "Whether or not you're his nephew. Family ties are nothing when they give no advantage to him."

Cade grunted, not necessarily his assent, Goronwy thought, but his understanding. Ahead of them, the rest of the stragglers passed through the higher gate, inset into the inner wall, that protected the next level of the fort. Goronwy and Cade were the last.

"Hurry!" Geraint waved at them from above the gate. He held a bow, ready to shoot at the Saxons as they leapt off their scaling ladders and onto the path behind the now undefended rampart.

Just as they turned into the doorway, Goronwy checked behind them one more time. A wiry Saxon had crested the wall to Goronwy's right. He whipped out a bow from its rest at his back—

"Watch out!"

—and loosed a shot at Geraint whose attention was elsewhere.

The cry stuck in Goronwy's throat. The arrow hit Geraint full in the chest. He folded over it and fell forward off the rampart, plummeting the thirty feet to the pathway below. The Saxon gave a cry of triumph, and suddenly two dozen Saxons were at the top of the wall and leaping down to the pathway.

"Inside!" Cade shoved at Goronwy, who couldn't move for shock. "I'll get him!"

Cade raced to Geraint's crumpled form while Goronwy screamed at those who guarded the gate to keep it open, even as the Saxons seized on their inattention to try to beat them to the open door in the inner wall. Goronwy planted himself in front of the gate and with a flurry of sword strokes fought three of them off long enough for Cade to slip through behind him.

Once they were safe, with the gate slammed shut, Cade laid Geraint against the wall near the great hall. The arrow was grotesque as it protruded from his chest, and his eyes sightless.

"I can't help him." Cade eased to his feet as he stared down at Geraint. "He's gone."

Goronwy rested with his head in his hands. Then, filling his lungs with air, he tipped his head back to gaze up at the sky. The rain had stopped just after they'd retreated to the second rampart and a few stars had come out, interspersed among the clouds. They had perhaps two hours to dawn.

"If it affects our next course of action, it looks like the morning will dawn clear, Cade," Goronwy said.

Cade nodded. "It would, today of all days. But that actually makes the decision easier, doesn't it?"

32

Cade

"**G**et up!" Cade toed Dafydd's prone form with his boot.

"I'm awake!" Dafydd had fallen asleep with his back to the wall. He sat near other archers who'd come through the doorway and collapsed to fall asleep where they lay. Angharad lay curled up next to him, her head on his thigh. The sky had lightened. Somewhere it was dawn, but the sun hadn't yet peeked over the eastern horizon. "How long have I slept?"

"Not long enough, I'm sure," Cade said. "There'll be plenty of time for sleeping when this is over, or none of us will ever sleep again."

Dafydd stroked the hair from Angharad's face and wiggled his legs to get her to wake up. She sat up, gazed at Dafydd with a completely blank stare that told Cade she wasn't really awake. She then leaned back against the wall and closed her eyes again. Dafydd got to his feet.

"I apologize for earlier, my lord," Dafydd said. "I said some things I shouldn't hav—"

Cade held up his hand to stop him from speaking further. "Two friends had a difference of opinion. That is all. That's not what this is about." At the same time, he was glad that, like him, Dafydd hadn't wanted to let the argument fester.

Dafydd blinked, opened his mouth, and then closed it. Cade knew how his friend felt: confused but too tired to try to guess what Cade wanted.

"I have many noble men among my companions," Cade said. "But only one has ever held the sword of the White Hilt. That man is you." Cade had been holding Dyrnwyn, hidden in a borrowed sheath with the belt wrapped around it, behind his back. He brought it out and showed it to Dafydd.

"But I thought it wasn't the real Dyrnwyn?" Dafydd gazed at the sword in clear disbelief and didn't take it.

Cade stepped closer and lowered his voice. "We were mistaken. Put it on."

"You want me to wear it?"

"Wear it and wield it. At first light, we ride. We will scatter the Saxons before us—and you will lead the men."

"Why not Goronwy? Or you for that matter? With Caledfwlch and the cloak you can fight in the sun, just like you did yesterday—"

"With the cloak, I am invisible, and Caledfwlch along with me," Cade said. "How do I lead my men when they can't see me? If I tell them that I am fighting among them, they will follow you."

Dafydd stared at the sword. Cade didn't urge it on him, just held it out to him. As far as Cade was concerned, the decision was the right one and the more he thought about it, the more sure he was. But Dafydd had to come to that himself, for by accepting Cade's challenge, not only would he lead the men, but make himself the center of all the action on the battlefield. A man had to choose that, not have it thrust upon him unwilling.

"Go ahead." Angharad spoke from behind Dafydd and he turned to look at her. She pushed to her feet and came to stand beside him, her hand on his arm. "I don't want you to fight, but given that you will whether I want you to or not, you should be the one to carry Dyrnwyn."

Dafydd gazed down at her for a long count of five. Then he turned to Cade. "I will do it."

"I'll be the unseen hand beside you." Cade clapped a hand on his shoulder. "Ready yourself. We ride within the hour."

Cade walked away from Dafydd and Angharad, leaving them to sort themselves out as they saw fit. Back inside the hall, he found Rhiann consulting with Catrin. "I need to speak to you, Rhiann," Cade said.

Rhiann gave him a long look in which he read more understanding than he necessarily wanted. "I already know what you're going to say."

"And what is your answer?" he said. "I know you're as skilled in the use of the bow as any of us here, but I can't let you fight this time—not from the walls—not with the chance that the Saxons will come over them."

Rhiann gazed at him steadily.

Cade tried again. "Enough men have already died today without losing you."

"What do you want me to do?" she said. "Defend the retreat again?"

"There will be no retreat," Cade said. "Every man capable of sitting on a horse—and that means every man here—will ride out to face the Saxons. You, the other women, and the servants, will remain inside the keep. If the Saxons get this far, we will all be dead and Caer Fawr will be theirs. If I am dead, Penda will spare your lives."

"Are you sure about that?" Catrin said. "Why would he?"

Cade stared past her, unseeing. Penda would spare Rhiann so he could marry her to Peada, but Cade couldn't bear to say that. "So Taliesin says," he said.

"He's awake?" Rhiann said.

"Awake and insisting he is well, for all that he's lain unmoving on a pallet since I brought him inside."

"A temporary thing only," Taliesin said.

Cade turned and couldn't help smiling to see the bard crossing the floor of the hall with long strides.

"Rhiann and I will watch from the top of the keep," Taliesin said. "We will be able to see the action well enough from there."

Cade looked down at Rhiann. "I saved some arrows, just for you, Rhiann. You'll have an even dozen, plus the one that Arianrhod left you."

Rhiann took the quiver from him, looked down at it, and then back up at him. "I suppose you didn't have to be a seer to see this coming."

"If you do end up needing them, make them count."

"I always do," she said.

"Ach, Rhiann, how can you laugh?" Cade pulled her into his arms. "I fear the world is ending, and we with it."

"I don't believe it," she said. "I can't believe it." She hugged him once, and then with a whirl, she strode away, Taliesin beside her, heading for the stairwell that led to the top of the keep and the battlements that would allow them to keep watch on the course of the battle.

Cade gazed after them. And then Catrin gasped. "My lord! Rhiann is—" She bit off the words.

"You do have a gift, then," he said. "For I saw it too."

"I saw two heartbeats where there should be only one," Catrin said.

Cade put a hand on Catrin's shoulder. "Tell her for me, if I don't survive this day. She will have a future King of Gwynedd to live for and protect."

"Of course, my lord." Catrin's voice trembled as she spoke, and then firmed. "Is that what you fear? Has Taliesin seen it?"

"Taliesin will not say."

33

Goronwy

Goronwy steadied his horse and pulled up beside a man who had a swath of blood coating his chest. Moments earlier, he'd been bleeding out on the floor of the hall.

The man saw Goronwy inspecting him and shot him a beatific grin. "Rhys ap Morgan was my lord. I'd followed his father since I became a man, and then him." He gave a short laugh. "I've died twice today already, and been resurrected by King Cadwaladr. Now I'm alive and well again, and about to die for a third time."

"King Cadwaladr doesn't actually bring men back from the dead." Goronwy checked the front of the line to see what kind of time he had before they would ride. Dafydd mounted his horse and leaned to the right. It looked odd until Goronwy realized that Dafydd was listening to Cade, though neither man, sword, nor horse were visible.

Cade had promised to act as a guard for Dafydd, and that was the only reason Goronwy hadn't tried to prevent it, or laughed at the absurdity of his brother leading their host of men. Goronwy still had trouble seeing his brother as a man, much less a knight upon whom all depended.

"Doesn't he?" the man said. "If Rhys had listened to him perhaps I would never have died at all." He moved away and fell into line on the right flank of the line of men.

The pathway down from the main gate was so narrow that only two men could ride abreast in places. Goronwy found a spot in the left column, and then Bedwyr pulled up beside him on the right.

"I like her," he said, by way of greeting.

"Who?" Goronwy said.

"Angharad. I like her. Your brother chooses well."

Goronwy coughed a laugh. "I do too, though I find it disconcerting that my little brother has such a way with women. Angharad has already helped him forget Rhiann."

The two men glanced to the top of the keep, where their queen stood behind the balustrade with Taliesin. The risen sun shown full on their faces and Rhiann shaded her eyes with one hand. Meanwhile, Taliesin held his staff aloft. That had Goronwy scoffing again—or almost—before he swallowed it. Who was he to question whether Taliesin's entreaties would do them any good? The world of the *sidhe* was far closer to this one than Goronwy was comfortable admitting.

Dafydd stood in his stirrups at the head of the company. He held Dyrnwyn above his head and Goronwy hoped that only his closest companions noted how white his brother's knuckles were around the hilt. Suddenly, the sword burst into flame from hilt to tip.

"We ride!"

Goronwy thought the call came from Cade, though the roar from the men that followed drowned out his certainty.

A shout echoed throughout the courtyard: "Hail Cadwaladr! King of the Cymry! The King shines forth!" Sure enough, the glow that even the cloak couldn't hide suffused Cade's position, Dafydd, and the half dozen men around them.

The gate opened and they urged their horses forward. The narrow causeway between the ramparts was full of Saxons, milling about uncertainly. They must not have understood the words the Welsh had shouted, or if they did, not understood what they meant. Several of the ladders from the outer ramparts had been brought forward, but the time Cade had given his men to prepare wasn't enough for the Saxons to organize their attack.

The riders swept down the pathway, their arms swinging and their horses taking out every Saxon within reach. With each foot they progressed, they picked up speed. All the way down from the fort, the hapless Saxons fell under the hooves or—those who were less lucky—to one side, where a Welsh sword sliced through them. At the front of the line, Dyrnwyn rose and fell. Many of the Saxons succumbed to Cade's invisible sword as well.

Those ahead of Goronwy had killed so many Saxons, that Goronwy found himself with little to do. Until he swung around the corner of the last rampart, past the Annex that they'd fought so long to defend, and straight into the bulk of the Saxon army on the field that hadn't yet channeled between the ramparts.

"My God!" That was Bedwyr from beside him.

Just ahead, Hywel checked his horse, which gave Bedwyr and Goronwy time to flank him. Dafydd and Cade cut a swath forty yards in front of them, still buttressed by nearly twenty knights, but the hundreds of Saxons had slowed their momentum. The three friends exchanged a glance, and in half a heartbeat, they all understood that their heroic charge had been exactly that: heroic, but ultimately fruitless, even if the immortal King of Gwynedd rode at their head.

Against all expectation, Goronwy's heart lightened. He threw back his head and laughed, and then spurred his horse into the fray, with Hywel and Bedwyr close behind. Even if this meant his end, he would die with his friends on every side, and wouldn't be among the living when the Saxons finally overran his country. He prayed that the Saxons would spare the women as Cade hoped, though Goronwy himself had no such expectation. Then he put everything from his mind but his sword and the men he intended to kill with it.

He met a Saxon axe with his blade and ripped it away. He turned to the other side and thrust the point through another man's throat. But then a third man buried his axe in his horse's chest and he went down. Goronwy cleared his feet from the stirrups, leaping just in time to a vacant spot of what had once been grass. Back to back with Hywel, with hardly a pause for breath, he continued to fight.

Goronwy lost track of the men he'd killed; lost track of all of his friends but Hywel. Sweat pored down his face, from the effort, rather than the heat of the day, since it seemed that the promise of sunshine had been a faint one. Better for Cade, perhaps, were he to lose the cloak. Better for Rhiann standing on the battlements. Goronwy glanced upwards. In the time since they'd left the fort, clouds had massed above them, dark, black, and menacing.

Only from the light that still shot from the center of the field did Goronwy know that Dafydd and Cade were alive. The light grew brighter, almost blinding him with its intensity when he looked towards it, and still the Saxons didn't give way. Goronwy shoved his sword through the midsection of one Saxon, pulled it from his belly and in almost the same motion, slashed through another's thigh. He spun, meeting a third man's blade. The Saxon's red beard covered his face and a grin split it. For the first time, Goronwy felt weakness in his arms and found himself giving way under the onslaught.

And then the point of an arrow punched through the man's ribs. The Saxon had been lunging at Goronwy, his axe held above his head, readying for a killing blow. Now, he stared down at the arrowhead that seemed to come from nowhere. Goronwy looked past him. Rhiann had shot him from the top of the keep.

He wanted to shout at her, to tell her that they were a lost cause and that she was to save her arrows for the last end of need. Which forced into his mind the sickening thought that maybe they'd reached that point, that Rhiann had seen the end coming and was prepared to use her last arrows if they would give her friends a few more moments to live. Behind him, Hywel still fought as one possessed and Goronwy resumed his place, at his back. Sweat mixed with blood ran into Goronwy's eyes, and he swiped at it with the back of his hand.

Or maybe those were tears.

34

Dafydd

When Cade had offered him Dyrnwyn, Dafydd hadn't taken it. Standing before his king, he'd felt like someone had stuffed cloth inside his skull, like Angharad's pillow, he was thinking so slowly. But now—now that he was on the battlefield—he'd never felt more glorious than he did in this moment. He didn't know if it was the sword, his position at the head of the company, or that King Cadwaladr rode beside him, bringing down one man after another. Dafydd fought as if this was the only reality he would ever know. His sword flaming higher than ever, Dafydd followed its lead, as if it had a mind of its own and Dafydd was a slave to its will.

Saxons scattered before him and he envisioned himself fighting just like Cade had fought against the demons outside Caer Dathyl. He would turn and they would flee before him; they would throw themselves upon their own blades; Taliesin would compose songs to his greatness...

"You're getting too far ahead."

Cade's sharp rebuke brought Dafydd back to reality. He didn't let up the motion of his sword arm, but it was like Cade had thrown a bucket of cold water over his head. He could sense everything around him again and was no longer wrapped in a muffling wool that prevented his senses from working. He felt it all: his muscles clenching and unclenching, his knees signaling to his horse, the ache in his shoulder from the effort of wielding the sword, the whistling of the wind through his helmet, with a high-pitched whine until he wanted to rip it from his head at the incessant noise.

"This way," Cade said.

Cade had been giving orders all along as they fought. Dafydd had just been ignoring him. Now, he did as he was told, working his way back towards their own men, instead of following a suicidal course towards the center of the mass of Saxon men.

Nonetheless, Dafydd had allowed too many Saxons to get between him and the Welsh line and because of it, three Saxons converged on him at once. Though he took out one, and Cade another, the last sliced through the meat of his thigh.

The pain was so unexpected, he screamed. To make matters worse, his moment of inattention allowed a fourth Saxon to bury his axe in his horse's neck. The horse went down and Dafydd just managed to leap free.

"Stay with me!"

Dafydd's stomach curdled at how exposed they were, even if the push and pull of battle had ebbed for the moment around them since Cade had severed the neck of three Saxons in succession to get to Dafydd. He gaped at the blood that poured out of his leg and he scrabbled with his free hand to stop the flow.

And then to Dafydd's horror, Cade dismounted and ripped off the invisibility cloak. He held out Caledfwlch. "Trade me."

When Dafydd looked at him stupidly, Cade thrust Caledfwlch into Dafydd's hand, took Dyrnwyn from him, dropped the invisibility cloak over Dafydd's shoulders, and pinned it around his neck.

"Will it heal me?" Those were the only words Dafydd could think to say.

Cade planted his feet, his back to Dafydd and his power shining out. It reflected off the black clouds above them, even if he wielded less than he might have were it night.

"Damn well better," Cade said.

And even as Dafydd watched, his wound closed. Another dozen heartbeats and he could stand and take his place, back to back with Cade, though this time it was Dafydd's sword that was invisible and he who dispatched would-be attackers who thought they would take out the King of Gwynedd from behind.

In truth, for all Dyrnwyn's glory, Dafydd was glad to fight with Caledfwlch instead. She didn't require some kind of test to wield her, and even if she wasn't as mighty as Dyrnwyn and didn't flame from hilt to tip, she felt more comfortable in his hand.

"I'll want her back when we're done here," Cade said, reading Dafydd's mind. "And the cloak."

Dafydd's heart lightened further when a moment later, from three different directions, Bedwyr, Goronwy, and Hywel appeared to join their circle. They were invincible now, no matter how many men came against them.

"Hold!"

The command echoed around the field and the Saxons obeyed, falling back from Cade's ring of men. Even Dafydd's countrymen faltered. Stunned, Dafydd saw a man wearing Hywel's crest remove his helmet and sit on it, his head bent and his sword lose in his hand. No Saxon took advantage of his capitulation because the Saxon warrior beside him did the same thing.

Through the faltering forces strode two dozen men in black. They converged on Cade's small ring of five from every direction. Dafydd barked a laugh at how unsurprised he was at this turn of events. Part of him had been expecting something like this from the start. Mabon was late to the party, but that didn't mean he wasn't eventually going to show.

"I thought we killed them." That was Bedwyr, deadpan as usual.

"Apparently not," said Hywel, having obviously spent too much time in Bedwyr's company.

"They killed King Arthur on the road to Caer Fawr," Goronwy said.

"And the men of Castell Clydog, back in Ceredigion," Dafydd said.

"They are here now; that is all that matters," Cade said. "And if they are here, then Mabon can't be far away."

The five companions backed towards each other, narrowing their circle so fewer of Mabon's men could attack them at once or isolate them, one from the other. The first man to appear in front of Dafydd was clean-shaven, his nose a fine point. He didn't see Dafydd, of course, since he was invisible and that was all Dafydd noted of him before Caledfwlch skewered him through the belly. Dafydd didn't remember even thrusting the sword.

But he didn't have time to think about it before another set upon him. And another, and he lost track of anything but these men in black who shouldn't be here, and yet were.

He'd killed four men and had countered the blade of a fifth when he sensed commotion to his right. He strained to see what was happening out of the corner of his eye, while still taking care of his opponent. Dafydd managed to dispatch him, and then turned to see Cade holding off two men at the same time. One was enormous, built out of solid rock it seemed, and the other was Mabon.

Sick to death of Mabon and all the damage he'd done, Dafydd moved towards Cade, stumbling over a body on the ground as he did so. Cade held out a hand, however, to stop him, despite the fact that Dafydd was still wearing the cloak so Cade shouldn't be able to see him. With that motion, it seemed like the entire battle slowed, just for this moment. Maybe it was some new magic of Cade's. Perhaps Mabon was disturbing the passage of time. Dafydd pulled up just behind Cade and glared at Mabon, but the god had eyes only for the King of Gwynedd.

"Put up your sword. You have lost." The familiar sneer was plastered to Mabon's face.

Dafydd opened his mouth to deny Mabon's words, but then couldn't. Where earlier Dafydd had seen Welshmen and Saxons sitting together, now they set upon each other again. Every man moved so slowly, however, it was as if their swords weighed a hundred pounds. Right in front of him, a Saxon killed one of Tudur's men. Gagging, Dafydd looked away, towards the west and Caer Fawr. The castle was in flames. Tears pricked his eyes.

A moan came from behind him. He spun towards it, terrified of what he might find, and it worse than he'd imagined. Goronwy lay on the field, about to lose his head to one of the men in black. Hywel and Bedwyr were already down.

"No!"

Dafydd threw himself at Goronwy's attacker. He wrapped his arms around his waist and brought him to the ground with his full weight. As they hit the grass, the fall knocked Caledfwlch from Dafydd's hand, but he didn't care. He sat up, straddled, the man, and punched him in the face. The man tried to defend himself, but Dafydd gave him a sharp cut that broke his jaw and Dafydd's hand.

"Dafydd!"

The word came sharply and again, because it was the voice of someone he loved, he came to himself. Goronwy had crawled to the spot where Dafydd had dropped Caledfwlch and fallen flat on it.

"Thank God," Dafydd said.

He staggered to where his brother lay healing from the gash Mabon's man had put in his side. Dafydd collapsed next to him and swung the invisibility cloak over both of them. Goronwy

- 339 -

would live. Many wouldn't. Dafydd swallowed his tears at the loss of his friends, and put one finger on the top of Caledfwlch's hilt. His broken hand began to heal. But from this battle, the Welsh would never recover.

35

Rhiann

Rhiann fired off an arrow, adding to the carnage in the fields below Caer Fawr. Wind had whipped around them almost from the instant the battle started and chilled her to her core. The battle raged right in front of them, right up to the lowest rampart. The main Saxon force had gathered in the field on the near side of the little creek. Penda must have thought they would soon be entering the fort, once they'd figured out how to breach the final rampart.

Her heart rose to her throat as she watched, such that she could hardly breathe around it. Taliesin had remained beside her as the morning wore on and the number of bodies of the fallen, already too numerous to count, grew ever larger. It was easy to think *why doesn't he* do *something*, but Taliesin's magic could not save their army.

She'd seen, long before the men possibly could have, that the Saxons were going to win. She shot another arrow at a man who'd been about to decapitate Hywel. Every time she aimed her bow, her hands trembled in the moment before she fired. She had to swallow hard and still them, trying to capture the calm that was required for the task. And failing. But then all of a sudden, she knew what to do, and she wasn't going to do it standing here, too far from the fight to see it properly or make a difference.

She ran for the doorway to the keep. Taliesin grabbed her arm but she shook him off. "I'm not close enough. Stay or come, I don't care which."

She barreled down the stairs from the battlements, skidding down each step since she was moving so fast. Taliesin came on behind her, no longer protesting. Rhiann burst into the great hall. A dozen women looked up as she entered—mostly camp followers and hangers-on—along with Angharad and Catrin, who lifted a hand to her as she passed them.

"What—" Angharad said.

Rhiann waved back, not wanting to alarm them since it would do no good. She simply told them the same thing as she'd told Taliesin: "I need to get closer."

It wasn't that she couldn't shoot an arrow four hundred yards. Of course she could. Even with her smaller bow, she could make one fly that far. But accurate? She'd almost killed Hywel with that shot. She'd never been so nervous to loose an arrow in her life, not even at the battle at Caersws where she and Dafydd and defended the retreat of the women and children.

Maybe she'd been naïve then. Maybe she hadn't known enough. Now she did, and it brought her to her knees.

Rhiann crashed open the door leading from the great hall, passed a few men who'd made it back inside the fort, and headed for the gate. The door had been left partially open and she ran through it.

"Rhiann, it isn't safe—" Taliesin said.

"Safe enough," Rhiann said.

Taliesin let it go, since they were already on the path. As she'd seen from her position on the battlements, the Saxons who'd surged between the ramparts in their initial victory had been decimated by the Welsh charge. Those that remained had given up trying to get into the keep. Their ladders didn't reach, and the battle had moved outside. The Saxons had gone with it, unaware that the Welsh hadn't even bothered to close the door.

At last she reached the Annex—the defense works that Goronwy had defended in the initial assault. It had a twenty-foot high rampart, augmented by walls that encircled an area fifty feet wide and twenty deep. Though it protected the main gate at the bottom of pathway, once the Saxons had come over the walls and opened that gate from the inside, they'd abandoned it as a post.

Taliesin closed and barred the gate to the annex, effectively locking them into this small, raised haven amidst the turmoil below them. The ancients had built it for just such an occasion, if the annex was all that was left of a defense, rather than the keep.

Rhiann climbed to the top of the wall. If anything, the roiling mass of men had moved closer to the ramparts in the time she'd taken to get here. Twenty feet away, a Welshman lost his head to a Saxon axe. She'd seen so much carnage, it shouldn't have surprised her, but tears sprung to her eyes anyway. She brushed them back.

Goronwy, Bedwyr, Hywel, and Cade, who'd thrown off his cloak, stood in the center of the battlefield. Rhiann didn't see Dafydd and her heart fell, until she realized that he must be filling the gap in their ring. The companions fought in a circle, their backs to one another facing outward, as a phalanx of attackers in black surrounded them.

She turned to Taliesin, her gaze imploring. She couldn't help it. Druids had spoken to the gods for thousands of years and he was the only one with any answers here at all. "Are you sure—"

"This is a long way from over."

But for once, Rhiann didn't believe him. Couldn't believe him. He'd been right so many times before, but ...

"Stand your ground, Rhiann, and don't waste your arrows," Taliesin said.

"I'm almost out."

"I'll get you more." He left her to scavenge arrows from the quivers of the dead archers who had fallen in the initial defense of the fort.

Rhiann set her feet and began loosing arrows into the Saxon army. *One, two, three* ... She trusted that Taliesin would find replacements, and as promised, before her remaining ones were spent, he appeared beside her with fistfuls that he stuffed into her quiver.

She had to pause in her shooting as he filled it, and their eyes met. A light grew behind Taliesin's eyes that she hadn't seen since that day they'd met, months ago on the battlements of Dinas Emrys. Taliesin then stepped away. He raised hands above his head and focused all his attention on a point over the center of the battlefield where Cade and his friends fought.

Earlier, at the start of the battle, he'd chanted words she couldn't understand, but now he lifted his chin and his voice rang out above the howl of the wind and the clash of men:

> *A knight on a swift horse*
> *creates turmoil among his enemies*
> *Thither will come an ancient enemy,*
> *Grief will he know.*
> *Sin and treason follow*
> *And old hatreds are renewed*
> *One stroke of his sword*
> *And our war-lord comes*
> *He remakes us*
> *and brings to us a new Eden.*

And as Taliesin finished, the most beautiful sound Rhiann had ever heard came from the west, wafting across the hills and fields. It was a horn. Not a Saxon horn, but an old-fashioned Welsh one. She knew the sound, even knew the horn, though she'd only heard it once before, in the setting out from Bryn y Castell before the ride to Caersws. A lifetime ago.

Rhun, Siawn, and their men had finally come.

SARAH WOODBURY

With their coming, the storm that had threatened to unleash its rain, ever since their men had ridden out of the fort, broke over the battlefield.

Wind and rain whipped into her face as Rhun's men crashed into the side of the Saxon lines. What had been a cohesive force collapsed. Rhun's sword rose and fell, slaying every man within reach. But there were so many, and Rhun had two hundred Saxons to fight before he could reach Cade and his friends. The hope that had briefly flared in Rhiann's heart drained out again, even as she shot one arrow after another, refusing to stop until either there were no more Saxons, or she ran out of arrows. Then to her horror, the ring of fighters broke apart. Every one of Cade's men had gone down, and Cade himself faced the last man alone.

Except it wasn't a man. She couldn't see his face, but she knew that stance. She knew that glow that emanated from him and told her the god confronted her husband again.

Mabon.

How she hated him.

Taliesin put a hand on her arm. "You see him? That means it's time."

Rhiann swept her rain-soaked hair out of her eyes and raised her bow. Lifting her eyes to the heavens for one last prayer, she focused all her attention on this last chance for some kind of victory. Her hands trembled and her wet bowstring didn't respond as it should. She would have replaced it earlier if she'd had any to spare. But even so, she pressed the black arrow, the one she'd been saving, the one that Arianrhod had given her by the river, into it—and then loosed it.

It hit Mabon in the center of his mass.

And with that shot, power exploded in the center of the field. It burst from the place Mabon had been standing and surged outward like waves from a boulder lobbed into a pool of water. The force pushed men and horses with it, laying them flat to the ground as it passed. It reached Caer Fawr and blew past and through Taliesin and Rhiann, who herself was thrown backwards off the top of the rampart.

Rhiann came to herself, flat on her back below the wall. Her bow lay ten feet away. Even Taliesin, whose composure had never wavered throughout their vigil, was on his knees, though still on the top of the wall.

He reached down a hand to her. "You'll want to see this."

Coughing, she got to her feet and clambered back to Taliesin's position. The field lay before her, still rain-soaked, though the downpour seemed to have lessened slightly. The five companions stood together. Cade held Dyrnwyn point down, its fire out.

Here and there, the Saxons they'd been fighting staggered to their feet, their swords and axes forgotten. Rhiann's jaw dropped to see half as many as there had been a moment before. Cade himself reached out a hand to a helmetless Saxon soldier to help him to his feet. Even from this distance, Rhiann recognized him by his ornate armor and the black swath of beard across his face. He'd visited Aberffraw when she was a girl. It was Penda, the King of Mercia

"What has happened?" Rhiann said. "Where did all of Penda's men go?"

"The gods fought with us and against us," Taliesin said, "just as I had foreseen."

"I don't understand," Rhiann said. "Mabon ..."

"He is gone for now, as are his troops."

"But he had no demons at his command," Rhiann said. "We faced real men."

"And almost were overcome by them," Taliesin said. "But as with the *glamour* he affects in our world, the size of the Saxon force was an illusion. Penda had many men, but not as many as we believed. If Penda had defeated us, it would have been in part because we defeated ourselves. We believed Penda had thousands more soldiers than he did."

"But we lost so many men!"

"Did we?"

"But Rhys! And Geraint!"

Taliesin nodded. "Yes, they are dead, but look around you now and tell me what you see."

Rhiann had a hand to her mouth. Many of the men who lay on the field of battle were dead, but here and there, men stirred and shook their heads. Could it be they'd received blows from which they were only now recovering? Could so many really still live?

"I don't believe it!" Rhiann said. And then the tears began to fall in earnest as all her fears and hopes coalesced into a potent mix of joy and pain, sorrow and gladness. They hadn't lost all their men. Wales would not be left defenseless. Her heart rose in her throat, along with hope. "But—" Rhiann swallowed and tried again. "And the arrow I shot at Mabon? Is he truly dead this time?"

"Arianrhod's arrow, his mother's arrow, ripped away the glamour and the links that anchored him to our world. My hope is that in Mabon's moment of weakness, Arianrhod would have tied him to her in the world of the gods. She couldn't find him—couldn't contain him—and was relying on you whom she deemed worthy to find him for her. If what I believe is true, he is trapped now in his mother's keeping."

"But for how long?" Rhiann said.

"That I cannot say," Taliesin said.

Rhiann stared at Taliesin for the time it took to take a long breath, and then threw whatever caution she still had—which wasn't much to begin with—to the wind that roared down the valley from the west.

The battle might have been over, but the storm hadn't spent its fury. The rungs of one of the ladders the Saxons had left propped against the rampart were slippery. She almost fell off at the end and landed hard. Once on the ground, it was difficult to see past Rhun's men and horses, but most of the men had dismounted by now and she found a path through them to Cade.

He hadn't seen her coming so when she launched herself at him, she almost knocked him over. But he weighed more than she did and he steadied himself, lifting her off the ground and clutching her to his chest. "*Cariad...*"

"I didn't see how we could win," Rhiann said into his collar. "It seems as unlikely now as it ever did."

"So this is the girl who has caused so much trouble."

Rhiann turned in Cade's arms. Penda stood before them, his hands loose at his sides. "I'm the girl who causes trouble?" she said. "Who encroaches on our lands with every day that passes? Who took advantage of my father's death to—" Rhiann broke off, so angry she couldn't finish her sentence.

Cade whispered in her ear. "Mabon visited Penda too, weeks ago."

Understanding dawned in Rhiann. She narrowed her eyes at the King of Mercia. "He told you that you could win."

Penda bowed. "As you say."

And that was all the apology they were going to get. The Welsh had fallen again and again to the Saxons, but rather than live under a foreign rule, they'd retreated west, into Wales. Penda had waged a war against his own nephew, over rocks and trees he didn't care for anyway and would have had a hard time controlling even if he did win.

Penda eyed Cade now. "Your emissary told me the truth about Oswin of Northumbria?"

"He did," Cade said.

Penda surveyed the battlefield. "I suppose you wouldn't consider fighting beside me against him? You've not lost as many men as you feared. You would be welcome."

Rhiann gaped at him, but Cade answered civilly. "Better an enemy I know than one I don't, is that it?"

Penda shrugged. The gesture was so dismissive—so casual—as if none of what he'd done mattered, that Rhiann wanted to launch herself at him like she had at Cade, except she would then scratch his eyes out. All he cared about was his own power and if Cade agreed to fight beside him—as Cadfael and Cadwallon had before him—it would be a victory of a sorts.

Cade studied him, still not answering, and Rhiann was struck with a sudden vision of Penda, lying on a field in the sun, his lifeblood flowing into the grass from a wound to the gut. She'd never *seen* before, but this felt like a sudden truth. If Cade denied Penda's request, he would not live out the year, just as Taliesin had foretold.

"I'm sorry, Uncle. I cannot fight for you today," Cade said.

36

Cade

Cade sat behind his desk, gazing at the chess piece Rhiann had brought him, turning the little king around and around in his fingers. The knife and the whetstone were to one side, and the cloak in a chest behind him. Dafydd still had Dyrnwyn in his possession and Cade had seen no reason to ask him for it. A cold anger still burned in Cade that he'd needed to use it, and at how close Cade had come to winning the battle but losing the war. If all had happened as Mabon desired, Cade's army would have been so weakened and diminished, it would have been left open to an attack from anyone who could marshal enough men.

But once Mabon was gone, the *glamour* he'd created had vanished. The veil had lifted and the trauma of the day had lessened. Cade had reached Bedwyr and Hywel soon enough to help them. Them and others, through the power of Caledfwlch. Many hadn't lived to fight another day and Cade mourned the loss of every man. Still, he had to be grateful that there were fewer widows to accuse him with their grief.

"I'm glad that Caer Fawr wasn't really on fire," Rhun said.

"*Glamour* again." Taliesin closed the door to the room, stumped over to a bench set against the far wall, and settled himself onto it. "I would give much to ensure a way to see through it."

That was quite an admission, coming from Taliesin. Cade gestured in the general direction of the hall, where his other friends were dining. "So many were sorely wounded. That was no lie."

"I for one, dislike intensely that I cannot trust my own eyes," Rhun said. He'd turned his chair around and sat with his arms resting on the back rail, cushioning his chin with his fists.

"Even I can't see through it," Cade said. "Maybe that's the next gift I will ask of Arianrhod."

"I wouldn't," Taliesin said.

Cade laughed under his breath. "No more gifts, eh? I suppose that's wise."

The three friends fell silent. In the aftermath of the battle, Taliesin and Cade had already talked for hours about the gods, about the battle, about the war that could rage in the world of the *sidhe* if Beli and the *sidhe* council learned of Mabon's actions. And at this point, how could they not?

Cade pointed to the Treasures in front of him. "What are we going to do with these now?"

"With Mabon gone, do we need to worry about them?" Rhun said. "Arianrhod has him contained, right? Isn't that what you said, Taliesin?"

"It is," Taliesin said.

"But for how long?" Rhun said.

Taliesin grunted his assent. "That is the question."

"We have to assume the worst," Cade said. "And plan for it."

"And that means collecting the Treasures ourselves," Rhun said. "If nothing else, it will spare their owners the danger inherent in them."

"And the cup of Christ?" Taliesin said. "Your holy grail of Christendom?"

Cade glanced at his friend. "You know about that? Underneath Dinas Bran you said it was *just a cup*."

"I didn't *see* as clearly then," Taliesin said. "It isn't one of Mabon's Treasures, but surely it is one in its own right."

"The monks say it bestows immortality on those who drink from it," Cade said. "Just like the drinking horn in your poem."

"You could go get it," Taliesin said. "Give it to Rhiannon."

Cade's eyes narrowed. Rhiann was asleep in the room behind them. In the weeks since Caer Fawr, her pregnancy had taxed her strength such that she slept more often than she was awake. "And keep her with me always? Of course I want that, but it would not serve."

"You could ask her," Taliesin said.

"You're tempting me," Cade said. "And I will not be tempted."

"As you say." Taliesin sat with his staff propped against his shoulder, gazing down at the floor. The workman had come a long way on the project of restoring Dinas Bran to its former glory. Another month and they'd finish the curtain wall. Provided nothing happened in the interim to stop the work.

Cade fingered some of the papers on his desk, the Treasures always at the edge of his vision, as if individually they might leap up and talk to him at any moment. He took a deliberate breath and let it out. "Will you find the rest for me? I need to know how close Mabon was to his goal to unite them all. We must know where they are and if they are safe."

Taliesin bowed his head. "You are confirmed in the idea that you won't keep them for yourself, then?"

"Of course," Cade said.

Taliesin nodded. "If you had not given me this task, I would have asked for it." He walked to the table and picked up the sacred knife from its spot.

"And the dark force that rose from the cavern?" Cade said. "You have not mentioned it since we rode for Caer Fawr, but I can see that it haunts you."

"It is pure evil," Taliesin said. "The druids have always drawn their power from the earth itself, but not all power is good. And some of my kind spent too much time in the dark." Taliesin met Cade's eyes. "I will be careful."

"Please do."

"I will attend your crowning at the summer solstice, my lord."

"I will expect you," Cade said.

Rhun stood too. "He wouldn't really be High King if you weren't there to keep him humble, would he?"

Cade shared in the laughter and sketched a wave as Rhun left the room.

Silence. Taliesin and Cade gazed at each other. Their eyes said a great number of things that they chose not to put into words.

Finally, Taliesin spoke. "I leave you in good hands."

"I'll try not to be too reckless in your absence," Cade said.

That brought a rare smile to Taliesin's face. "Blessings upon you, and upon your House, my lord."

And he was gone.

Blessings upon my House. Cade got to his feet. Political power had come to him through right of birth and strength of arms. Love, however, was something that could only be earned. Something else that Mabon would never understand.

Cade followed Taliesin out the door and turned toward the room he shared with Rhiann. *His House.* He had a wife and child waiting for him.

The End

Thank you for reading *The Pendragon's Quest*. For more information about Wales in the Dark and Middle Ages, please see my web page: www.sarahwoodbury.com

Acknowledgments

I have many people to thank, not only for their assistance with *The Pendragon's Quest*, but who have helped make my books better and my life sane for the last five years.

First and foremost, thank you to my family: my husband Dan, who five years ago told me to give it five years and see if I still loved it. I still do. Thank you for your infinite patience with having a writer as a wife. To my four kids, Brynne, Carew, Gareth, and Taran, who have been nothing but encouraging, despite the fact that their mother spends half her life in medieval Wales. Thank you to my parents, for passing along their love of history, and particularly to my father, who died only a few days before I published *The Pendragon's Quest*. I couldn't finish it fast enough and he faded away before he had a chance to read it.

Thanks to my beautiful writing partner, Anna Elliott, who has made this journey with me from nearly the beginning. Thank you to the many support groups to which I belong, including the Indie Chicks, Indie Writers Unite, Writer's Café at the Kindle Boards, among others (you know who you are!).

And finally, thank you to my readers. You make it all worthwhile.

About the Author

With two historian parents, Sarah couldn't help but develop an interest in the past. She went on to get more than enough education herself (in anthropology) and began writing fiction when the stories in her head overflowed and demanded she let them out. Her interest in Wales stems from her own ancestry and the year she lived in England when she fell in love with the country, language, and people. She even convinced her husband to give all four of their children Welsh names.

She makes her home in Oregon.

Printed in Great Britain
by Amazon.co.uk, Ltd.,
Marston Gate.